TELEVISION FOR

Also by Danit Brown

Ask for a Convertible

TELEVISION FOR WOMEN

A NOVEL

DANIT BROWN

MELVILLE HOUSE
BROOKLYN · LONDON

Television for Women

Copyright © 2024 by Danit Brown
All rights reserved
First Melville House Printing: April 2025

This work was supported by a grant from
the Hewlett-Mellon Fund for Faculty Development
at Albion College, Albion, MI.

Melville House Publishing
46 John Street
Brooklyn, NY 11201
and
Melville House UK
Suite 2000
16/18 Woodford Road
London E7 0HA

mhpbooks.com
@melvillehouse

ISBN: 978-1-68589-183-1
ISBN: 978-1-68589-184-8 (eBook)

Library of Congress Control Number: 2024950734

Designed by Beste M. Doğan

Printed in the United States of America

10 9 8 7 6 5 4 3 2 1

A catalog record for this book is available from the Library of Congress

For Ziv, Nadav, and Shai

TELEVISION FOR WOMEN

1

THE WHOLE MESS STARTED WHEN Owen was fired at the end of summer term. Estie had been right at thirty-six weeks and two days when he came home and announced that his position as an English professor at Norton College had been terminated. "Financial exigency," he said, his eyes puffy. It was a good hour-and-fifteen-minute drive from Norton to Briarwood, where he and Estie lived, and Estie guessed he'd cried all the way home.

He spent the next thirty minutes hauling in boxes of books from his car and stacking them neatly in the closet of what was going to be the baby's room, and the ten minutes after that cleaning up cat vomit. The cat, Herbert, disapproved of strong emotions.

"So what happens now?" Estie asked. "Do you look for another position?"

"I don't know," Owen said. "No. Not yet. They don't post English jobs until October."

Estie felt her stomach clench, or maybe that was just Braxton Hicks. It was the end of July, and the baby was due in late August. "What are we going to do?"

"I don't know," Owen said again. "It just happened. I need time to think."

Estie nodded, ignoring the baby's kicks of protest against her ribs. The truth was, she'd been waiting for something like this to happen ever since she'd gotten pregnant, possibly even before. Estie knew she'd been lucky so far: the major disasters of her life up to this point—her parents' divorce, the not-quite-breakup with her college boyfriend, Dan—had been relatively minor. But if reports of tornadoes and school shootings had taught her anything, it was that luck was fleeting and complacency dangerous: the other shoe was out there, dangling, ready to drop, and it was important not to be caught off guard. Except that Estie *had* been caught off guard. Owen losing his job felt like a failure of imagination on her part: it had never occurred to her that a tenured professor could be laid off. How had she not considered this possibility? Why had she not made any backup plans?

Then again, it wasn't as if much *had* been going according to plan lately. Take, for instance, the pregnancy itself. Yes, Estie was glad she was pregnant—she was; she really was—but she'd always imagined that she would be the one setting the schedule, the one who would someday find herself weeping in the diaper aisle at Target, triggered by a passing stroller or the photo of some celebrity's sleeping baby, and then rush home and declare it was time. Instead, it was Owen who had made the decision back in January, after they'd gone to one of Estie's coworker's baby shower. The coworker, Jillian, was the receptionist at Big Earth, the artisan tile factory where Estie worked as a glazer, and she was the kind of person who emailed everyone photos of her positive pregnancy test, then separately cornered each of her coworkers and forced them to place a hand on her small mound of belly while, flushed with pride, she asked, "Can you feel the peanut kick? Now? And now?" When it had been Estie's turn to feel the baby move, Jillian had guided her hand so far down along her abdomen that Estie's fingers had brushed against the waistband of Jillian's underwear. "Okay, I feel it, I feel it," she'd said, even though the only thing she'd felt was Jillian's hot skin. "She could've at least bought me dinner first," Estie complained to her best friend, Alice, and Alice, who worked at a start-up in Chicago that was developing a tartar-detecting smart toothbrush, had laughed: "At least there's only one of her," she'd said. There were four pregnant women in Alice's unit alone.

Jillian's shower had been held at Precious Insights, a converted movie theater that specialized in big-screen 4D gender-determination ultrasounds that you watched from "luxurious stadium seating" while sipping mocktails from a sippy cup. According to Jillian, vanity ultrasounds were all the rage and women-only baby showers were passé, but then again, Jillian also liked wearing maternity tees that said things like "Don't eat watermelon seeds" and "You're kicking me, smalls." Still, there were going to be cupcakes, so Estie had figured that she and Owen would spend a pleasant afternoon rolling their eyes at each other and feeling superior. And the afternoon had certainly started out that way, with Owen grimacing at the Precious Insights slogan, which was painted on the wall in a precious, impossible-to-miss script: "The Largest of Blessing's Are Those That Are Small." Nothing set Owen off like apostrophe errors in corporate logos.

"See," he said, pointing to the same error in the program the hostess handed them. "If you're not careful, these mistakes just perpetuate themselves."

They'd found seats in the right corner of the theater, near the emergency exit because you never knew, and looked on as Jillian hoisted herself up on the cot in the center of the room and hitched up her maternity blouse without hesitation. The ultrasound tech, a woman in blue scrubs and lots of blue eye shadow, smeared jelly on Jillian's abdomen, which, unsheathed, looked plastic and fake, crisscrossed by pale stretch marks and so taut with baby that her belly button appeared to be turned inside out, like one of those pop-up timers people used to cook turkeys. Then the lights dimmed, Jillian and her husband clasped hands, and the Dolby Surround Sound speakers began blasting the whooshing of the baby's heart into the observation area. A few seconds later, the large screen behind Jillian flickered to life and there was the baby in all its yellow three-dimensional glory. Next to Estie, Owen exhaled loudly, as if he were the one who was nervous.

"Here is Baby's foot," the ultrasound tech said, pointing. "Here are Baby's little toes." She moved the wand a little, then announced, voice bursting with pride, "And here's Baby's little boy part," as if she'd just attached the penis to the baby herself.

Estie had expected Owen to make some sort of crack about the solemnity of it all, but all he did was lean closer and squeeze her knee. The tech slid the wand over a little more, and on the monitor, the baby's blurry yellow face filled the screen, shifting in and out of focus as if he were pressing himself against a fleshy yellow wall, a tiny Han Solo trapped in carbonite. You'd make out the orbs of his eyes and his flat little baby nose, and then they would recede and melt into the background, or worse, transform into dark hollows as if the baby were all skull, as if he'd forgotten to grow muscle and skin. "It looks like an alien," Estie started to say, but just then the baby yawned and rubbed his eyes with a small fist, looking as aggrieved as any human interrupted in the middle of a deep sleep.

"Wow," Owen had whispered, his voice reverent. "I mean, wow." And just like that, getting pregnant became yet another milestone in a long list of milestones that refused to unfold as seen on TV—a first kiss full of spit and onion rings, a first high school party without beer or weed, first-time sex without soft lighting or simultaneous orgasms. Instead of swelling violin music and a gentle baby wakeup call, what Estie had gotten was Owen shuffling her off to the bedroom the moment they got home, then undressing her from top to bottom, all business, no kissing. "Sheesh," Estie had said, "what's your hurry?" Her fingers were still sticky from the cupcakes, and there was a smudge of blue frosting at one corner of Owen's mouth, but his urgency had made her feel irresistible—he was usually so calm, so measured in everything he did—and so she'd helped him with the clasp of her bra, with her zipper, with her socks, with his, and tried not to feel self-conscious and fat when he lifted her onto the bed and climbed on top of her.

"Feel my heart," Owen had said once he was inside her, and Estie *could* feel it, beating rapidly against her own chest. She waited for Owen to pull out and put on a condom, and when he didn't, she'd said, "Wait." Owen paused, resting his full weight against her so that she was pinned. "I really really love you," he told her. "We're adults. It's time."

"Be serious," Estie said, squirming.

"Come on," Owen whispered, still on top of her, his lips against her ear. "I want you. I want you and me and a baby of our own."

Estie swallowed hard, suddenly aware of Owen's bony ribs against her chest, his jutting hips against her inner thighs. She could have told him to stop, but doing so felt pointless—she didn't know what she wanted, just what she ought to want. She was thirty-two. She was married and gainfully employed. She'd always figured she'd have a baby *someday*. She closed her eyes and tried to relax. Of course she wanted a baby. Of course she did. "Okay," she told Owen. "Okay. Let's do it."

———

Even though only high school girls got pregnant the first time they had unprotected sex, Estie had gotten pregnant right away. "That's some good sperm," Owen said proudly when she showed him the first positive pregnancy test, and then the second and the third, because what if the first and second tests were defective? They waited until they had the doctor's confirmation before telling Estie's mother, who for months had been campaigning vigorously for Estie to have a baby before her eggs shriveled up and her uterus rotted, never mind that Estie's brother, Sammy, had already provided her mother with two perfectly good grandchildren. "Nobody wants a perimenopausal mom," Estie's mother had pointed out helpfully time and again, although now that Estie was finally pregnant, instead of shrieking in delight or bursting into tears of joy, her mother contented herself with eyeing Estie's waistline and saying, "I thought as much." Then, after some further consideration, she added, "You'll have to get rid of the cat. Cats suck the breath out of babies."

"That's ridiculous," Estie said, or maybe even snapped, although later that evening, while Herbert was using the litter box, she surreptitiously asked Google, "*Do* cats suffocate babies?" and Google answered ominously, "Not purposely," which wasn't as comforting as it could have been.

But even though her mother's reaction to the pregnancy had been disappointing, it had still been far better than Alice's response, which had been a pause so pregnant it put Estie's actual pregnancy to shame. Estie knew what the pause meant: Alice was trying to think of something nice to say. She'd done something similar back when Estie told her she was marrying Owen, but that had been because Alice had impossibly high standards for marriage, and so that silence had been easy to dismiss. Alice's hesitation about the pregnancy, though, rattled Estie. She cleared her throat. "You're not happy about the baby?"

"That isn't it," Alice said. "I just didn't know you were trying."

"We weren't," Estie said, "and then we were."

"Huh," Alice said. "That's the biological imperative to reproduce for you. You couldn't help it."

"No, I could have," Estie said. "It's not like that." She put a hand on her belly, which felt, at four weeks, no different than it ever had—soft and paunchy—and for a moment she wondered if maybe she was mistaken and she wasn't pregnant after all. Please, she caught herself thinking, please. She didn't let herself finish the thought, but after she hung up, she found herself taking the final pregnancy test in the four-pack she'd purchased, blushing in embarrassment when the second blue line showed almost immediately. She was still pregnant. There was no reason to think otherwise. The whole thing, she reminded herself, was going exactly according to plan.

2

AFTER HE FINISHED STACKING THE boxes of books from his office in the nursery closet, an exhausted Owen told Estie, "I don't think I can go to childbirth class. Not tonight. Tell them I'm sick?" Then he lay down on the couch, head down, arms and legs drawn inward, and fell asleep almost immediately, Herbert curled up behind his knees.

"Okay," Estie said, mainly to herself. She considered staying home too, but that night's topic was diaper changes, and those seemed important. Plus, she needed time to think, or to not think, or to do or not do *something* that would soothe the panic rising in her throat. Maybe a class full of pregnant women led by an instructor who kept reminding them to trust their Inner Wisdom was exactly what she needed.

Except that it apparently wasn't. Class was held in a yoga studio with mirrors on two walls, which meant that the instructor, Rita, with her flowing skirts and jangly bracelets, spent most of class addressing her own reflection while the parents-to-be sat in a semicircle in front of her, bobbing up and down on giant inflatable balls. While Rita lectured about the evils of absorbent gel beads—"I'm not against Pampers or Huggies per se," she explained—Estie tried to convince herself that Owen getting laid off was a good thing, a kind of parental leave that would enable him to be fully present for the birth and the first couple months of the baby's life. This was *not*, she told herself, the beginning of a downward spiral that would have them living out of their car by Christmas. Her mom still lived in town. Her brother worked for Google. Nobody would let them starve. She forced herself to focus on Rita, who was passing out baby dolls to everyone. The doll she handed Estie was naked except for a diaper and made of yellowing plastic that made her appear jaundiced. Her hair was blond and matted, and her eyes didn't shut properly, as if she instinctively understood that Estie wasn't to be trusted.

Rita returned to the front of the classroom and clapped her hands sharply, then announced, "Rule number one: If there's no changing table, place your baby on the floor. Babies can't roll off the floor."

Obediently, Estie heaved herself off her yoga ball and began the arduous process of getting down on her knees.

"Now remember—" Rita began, and that was when it happened: Estie, still making her way down to the floor, lost her balance and tipped forward—stupid shifting center of gravity—her knee landing squarely on the doll baby's sternum. The doll baby crumpled with a high-pitched squeak, and the pressure of the escaping air launched her head across the room. The other parents-to-be gasped, then watched in horror as the head rolled to a stop at Rita's feet. Estie watched in horror too, too mortified to laugh when Rita picked up the head and quipped, "Okay, start over. The *actual* first rule of parenting is: do not crush your baby." She walked over to Estie and pried her trembling fingers off the doll's torso so she could shove the baby's head back onto her little stump of a neck. Then she straightened up and checked her reflection in one of the mirrors. "Reattaching limbs," she cautioned, tucking a wayward curl behind her ear, "isn't nearly this easy in real life."

Estie knew that, and she also knew that a head wasn't a limb, but she was too busy blushing and sweating to say anything. And that was pretty much how she spent the remainder of class: cringing and sweating and using a wet wipe to clean up the yellow mustard Rita had thoughtfully squeezed into each doll's diaper in what she called "a touch of realism," then cringing and sweating some more. When class finally—at long last—ended, Estie was the first one out the door, the first one screeching out of the yoga studio's parking lot: she was going to have to find another childbirth class in another town.

AC blasting, she drove around in circles until she felt calm enough to go home, or at least calm enough to stop at the Creamery for some ice cream—two scoops of chocolate chip for her, a mint Oreo shake for Owen. She parked, then hoisted herself out of her car, and, because apparently having your husband get laid off and accidentally crushing a doll baby wasn't portentous enough for one day, she spotted Penny Smilovitz standing three people ahead of her in line. Estie hadn't seen Penny since their freshman year in college, but she still recognized her immediately in much the same way that she recognized her own foreshortened reflection in the funhouse at the annual Kiwanis Fair. The acne was gone, thank goodness, but Penny still had those liquid brown eyes and the nose that, during puberty, had broadened and lengthened at an alarming rate but had now finally settled into the right size for her face.

"Oh my God," Estie said. "Penny." Almost immediately, she wished she'd kept quiet. She wasn't proud of the way she'd handled her friendship with Penny, a friendship she'd resisted for the first two months of ninth grade, put off by Penny's frizzy hair, her braces, her giant grown-woman boobs. You had to dress for the job you wanted, not the job you had, and the job teenage Estie had wanted—being popular—didn't allow for (and here the grown-up Estie had to wince, because there was no good way to put it) ugly friends. Then again, at fourteen Estie had been no prize herself—sallow and plain, with greasy bangs and cold sores that showed up like clockwork two days before her period—and it didn't take her long to understand that high school was much easier to navigate with a partner at the ready for science lab, for gym class, for group projects, a partner who didn't reek of sweat and cigarettes or spend most of class drawing lightning bolts on the soles of their shoes. And so she and Penny had settled into a friendship of sorts, an arrangement of convenience, maybe, which was fine. More than fine, actually, because going over to Penny's to do things like bake cookies or thumb through the dirty parts of Penny's mom's romance novels turned out to be kind of fun, even if it hadn't been the *right* kind of fun. And even that didn't matter because, as Estie kept reminding herself, nobody actually *wanted* high school to be the best years of their life, not when there were a good sixty years to get through afterward. And so her arrangement with Penny had lasted right up until they'd graduated and gone to different colleges and "drifted apart"—which was how Estie liked to think of it—and the last Estie had heard, Penny had moved to California.

Except now Penny was back and standing in line for ice cream. "Oh my God, Estie," she said, dropping back to stand beside her. "Look at you!" She gestured at Estie's ginormous belly. "Do you know what you're having?"

Estie did know. "A boy, thank God."

Penny patted her own flat stomach. "I just hit twelve weeks, so we don't know yet."

"I swear," said the ponytailed man who was eavesdropping behind them, "you pregnant women are everywhere." He winked at Penny. "If only there were some kind of pill . . ."

"Har har," Estie said, and Penny gave him a withering look, and apparently the shared bond of being pregnant among idiots trumped twelve years of silence. "It's so weird to see you," Penny said after the server handed them their ice cream, "and also not weird at all. We only moved back, like, two weeks ago."

"That's so great!" Estie said, although she wasn't sure if it really *was* all that great. Standing next to Penny after all these years was making her feel dowdy and fat. Had she always been shorter than Penny? Had Penny always looked better in jeans? And then there was the matter of the square-jawed and massively forearmed man who was saving Penny a seat at one of the few shady tables outside.

"Wow," Estie said when Penny introduced the man as her husband, Jack, "you're huge."

"I know," Penny said. "I thought it was cute, but now I'm going to have to push out his giant baby." She pretended to shudder, and Jack rolled his eyes.

They spent the next few minutes exchanging headlines—Jack was an accountant, Penny worked at Briarwood Speech and Language out by the mall, and they'd just bought a house on the Old West Side, a neighborhood full of stately Victorians with gingerbread trim. "I'm at Big Earth," Estie said when it was her turn. "And Owen is a professor at Norton. Or he was. He just got laid off." She thought it was a good sign that she managed to say this last part without her voice cracking, although she did have to blink a few times when Penny said, "Oh no. Poor him. And poor you."

"Oh, we're fine," Estie said, careful to keep her voice light. "He'll find something else—there are, like, a million colleges between here and Detroit." Then, as if suddenly remembering, she added, "Speaking of Owen, his ice cream is melting. So great to run into you. I'll see you around?"

Penny nodded, and that would have been the end of it, but Jack had apparently never heard of Michigan invites and how everyone knew they were only for show, and so, just as Estie turned to leave, he pulled a pen and a crumpled receipt out of his pants pocket. "Wait a second," he said, tearing the receipt in half. "You two should exchange phone numbers."

Back in the duplex, Owen was still asleep, so Estie slid his shake into the freezer, then worked herself up into a state of righteous indignation on his behalf—because anger had to be better than panic—before calling Alice to fill her in. "All those weekends of grading," she said, "and for what?"

"But I thought he had tenure," Alice said.

"I know!" Estie said. "Can you believe it?"

She waited for Alice to say something else, something equivalent to Penny's "Poor you," or "I'm sorry," or "Those assholes." But instead, what Alice said was, "I didn't think colleges worked like that."

"Well, they do," Estie told her. "They can lay you off if they run out of money." She felt incandescent with rage, so much so that even the warm purring weight of Herbert on her chest was doing nothing to settle her down.

"Did they have to lay off a lot of people?" Alice asked.

"I don't know. Probably? I didn't think to ask." Even Estie could hear the whine in her own voice. She loved Alice, her logic, her ability to advise Estie through flight delays and corrupted Word documents, but this—Owen losing his job—was different. There was no logic to it, at least no logic that didn't involve moving numbers from one budget line to another. "I mean, we just found out."

Alice was quiet for a few seconds. "I'm sorry. Is there anything I can do?"

By then, it was too little, too late—everyone knew that a *sorry* you had to solicit didn't really count—so Estie just said, "Thank you. I don't think so." And then, because she didn't want Alice to hang up mad, she said, "At least Herbert is having a good day." Alice was the one who had given her Herbert, the one who had driven all the way from Chicago to Briarwood with kitten Herbert in a soft-sided carrier after Dan, Estie's college boyfriend, had ghosted Estie. Up until then, Estie hadn't even known she'd wanted a cat, but after that first night of Herbert sleeping between her knees like a small, thrumming hot-water bottle, there had been no question she was keeping him. "How'd you know?" she'd asked Alice over breakfast, and Alice had shrugged: "I just did."

Now, Estie held the phone to Herbert's neck so that Alice could hear him purr, and maybe that in itself was enough, because by the time they'd hung up, Estie felt calmer. It wasn't as if the world was ending. Somehow, she and Owen would be fine.

3

ALTHOUGH NORMALLY ESTIE DIDN'T WORK Saturdays, that Saturday had been Big Earth's Boneyard Sale. The Boneyard Sale happened twice a year, in February and in August, when Big Earth freed up storage by selling remnants by the pound to people who normally couldn't afford hand-crafted midcentury modern tiles. Back when Estie was in high school, it had taken her mother three years' worth of Boneyard Sales to collect enough tiles to reface the fireplace, and then, before the weather got cold enough to actually build a fire, her parents divorced and sold the house. In the public version of the story, the one Estie told at her job interview all those years ago, her mother had wept upon exiting the living room for the last time. In real life, she'd merely muttered, "The new owners better fucking appreciate this," before slamming the front door behind her. By that point, Estie's mother rarely cried—swearing, she told Estie, was infinitely more satisfying and effective. Either way, it made for a good story, and Estie had gotten the job.

While Estie got ready for work, Owen sat at the kitchen worrying, his mouth pinched, his stare unfocused. She set a box of cornflakes and milk in front of him. "You've got to eat something," she said. When Owen didn't say anything, she brought him a spoon, then reached for his hands and placed them on her belly, where the baby was doing his morning stretches in a bath of cortisol and Owen's milkshake from the previous night, which she'd ended up drinking. "Don't worry so much," she told him. "We're smart. We can figure out health care and unemployment and all that stuff."

For the first time that morning, Owen looked at her directly. His eyes were wet and rimmed with red, but that might have just been the cat allergies. "You can't get unemployment for academic jobs. I checked."

"Okay," Estie said. "Then we'll just figure out health insurance." And really, that part was already figured out, because she'd just add him to her policy at Big Earth. "See?" she wanted to tell someone—Her mom? Alice? The former classmates she occasionally ran into at Kroger?—"See? It's not such a dumb job after all." Not that people thought her job was stupid, but they did seem to regard it as a passing whim, a temporary reprieve from the life Estie was supposed to be living, a life in which she'd have to wear business casual clothes and sit in front of a computer. To be fair, Estie had thought so too, at least initially, except then it turned out that she loved her work, the precision of glazing, the steady hands it required, the way that, at the end of the day, she could literally see all the work she'd done: geometric orange sunbursts, lineal hummingbirds, yellow poppies abstracted into angles. And thank goodness for that, because what if she'd quit Big Earth to move to Norton and work in some kind of minimum-wage admin job with no benefits, and *then* Owen had been laid off?

The Boneyard Sale was always a zoo, crowded with people sorting frantically through factory seconds and lugging around heavy boxes with their quarry. Estie's job that afternoon was working the popcorn popper so that customers could fortify themselves for the long wait in line to pay. The popper was one of those red and white old-fashioned machines with wheels, and less than an hour into the sale, Estie's hands were slick with oil and she desperately wanted to sit down. She abandoned her station and went to get a chair from the lunchroom, crossing the line of waiting people that snaked through the building, skirting the tile presses and kilns and weaving its way through the racks of tiles awaiting firing. She led with her belly, holding the chair way up high over her head, but nobody offered to help her—shopping for handmade luxury items apparently blinded people to pregnant women carrying heavy objects. "Excuse me," she said to a woman with a sensible mom haircut who was blocking her way. The woman turned and gasped, and that's when Estie realized it was Cathy, the English department secretary from Norton, holding a box of green field tiles.

"Oh, Estie," Cathy said—stammered a little, in fact. "I forgot you work here."

Norton was far enough away from Briarwood that Estie didn't usually run into people Owen knew from work unless they were making the trek to Costco—Briarwood, with its two Targets and a Trader Joe's, was a bustling metropolis compared to Norton and its sad little FreshMart. Still, people came to the Boneyard Sale from as far as Indiana, so it wasn't all that weird to run into Cathy, whom Estie had always liked because she sent her e-cards on her birthday.

Cathy cleared her throat. "How are you? How's the—" She gestured at Estie's belly.

"We're good," Estie said. "Except, well, the whole thing with Owen."

Cathy hesitated, and Estie could tell she was choosing her words carefully. "For what it's worth," she said finally, "I'm really sorry."

Estie nodded. "Yeah, I had no idea that the college was in that much trouble."

"Trouble?" Cathy looked surprised.

"You know," Estie said, "laying people off."

"Laying people off?"

Estie stared at her. Was it possible that Cathy didn't know? And if she didn't, why exactly was she sorry about Owen? The noise in the room seemed to recede, and Estie could feel sweat gathering at her hairline and pooling in her armpits. "Owen was laid off," she tried again, "because the college is in financial trouble?"

A mix of emotions flashed across Cathy's face—confusion, surprise, understanding—before she settled on something resembling embarrassment. "Oh, Estie, sweetie," she said finally, her voice so full of pity that Estie could feel her own breath catch. "I don't know what Owen told you, but he wasn't laid off. He was fired."

Estie didn't know what it said about her that the first reaction was humiliation not just for Owen, but also for herself, for the fact that she now owed Alice an apology. She poured another cup of kernels into the popcorn machine's pan and watched Cathy work her way to the front of the line and pay for her tiles, careful to avoid so much as a glance in Estie's direction. Not that Estie could blame her. Owen must have done something awful, like embezzling or having an affair with a student, except that Owen was too honest to embezzle. Owen having an affair, on the other hand, made sense: How many times had Estie driven to campus to meet him for an evening event only to spend a few minutes sitting on the bench outside his office while he finished up with an overly earnest girl in a low-cut tank top and too much eye makeup? Sure, his door had been wide open, but that didn't change the fact that Owen was the youngest and most crush-worthy of the three men in the English department, the other two of whom were already well into the too-much-nose-hair stage of life.

Somehow, Estie managed to finish working and drive home, but when she walked into the duplex Owen took one look at her and immediately leaped into what she privately considered his superhero stance—legs wide, arms crossed, jaw tightly clenched—and demanded to know what was wrong.

For a long moment, they studied each other, and then Estie said, "Did you have an affair with a student?"

Owen gaped at her. "God no, Estie," he said. "Who do you think I—"

"Cathy was at the sale. She said you were fired."

"Oh," Owen said. "Oh." He relaxed his stance, then closed

his eyes as if the truth were too awful to bear. "That's not what happened."

"Then what *did* happen?"

Owen sighed. "They found out the truth."

"Found out what truth?"

"That I don't have a Ph.D."

It took Estie a few seconds to process what he was saying. "You don't?"

Owen shook his head. He looked so miserable, so worn out, that Estie could feel her heart contract. Poor Owen. "I never finished my dissertation," he said. "I guess everybody just assumed." Then, much to Estie's horror, he covered his face with his hands and began to weep. She guided him over to the couch, then sat down next to him, rubbing his back. Although she suspected she should've been upset that he hadn't told her the truth up front, more than anything, she felt relieved: it hadn't been an affair, just a misunderstanding. "It's not your fault," she said, trying to console him. "It's all just a mix-up. Can't you just finish your degree now?"

"Oh, Estie," Owen said, sounding so wistful that Estie stopped breathing. "That's not how it works."

"People drop out of school and go back all the time," Estie said, and when Owen didn't answer, she added, "And everybody gets fired at some point. I got fired from Arby's in high school. For failing to properly secure the slicer."

Owen sniffled. "Like that's even the same thing."

"I know it isn't," Estie said, because clearly it wasn't. She'd still been living with her parents then. And she most definitely hadn't been pregnant.

That evening, she and Owen sat down with the laptop and a list of expenses, Owen patiently adding everything up to a number far greater than what Estie made at Big Earth. He checked their savings account and did some quick division. "We have enough for six months," he told Estie, "more if you don't take all twelve weeks of your leave."

"But no house," Estie said. It wasn't fair. What did Owen's degree even matter? When you typed "Are Ph.D.s" into Google, autocomplete suggested: ". . . a waste of time." You didn't need a Ph.D. to get a job, or make a decent salary, or join a country club. And Estie had read some of the papers Owen was always grading: you didn't need a Ph.D. to teach freshmen either.

For the millionth time that evening, Estie thought back to when she'd first met Owen, at the Burger King off I-94. He'd been on his way to a conference in Cleveland, and Estie, somewhat out of practice after three and a half years with Dan, hadn't been sure if he was flirting with her while they waited for a tired-looking woman in a hairnet to fry up some onion rings. But he *had* been flirting with her, and two days later, on his way back to Norton, she'd agreed to meet him for Chinese. The restaurant had been busy, and while they waited for a table, Owen told Estie about the time he'd been nine or so and came home crying because he'd hit Amy Johnson, the love of his young life, and she'd stopped speaking to him. Owen's mother had listened to kid Owen's tale of woe, then gone to one of the bookshelves, pulled down *Anne of Green Gables*, and handed it over. "I loved that book *so much*," Owen told Estie, and Estie suddenly understood what people meant when they said someone was a keeper. Something must have shown on her face, because Owen said, "What? You don't like Anne?" And later, after kissing her sweetly and without tongue, he said, "You should probably know that I'm looking for something serious." His hands were warm on her shoulders, and his mouth tasted like the wine they'd had along with dessert, and Estie was surprised to discover she felt charmed.

Now, watching Owen move numbers from one column to another, Estie tried to remember when, in those early days of falling in love, they might have talked about his degree, but she couldn't imagine when it would have even come up. There was no way around it: she must have assumed he had a Ph.D. just like everyone in his department.

Still, the whole ordeal felt like a dirty little secret, something that required euphemisms if not outright dishonesty. The following day, when Estie called Alice to tell her she'd been right, that Owen hadn't told Estie the entire truth about losing his job, at least not right away, the words caught in her throat and she couldn't do it. "Come visit," she'd said instead, even though Alice didn't like coming to Michigan, hadn't been to Michigan, in fact, since Estie and Owen's wedding three years earlier.

"I wish I could," Alice said, "but there's an update due in at the end of the month."

"Just like the baby," Estie pointed out.

"Actually," Alice said slowly, "not at all like the baby."

Why did Estie keep doing this, insisting that they talk about the baby even though Alice couldn't be any less interested? "Promise me," Alice had said early on in the pregnancy, "that you won't be like those mommies who can't talk about anything except their babies," and Estie had promised, and she'd kept her promise *most* of the time, only slipping when the baby was kicking hard or she was irritated with Alice. And the baby *was* kicking hard and she *was* irritated with Alice, unfairly so. "I'm sorry," she said before hanging up. "I guess I'm just stressed."

"Yes," Alice said, her voice gentle. "Of course you're stressed. I'm sorry too."

Later that night, Estie texted Alice another apology, just in case. Although they'd been friends since freshman year of college, Estie still couldn't shake the conviction that their friendship was fragile and tenuous. Girls like Alice, with her peaches-and-cream complexion, her perfect nose, her gray eyes and pale eyelashes, didn't belong with ordinary girls like Estie. No. Girls like Alice belonged in a clothing catalog for rich, outdoorsy people who enjoyed standing alone in front of abandoned lighthouses, a golden retriever by their side.

Estie sat back on the couch and propped her feet up on a pillow, which Herbert took as an invitation to wedge himself between her ankles, and spent the next hour flipping through channels and waiting for Alice to text her back. Which she did, eventually, although all she'd sent was a yellow thumbs-up. *Whatever*, Estie told herself. She turned off the television and opened her browser and clicked over to babybelly.com, which featured picture after picture of women's pregnant bellies, belly buttons poking out as if ready to burst. At the bottom of the screen, there was a counter that measured website traffic, and Estie watched it tick up, then up again, as other pregnant women, women she didn't know and would probably never meet, sat down bleary-eyed in front of their own computers, unable to sleep as well.

4

AND THEN THEY WERE AT thirty-seven weeks, and Owen had somehow managed to line up five intro writing courses at three different colleges in three different Detroit suburbs, the closest one a full forty-five minutes away, but at least now, he explained, they'd be able to cover day care. The afternoon he signed the last set of HR papers, he marked the occasion by coming home with a crib from Target, this despite Estie's mother's insistence that it was dangerous to count a baby before it hatched if you didn't want to find yourself tearfully scraping bunny-and-giraffe wallpaper off the walls of the nursery. This was, her mother explained, why Jews didn't do baby showers, didn't wash and fold onesies, didn't assemble a crib in preparation for the baby's arrival—why ask for trouble? Not that any of this stopped her mother from stocking up on tiny T-shirts with slogans like "Boy: noun. A noise with dirt on it" and "Daddy's Little Wingman" and "I like big boobs and I cannot lie." God, how Estie hated baby clothes that took advantage of babies' indifference to dignity and, if low retail price were any indication, child labor, but her mom refused to stop: "*I'm* not the one having the baby," she pointed out, then added, "And I'm keeping all the receipts."

"Your mom's God must be really easy to fool," Owen had noted when Estie showed him a *Star Wars*–themed onesie that read "Storm pooper," but that had been before he lost his job, thereby proving Estie's mother's God wasn't so easy to fool after all, a fact that should have given him pause, but didn't: "We're full term," he said now. "We need to get ready."

Estie was tired, and her feet were swollen, and just standing up made her breathless. And here was Owen, going around jinxing everything with his impatience, practically guaranteeing the birth wouldn't go as planned.

As if reading her mind, Owen said, "It's just a crib. It's just a mattress." He blew his nose into an old Snoopy pillowcase that he'd cut up into squares. The pillowcase, he claimed, was softer than tissues and less expensive than handkerchiefs, which nobody even used anymore. He left the cloth squares, which he called snot rags, everywhere—tucked between couch cushions, tangled in bedsheets—but Estie couldn't complain: Herbert was her cat. She had to accept the consequences.

"Your allergies are getting worse," she observed.

"Don't change the subject."

"Fine," Estie said, too hot to argue. It was almost the end of August, and the duplex didn't have air conditioning, and, full term or no, it still wasn't clear to her how she was going to get the baby out of her body despite her father's repeated observations that every thirty-five seconds, in some "less nice" part of the world, a peasant woman squatted in the middle of a field, pushed out a baby, and immediately resumed thatching the roof of her cottage. "Women have been doing this for thousands of years," he liked to tell Estie, which really wasn't all that different in substance from the unwavering faith in Inner Wisdom touted by Rita, the childbirth instructor. Then again, Estie's father lived on a golf course in Florida and had never attended an actual birth, and Estie didn't really trust Rita, with her belief in the healing powers of essential oils and penchant for reenacting her own labor, which involved moaning, "Oh fuck! That hurts! Fuck!" with increasing volume. Not that giving birth was about dignity, Estie reminded herself. It was about getting out alive.

And so: "Inner Wisdom," Estie whispered to herself as she watched Owen assemble the crib. "Inner Wisdom." It didn't help. She was still too hot. The baby was still coming.

Now that Jillian was back from her parental leave, she had taken to pumping in the corner of the glazers' workroom, which was air-conditioned so that their sweat wouldn't mar the glaze. "It's either this or the bathroom," she explained, "and we're all women here." It wasn't the pumping Estie minded so much as the way Jillian talked, which made it seem as if motherhood were an endless cycle of feeding and pumping and not enough sleep, punctuated by the occasional blowout. "You don't know what you're in for," Jillian liked to say whenever her eyes met Estie's. "Just you wait." And then she'd say, "God, I'm starving. Anybody up for lunch?"

This was why, despite the hot, humid weather, Estie chose to eat her lunch outside. She sat at a table shaded by a couple of maple trees, and between the smell of freshly mown grass and the slight breeze, she felt her shoulders loosen, her breathing slow. She unpacked the lunch Owen had prepared—sandwich, carrot sticks, a hard-boiled egg, and a note with a heart and the words "We'll get through this"—and just for a moment, she allowed herself to feel hopeful. And then, as if on cue, her phone rang, and it was Alice, who rarely called rather than texted, and who certainly never called in the middle of the day. Estie felt herself stiffen—it had to be something bad, a car accident or cancer. "What's wrong?"

"Are you at work?"

"Yes," Estie said. "What happened?"

"Nothing," Alice said. "It's just, well . . ." She trailed off.

Alice found a lump, Estie thought.

"Okay," Alice started again. "So listen . . ."

Alice was getting married. Alice had eloped. "Just tell me."

"It's about Owen," Alice said. "About his job. Something wasn't sitting right with me, so I googled it . . . and . . . Well, I'm sending you a link."

"What?"

"Do you want me to stay on the phone while you read?"

"What?" Estie said again. "No. I'm fine."

"Are you sure?"

Estie hung up. For a moment, she considered not clicking on the link Alice had sent, but then she decided she had to. Anyway, what could Alice have possibly found? A student complaint? Owen's ratemyprofessor.com page? She waited impatiently for her browser to load, and when it did, it was to a recently published article in *The Jackson Times*, mean-spirited headline and everything: "Those Who Can't, Teach." Below the headline, in smaller letters, the bolded text read, "Local professor dismissed for faking degree." And there it was, Owen's picture straight off his faculty ID, along with a picture of a grim college president who, with her sleek bob and sleeveless navy shift, looked like she could be delivering the evening's weather. "We don't tolerate academic dishonesty in our students, and we certainly will not tolerate it among our professors," she was quoted as saying. "It goes against everything a top-notch liberal-arts college represents." According to the president, Owen had been hired on the condition that he complete his dissertation and defend it before the end of his third year of employment. When the deadline rolled around, he'd dutifully presented the college's Dean of Academic Affairs with a letter from his graduate school department chair saying that he had completed all requirements and earned his Ph.D., a letter which later turned out to have been faked. "We now request official transcripts from all our professors," the college president explained. "We never imagined someone would be capable of such deceit." It had only been freakish luck, in fact, that brought the whole fiasco to the college's attention: the chair of the English department at Norton was asked to serve on a panel with Owen's grad school adviser, and the two had gotten to talking.

Estie sat back and tried to process what she'd read, but she felt as if she'd been swaddled in thick, heavy cotton, as if the rumble of the garbage truck that was passing by right then was coming at her from very far away. She'd met Owen in November of his third year at Norton. It didn't take a genius to figure out that he must have faked the document after he'd already known her, after he'd begun spending every weekend with her in Briarwood, after she'd already cared about him and felt as if she'd just narrowly been rescued—as if *he'd* just narrowly rescued her—although she still wasn't sure exactly why she'd needed rescuing so badly, or from what. But in all that time, and in all the time since he'd been fired, Owen had been lying, telling the kind of lies that required sneakiness and planning and outright fraud, and Estie had been oblivious, as oblivious as oblivious could be.

Estie could feel a bout of ugly crying coming on, except that Ryan and Ben, the guys who ran the kilns, were also outside, sitting at a different picnic table, smoking and talking about baseball. She closed her eyes and tried to take what Rita liked to call a deep, cleansing breath, but her distress wasn't good enough for her mother's vengeful God, who apparently wanted to make sure she got the message loud and clear: when she opened her eyes, a doe was standing on the edge of the woods, head cocked as if testing the air. That in itself wasn't unusual—people at Big Earth regularly left out apples or carrots for the deer as a kind of last supper before they attempted to cross I-94. What was unusual was that this doe was ill, very ill, maybe even dying. Her neck and forelegs were covered by dark, fleshy growths, some scratched and bleeding, others dangling from her hide like freakish Christmas ornaments or stalks of cauliflower gone bad.

Ben and Ryan must have seen the doe too, because Ben gasped and Ryan said, "Holy shit," and adjusted the brim of his Tigers cap so that it covered more of his eyes. For a moment, all three of them gaped at the doe, and then Ben stammered, "Rabies?"

Ryan hurriedly stubbed out his cigarette. "Don't know. Don't care. Let's just get out of here." He gestured at Estie's belly. "You especially." Estie swept her lunch back into her bag, and the three of them bolted toward the back door and headed inside, and all that movement must have startled the doe, because by the time everyone gathered around the windows, it was gone.

She ignored the follow-up texts from Alice—"I thought I'd hear from you by now. You okay?"—because what could she say? Was there anything worse than hearing your husband had actively lied to you, that he was guilty of more than simple omission, from the one person who had been suspicious of him all along? How big of an *I told you so* did Estie even need? *Fuck it*, she told herself, and instead of returning to work, she told Sylvia she was sick. She wasn't ready to go home yet, so she drove to Target, where she walked up and down the bright aisles unseeingly until the baby elbowed her from the inside as if instructing her to stop. She looked up to discover she was in the baby section. "Fuck it," she said again. It wasn't as if Owen and her mother hadn't already jinxed the baby. She spent the next fifteen minutes buying a bouncy seat, a baby gym, a set of pale-yellow onesies, and, in a moment of weakness, two sets of novelty pacifiers in the shape of vampire teeth, one for her and one, she suddenly realized, for Penny. Penny? Yes, *Penny*. Because what Estie needed right then was someone exactly like Penny, someone who was also pregnant, who would understand what it meant to be tired and hormonal and so goddamn hot in a way Alice and Owen simply couldn't. And Penny had always been so *nice*, had held Estie's hand through Estie's parents' divorce, had told Estie which questions would be on the history exam she'd taken during first period and Estie would be taking during third. Penny. Estie searched through her purse for the receipt with Penny's number and, after several minutes of careful consideration, entered it into her phone, typing, "It's Estie. Want to have brunch sometime? Or more ice cream?"

"Definitely ice cream," Penny texted back. "I'm so hot I might combust."

"I made lasagna," Owen announced when Estie walked in the door. When he saw the Target bags, he added, "What's all this?"

Estie was starving and exhausted. She'd spent nearly $400 on baby gear, and another $20 on fuzzy socks in case it was cold in the hospital, but instead of a buyer's high, all she felt was dread. She collapsed on the couch, where Herbert, who had been grooming himself on the middle cushion, butted his head against her right thigh in greeting. "I saw the article."

"What article?"

Was it really possible that Owen didn't know? "Here," Estie said, handing him her phone. "This."

Owen glanced at the screen and—was Estie imagining it?—blanched. "It's in the paper?"

"It says they tried to reach you."

"Well," Owen said, "they didn't reach me." He gave her back the phone and crossed his arms over his chest. Then, as if thinking better of it, he moved his hands to his hips and assumed his wide-legged superhero stance. It wasn't a good sign.

"You lied to me," Estie said. She'd been practicing saying it all through Target and all the way home.

"About what?"

"It wasn't just a misunderstanding. You faked your Ph.D."

"Okay," Owen said. "But I didn't lie to *you*."

"How can you say that?" Estie started to ask, but just then there was a knock at the front door. She checked the time on her phone. "Shit," she said. "Yoga." Her mother had a habit of dropping by on her way to other places, the gym or the grocery store, to perform what Estie thought of as random inspections—Was the floor swept? Were the plants watered? Was Estie engaged in a meaningful and productive task like making soup? *"I can't,"* she mouthed at Owen because she really couldn't, but it was too late and Estie's mother was already unlocking the door. Why had they given her a key? Estie knew why—so her mother could stop in and feed the cat when they were out of town—but still. Stupid cat.

"Smells good in here," her mother said, then eyed Estie from bottom to top. "You're not picking at those pimples, are you?"

Estie and Owen exchanged glances. "Mom," Estie said, trying to keep her voice steady. "Please don't."

Her mother gave her an appraising look. "You okay? You look upset."

"I'm fine," Estie said, but it was no use. Her mother so rarely asked her how she was feeling that on those occasions she did, it had the same lachrymatory effect as cutting onions. How did her mother always manage to sense her at her weakest, and why did Estie always fall for it even though she knew what would happen next? Her mother's gaze, all that concentrated attention, would go straight to Estie's head, and she would tell her mother everything and feel fabulously unburdened for a second or two, at which point her mother would swoop in with an additional insight or some piece of advice that always amounted to the same thing—"There are children starving in Sudan. Get some real problems, and then we'll talk"—after which her mother would resume whatever it was that she'd been doing before she'd noticed Estie was sad and leave Estie alone to contemplate her own small-mindedness.

"Oh, Estie," her mother said now, offering her a Kleenex she'd magically produced from the opening of her left sleeve, "this is the worst part of pregnancy. The final stretch of waiting." She checked her watch—she was the only person Estie knew who still wore an analog watch. "I've got five minutes. Walk me out to the car?"

Estie swallowed a sigh and trailed her mother to the front door, where she slipped on Owen's flip-flops because her feet were too swollen for her own. "Your ankles seem to have gone missing," her mother observed, but once they were outside, she turned serious and said, "What's wrong? Is it the baby?"

"No," Estie said. "It's this whole thing with Owen's job."

"Oh," her mother said. "That."

"It isn't nothing."

"No," her mother agreed. "But this is Michigan. He's not the first man to lose his job and he won't be the last. And he's already found something else. You won't starve."

"But he . . ." Estie couldn't tell her mother. She couldn't. ". . . let everyone think that he had a Ph.D."

"And?" Her mother looked blank.

"So I thought he had a Ph.D."

"So?" Her mother checked her watch again, then began digging in her purse. "Look," she said, all business once she'd located her car keys, "he isn't cheating on you, right? Or hitting you? Or spending money you don't have?"

Estie shook her head no.

"Then you're fine," her mother continued. "Your job right now is to have that baby and keep it alive, and believe me, you're going to want Owen on board for that. The next few months are going to be hard, and this isn't the time for fights that don't matter." She glanced at her watch again. "I have to go or I'm going to end up in the back of the room where I can't see the instructor."

Normally, by this point in the conversation, Estie would have stopped crying and gone numb, possibly with rage, but that was before she'd gotten pregnant and hormonal. How could anyone cry so much, she wondered as she watched her mother drive off. Then she took a few deep breaths, dried her eyes on her T-shirt—the Kleenex had disintegrated by then—and headed back inside to Owen, who, Ph.D. or no, had made her lasagna from scratch and never asked her to contemplate other people's much greater pain.

"Good, huh?" Owen said after she'd downed two pieces under his watchful gaze. And then, after a couple of preparatory nervous swallows, he said, "You googled me?"

"What?"

"The article."

Estie stood up and began stacking dishes in the dishwasher. "Alice sent me the link."

Owen sighed. "Of course she did."

"What's that supposed to mean?"

"She never liked me."

For a moment, Estie stared at him in disbelief. His beard was coming in, and he was wearing the same clothes he'd worn the previous day, if not also the day before that. She wondered when the last time was that he'd brushed his teeth. "Well," she said, "good work. Way to prove her wrong."

5

THE BABY MUST HAVE TAKEN Estie's Target shopping spree as a sign that it was time, because at four a.m. that very night, Estie awoke to a deep, dull ache and a belly so tight it took her breath away. Then the pain dispersed, and she padded to the bathroom, peed, then whispered, "Mucus plug" to her reflection in the mirror, a woman who looked just like her but with a puffier face and larger breasts and an even bigger mound of a belly. Poor mirrored fool—she didn't know what was coming. "Sweet, sweet coffee," Estie whispered encouragingly to her reflection. "Sweet, sweet nonmaternity pants." She considered whether it was worth waking Owen up, but the pain wasn't bad and the contractions were still pretty far apart, so she let him sleep until six a.m., when she finally nudged him awake and said, just like all those women on TV and in the movies, "It's time." She was unexpectedly calm and exhilarated, actually looking forward to meeting the baby. "He's coming!!!!" she texted Alice, who didn't text back because she was probably still asleep, and then Penny. "OMG," Penny texted back. "Good luck!" By then the contractions were regular but nothing Estie couldn't handle. She clutched Owen's hand

and breathed through them, then ate the breakfast he made her—six scrambled eggs for the protein, four slices of whole wheat toast for the complex carbs—double-checked the contents of her hospital bag—clean underwear, that stupid baby hat that had taken her four months to knit, her new fuzzy socks—and called the Labor and Delivery triage nurse for instructions.

"I don't know, honey," said the nurse, "you don't sound stressed. Why don't you just stay at home for now? We're swamped anyways." It was what the triage nurse said every time Estie called, which she did at regular two-hour intervals. "Have you tried a warm shower?" the triage nurse asked. "Have you gone for a walk?"

"I might've spoken too soon," Estie texted Penny because Alice still hadn't texted her back. She looked at the duffel waiting patiently by the door and felt ridiculous for having packed it back in July: in the time since that first contraction, she could have packed seventeen bags, double- and triple-checked each one of them, and still been able to go out to lunch and to a movie, which was what she did. It was one of those warm end-of-summer days, and she and Owen sat at an outside table at the restaurant and ate extra-large meaty sandwiches on large brown rolls, for even more protein and even more complex carbs, then saw a film in which the main character went into labor, screamed for a while, and delivered her dead lover's son, his only legacy, in under five minutes, or was it under six? It was hard for Estie to concentrate, but it was harder not to be bitter.

"I guess they don't want us," Estie told Owen after calling triage yet again. Then she started to cry. It wasn't that the contractions were bad, but they were relentless, and she was ready for them to stop. Time slowed down to a trickle.

"Call again," Owen told her. "Maybe the nurse will believe you now."

The nurse didn't, but Estie made Owen take her to the hospital anyway. She lay on a cot, her legs spread, and waited for the nurse to exclaim, "You got here just in time!" But all the nurse did was poke around, then announce, "Two centimeters. Have you tried taking a walk?"

By the time she was finally admitted—around midnight—Estie couldn't muster up one ounce of Inner Wisdom. All that walking, all that laboring, and she was still stuck at two centimeters. "Do you want to get in the hot tub?" the L&D nurse asked. "Do you want me to dim the lights?"

"No," Estie said. "Just make it stop," and the nurse pursed her lips in what could have only been disapproval and ordered an epidural. And just like that, Estie was flat on her back, hooked up to four different IV drips. "Listen," she told the baby, "you're on your own now. Good luck." By then, the pain had subsided, and Owen was snoring in the recliner next to her. He could sleep anywhere. Estie watched him for a while, disgusted by all that gargling in the back of his throat, by the way his mouth hung open and lax. Who was this stranger next to her, this man who left her alone in what, she thought dramatically, was clearly her time of need?

At seven a.m., the doctor on call came by to break Estie's water. "Four centimeters," she reported. "It's time to move things along." The nurse nodded and hung another bag of fluid on the IV stand. "This'll get him out of there," she said. Then she went off duty and was replaced by a bouffant-wearing nurse who asked, "Did you try the hot tub?" and wrinkled her nose every time she changed the waterproof pads on which Estie was lying.

"Why does she have to be so *mean?*" Estie muttered. Owen patted her leg sleepily, but she couldn't feel his hand, not really.

To pass the time, Estie alternated between counting the ceiling tiles and watching the MedFlight helicopter take off and land on a nearby roof. Then, at ten a.m., bored, she called Alice, who still hadn't gotten back to her.

"I'm in a meeting," Alice said. "I'll call you back."

"I'm in the hospital," Estie said, but Alice had already hung up.

It wasn't as if Estie had expected Alice to drop everything just to come see her, but she'd hoped. There were plenty of precedents for this, after all: all the times Estie had driven to Chicago to help Alice move apartments, and the time Alice had appendicitis and her parents were in Europe and Estie had dropped everything and rushed to her side. And yes, all that had been years ago now, when Estie had still been single, and these days she and Alice were no longer each other's first call, but surely it wasn't unreasonable for Estie to expect an occasional "How's it going?" or "You can do it!" text. She was having a child, for God's sake, which was at least as big a deal as losing an appendix.

"I don't think Alice likes me anymore," Estie told Owen the next time he woke up.

Owen yawned twice, then said, "This maybe"—another yawn—"isn't the best time to evaluate your friendships."

"Better my friendships than my marriage," Estie said, glowering, and then resumed counting the ceiling tiles until the doctor stopped by, and, unimpressed by Estie's cervix's progress, suggested a Pitocin drip: "Now this will really get him out of there."

At noon, Penny walked in, eyes shining, holding a small stuffed bear. "I'm here for an ultrasound and thought I'd say hi. I can't believe it's finally happening!"

Estie glanced down at her legs, which she couldn't quite feel, but all she saw was her own gigantic belly and the tube connected to the catheter. Her hair, she thought, was probably all matted and greasy. "This is Penny," she told Owen. "We were friends in high school."

Penny reached over to squeeze Estie's hand: "How bad is it?" She looked good, Estie thought. Glowing, hair pulled back into a messy bun. If she was thinking anything about all the tubing and monitors surrounding Estie, she didn't show it.

"I had an epidural," Estie admitted. "So mainly it's just boring."

"Did they give you any morphine?"

Estie shook her head no.

"That's too bad," Penny said. "I heard it's awesome." She started to say something else, but right then the evil nurse walked in. "Time to drain the urine bag!" the nurse announced gleefully, then flipped up the edge of the sheet that was, presumably— because Estie couldn't actually see for herself, beached whale that she was—covering up the bag, which was hanging off the bed frame. Estie felt herself flush. "Oh God," she told Penny, "you didn't need to see that."

"See what?" Penny squeezed Estie's hand a second time before moving out of the evil nurse's way. "I better go—Jack's waiting down in the lobby—but you can do this. I know it."

Estie nodded. It wasn't as if she had a choice. And at least it was Penny who had seen her bag of urine and not Alice, who had always been nervous around body fluids, as evidenced by the fact that she never got wasted and hadn't given her first hand job until well into their senior year.

The evil nurse disconnected the urine bag from the catheter tubing and poured its contents into a large measuring cup, wrinkling her nose yet again. "How can a nurse be so easily grossed out?" Estie asked Owen after she'd left the room. "Especially in obstetrics?" She craned her neck to check the time. "Her shift better end soon, because I'm not giving birth in front of her."

Owen smiled but didn't say anything, at least about the nurse. "I don't think you've ever mentioned Penny."

"No," Estie said. "We grew apart."

Owen waited for her to say more, but she didn't. "Want some apple juice?"

"Sure," Estie said, because was there anything that tasted better than apple juice over ice when you were in the hospital and not allowed to eat on the off chance you ended up needing surgery? That small pleasure hadn't been covered in their childbirth class, although it wasn't as if Estie's labor was looking anything like the labors in all those videos they'd watched. You never saw the women in childbirth videos tethered to machines and baggies of fluids while a TV blared in the background. No, the women in those videos were focused, calm, quiet except for an occasional low moan, the kind of women who, if they ever deigned to turn on their hospital-room TVs, would no doubt choose to watch something that was critically acclaimed—*Citizen Kane* or *To Kill a Mockingbird*, or maybe, if they were Jewish, *Schindler's List*. Estie was nothing like those women, had never been like those women in the first place, and the thought filled her with despair. She was thirty-two; when, exactly, was she going to stop feeling like an insecure teenager? Wasn't bonding with Penny over pregnancy just as pathetic as bonding with her because Estie didn't want to sit alone in the cafeteria, especially given that there hadn't been one single day in high school when she hadn't longed to be sitting with someone else, someone more popular and more connected than Penny, someone who would sling an affectionate arm around Estie's neck and invite her to share a limo to prom? That hadn't happened, of course, and Estie ended up going to prom with Joseph Van Vranken, a skinny, big-headed kid who went on to become a wealthy hedge-fund manager in custom-tailored suits that disguised his lack of proportion. Naturally, Estie hadn't known that he'd end up doing so well, and so she'd spent most of the evening trying not to stare at his pimply skin, which was so tantalizingly close she could make out the individual pores even in the dim light of the disco ball. After the prom, instead of taking Estie straight home, Joseph Van Vranken parked his beat-up Ford Escort on a dark side street, then turned toward her and put a hand on her boob. Which was fine, Estie told herself. It was just a boob, and it was important to consider other people's feelings—unless, as Estie's mother warned her time and time again, you wanted to end up divorced and living on a golf course in Florida. After all, what if it had been Estie sticking her hand down an unsuspecting Joseph's pants? And what if he'd responded by telling her to stop? Wouldn't he in fact be saying that even though he was seventeen and spent all his free time thinking about girls doing things to his penis—"His *cock*," Penny would have corrected her—he found Estie so unappealing that he preferred to go untouched? No, thank you. If there was such a thing as karma, then Estie was going to do her goddamn best to be open-minded and generous, the kind of person who understood that awkward teenage boys with bad skin and greasy hair also deserved to feel that sex was within their reach. So she'd just sat there and waited it out until Joseph Van Vranken put his hands back on the steering wheel and took her home, where she brushed her teeth and washed her face and, when that didn't get rid of the smell of his saliva on her skin, took a full-on shower and never told anyone what happened because even though she'd done the right thing—she was certain of that much at least—she kept imagining how slutty and awkward she must have looked being groped by Joseph Van Vranken, her boobs hanging over the top of her dress. She would have rather died than invite anyone—even Penny, who would have probably been disgusted on her behalf—to imagine her in that position. And maybe that was the beginning of the end of her friendship with Penny, or at least the end of the part where they were close and told each other everything, because after that night, Estie completely gave up on high school and decided to just hunker down and bide her time until college, where she would finally be free, if not exactly to be herself—because who wanted that?—then at least to not be some awkward, geeky boy's consolation prize.

By day three of freshman orientation at her college, though, Estie discovered that she'd fundamentally misread the social dynamics of high school, that she hadn't, in fact, been unpopular, just unremarkable, the kind of person you glanced at and moved on. The truly unpopular, it turned out, were the kids who had spent high school developing heady intellectual interests—poetry, Marxism, acupuncture—and thick skins that now made them quirky and fascinating. "I can't do this for another four years," she'd whispered to Penny over the phone while her new roommate stuffed three condoms into her pocket in preparation for a night out (*Three condoms!* the virgin Estie had marveled), and Penny had whispered back, "Yes, you can." And then, like an answer to a prayer, Estie met Alice, who was sitting by herself in the dining hall, a copy of Jane Austen's *Persuasion* propped open in front of her, wearing a black Gap cardigan that Estie recognized mainly because she owned the navy version. Estie set her tray on the table and asked, "Can I sit here?" and Alice had looked up from her book and blushed so fiercely Estie imagined she could feel the heat radiating off Alice's face. Alice may have been beautiful, she realized, but she was also very shy, and something about that shyness disarmed Estie and she'd known, almost instantly, that with Alice by her side, she'd be okay.

And she *had* been okay, more or less, until this moment in the hospital, when Alice wasn't returning her texts and Penny had just seen a bag full of her urine, and she was on the verge of giving birth to a child who, for all she knew, could turn out to be a serial killer. No one in their right minds could consider this progress. Feeling desperate, she glanced over at Owen. "Listen," she said, "can you pass the remote?"

She settled on watching reruns of *The People's Court*. The way the judge yelled at the litigants—"Do I look like an idiot to you?"— suited Estie's mood and kept her from yelling at Owen, who, even though it was only three in the afternoon, kept dozing off in the visitor's chair or working on syllabi for his new courses. No wonder the baby inside her was reluctant to come out. "Cheerful thoughts," Estie whispered to herself, and still, time dragged on. It was five more hours before Estie was finally ready to push. Or maybe to poop. Who could tell? She imagined the evil nurse and the doctor recoiling in horror, then later retiring to a janitorial closet for a quickie straight out of TV. "I can't believe she thought she was pregnant," the evil nurse would say, exposing her pale neck to the doctor's kisses. And the doctor, his teeth against the evil nurse's skin, would say, "Fiber. Fiber fiber fiber."

"Push!" the doctor ordered from somewhere far away between Estie's legs. "Push!"

"No," Estie said. The epidural had worn off and she was crying again, and Owen, finally awake, was standing over her, dabbing at her face with a tissue. "Take it out. Can't you just take it out?"

The evil nurse laughed ominously, and Estie couldn't help but notice that she had lipstick on her teeth. "Mama, you're the only one who can get that baby out now."

"Pull up your legs," the doctor instructed. "Hoist yourself up on this birthing bar. Roll over on your hands and knees."

"I can't," Estie cried. "I can't." And it was true. She couldn't move. She was slippery with sweat, and her limbs, puffy with fluid, were heavy and useless. *C-section*, she thought. *Please. Anything.* She tried again to hold her legs up, to spread them wide, but she couldn't get her hands around them, and finally the nurse, pitying her, pressed against one thigh, Owen against the other, and a second nurse materialized out of nowhere to push on Estie's abdomen.

"Baby's crowning," the doctor said. "Here comes Baby!"

Estie felt the baby sliding away inside her, sucked by a tractor beam into an airless, much-too-small hollow surrounded by bone. It was a sensation so frightening, so beyond her control, that she froze, her ears roaring with blood.

"And there Baby goes," said the evil nurse.

Estie opened her eyes, which she had squeezed shut. "I can't do it," she told Owen. "I can't." But Owen wasn't paying attention to her. He was watching the doctor, a worried expression on his face. Somewhere in the room, a monitor was beeping a warning.

"One more push, Mama," the doctor instructed. "Just one more."

Estie closed her eyes again. She was done. She had nothing left. Any second now, they would wheel her into surgery and she'd have a C-section, and that would be that. But then she felt Owen lean in close, so close she could feel his breath on her face.

"Estie," he said, his voice low but firm, "listen to me. Just get him the fuck out of there." And when she hesitated, he added, "Now."

"How dare you?" she wanted to ask, but she gritted her teeth and pushed until she felt her body taking over once again, pulling the baby away, suctioning it out of her, all those nerves and muscles and bones be damned.

"You're doing it," the doctor said. "Almost there."

And then the baby was out, and the evil nurse placed a red, impossibly large, molting creature on Estie's chest. The baby was warm and dense, squirmy and unexpectedly strong, already mewling to register his complaints as a second nurse wiped him down, cooing, "So much hair! What a sweet baby girl."

Owen didn't seem to have heard her, but Estie had. "Girl?"

The second nurse placed a stethoscope on the baby's back. "Yes, a girl with a nice strong heartbeat."

"A girl?" Estie said again. And Owen said, "Are you sure?"

The nurse nodded. "See for yourselves."

"But we were told we were having a boy," Estie insisted.

"Mistakes happen," the nurse said. "The main thing is that you have a healthy baby."

"That's right," Owen said. He reached over and stroked the baby's hair with one finger. "Jesus," he said. "You did it. Our baby. Our baby girl."

The baby strained against Estie, and she realized her arms were trembling from the effort of holding her. "Can you take her?" she asked.

"Our baby girl," Owen said again, not hearing. "You really did it."

Estie tried to smile. She'd done nothing. The baby's appearance had been in spite of her, not because. Her Inner Wisdom had failed, and now here she was, her muscles shriveled and twitching, the baby's angry weight pressing against her ribs and constricting her breath, her body an old woman's body. What had ever made her think she could do this? With the last of her strength, she heaved the baby upward and off of her chest. "Take her," she told Owen. "Take her. Please."

6

EXACTLY TWENTY-SIX HOURS AFTER THE birth, Estie and Owen wrestled the baby into her bucket and the bucket into the car seat base and headed home. "Now what?" Estie asked Owen once they'd made it to the duplex safe and sound. Owen stooped to set down the baby, still in her carrier, on the floor, then changed his mind when Herbert came running in from the bedroom. "Easy," Owen told the cat, then tilted the bucket so Herbert could see inside. "Look," he said. "Your little sister."

Estie rolled her eyes, certain that if Herbert were human, he would have rolled his eyes too. But he wasn't human, so he made do with a couple of sniffs and a haughty glance before slinking off to his food dish in the kitchen.

"So much for that," Owen said. He set the baby down, this time on the coffee table, and then sat down on the couch, across from her. "Come here," he beckoned, and Estie lowered herself gingerly into the space beside him. For a few moments, the two of them sat there gazing at the baby, who somehow managed to be both unbearably cute and unbearably ugly at the same time: all those wriggling fingers and toes, all that newborn acne, the uncanny resemblance to Owen, with his long face and dimpled chin, which was apparently an evolutionary adaptation to keep the father in the picture. "Okay," Owen said, yawning. "Syllabi." Then he sneezed.

Estie nodded. The baby wasn't even two days old, and she was already more tired than she'd ever been. She leaned her head back against the wall and closed her eyes.

"Want me to call your mom?" Owen asked from the kitchen table, where he was setting up shop with the laptop and a couple of snot rags.

Estie didn't even bother to open her eyes. "No," she said. Earlier that morning, her mother stopped by the hospital briefly to exclaim, "I told you the ultrasound was wrong," loudly enough that everyone at the nurses' station could hear, and once that was done, she immediately rushed off again so she could get to the farmers market before it ran out of eggs. No. The last thing Estie needed now was her mother whooshing in and out of the duplex just to say "I told you so" and point out that the baby was covered with spit-up.

She must have drifted off after that, because the next thing she knew, the baby was snuffling in her little bucket, working her tongue uncertainly but in increasing dismay. Estie pulled up her shirt, then picked up the baby and tried to position her in the way the lactation consultant in the hospital had shown her, but the baby was too excited, so eager to start nursing that she missed the nipple entirely, her open mouth sliding right off of Estie's breast. The baby pulled away, surprised, and started crying, and Estie nearly keeled over in pain. She couldn't stand the baby's wails—she was frantic to make them stop—and when she couldn't, she started crying too. So much for nursing as a natural instinct. By then, Owen was standing over her, coaching: "Squeeze your nipple between your thumb and forefinger. Make sure you're supporting her head." Estie did her best to ignore him and tried to stuff her nipple into the baby's mouth. She tried and tried, over and over and over again, until the baby finally managed something resembling a latch and stopped mid-wail. Estie, though, kept right on crying. "I don't think I can do this," she told Owen, who was still standing over her, looking shaken.

"Want me to call your mother?" he offered again.

Estie shook her head no. Once the baby was done nursing, she handed her to Owen and stood up on wobbly legs. "I'm going to go lie down," she said and shuffled off to the bedroom only to discover that the cat had spent the twenty-six hours they'd been away revenge-vomiting on her side of the bed. At that point, they'd been home two hours and thirty-two minutes. Not that the passage of time mattered: once they got through the day, there was still the night to get through, and then another day, and another. "You fucker," Estie told Herbert and headed to the kitchen for some paper towels. After she was done cleaning up cat puke, she sat down on the carpet and leaned against the bed, the paper towels full of vomit crumpled beside her, Herbert in her lap, and that was how Owen found her twenty minutes later, tears streaming down her face. "I'm calling your mom," he said, and Estie nodded. While Owen called, she threw away the paper towels and began stripping the bed under Herbert's watchful gaze. "Is she coming?" she asked when Owen hung up. She was so tired her head hurt.

"No," Owen said, and Estie could tell he was trying not to scowl. "She's going to the movies with a friend."

"Naturally," Estie muttered and blew her nose into a paper towel. She took the baby and watched Owen remove the covers from the pillows, then made her way back to the living room, and when the doorbell rang a few minutes later, she almost cried in relief, except that when she opened the door, it wasn't her contrite mother but the UPS man with a box of diapers Alice had sent as a gift. Estie couldn't help but feel a little hurt. Diapers were useful, but they didn't make for the kind of gift that Estie would one day be able to show the baby, saying, "Mommy's best friend sent this when you were born."

"Okay," Owen said, "but at least she didn't send another toothbrush."

He was right about that, but still, the diapers reaffirmed Estie's suspicion that Alice didn't quite approve of the baby, or didn't quite approve of Estie having a baby with Owen, or—by extension—that she didn't approve of Owen, which was, in fact, true. Owen had rubbed Alice the wrong way almost immediately, or rather Estie had, when she'd explained to Alice Owen's theory of marriage. According to Owen, the good men—the handsome ones with lucrative jobs—were snatched up early, leaving everyone else, including Owen, waiting in the wings until the women, now older (read: more desperate) turned their attention to a second tier of men with stable careers (*Ha!* Estie thought now) and passable looks. "And that's where I shine," Owen had said. "I'm top of the middle."

Estie thought Alice would find this funny and true, but Alice didn't tolerate mediocrity, not in herself, not in others, and definitely not as a way of being in the world. "He's implying we're Grade B women," Alice had said stiffly. "That *you're* a Grade B woman." She had a point—Estie recognized this even then. Those Grade A men had to marry *somebody*, and they certainly hadn't married Estie or Alice. But then Owen had asked Estie to marry him and Alice had softened, finally conceding, "I guess you just love who you love." Or maybe that was wishful thinking on Estie's part and Alice hadn't softened after all, because she'd sat unsmilingly through the wedding, and Estie had been so distracted by her pinched expression that in the photos she looked bewildered, a lost tourist who had accidentally stumbled into someone else's wedding only to be mistaken for the ecstatic bride. At the time, Estie had blamed this on Alice's shyness, but apparently it had been disapproval, disapproval that lingered and extended, it seemed, to the baby. No, Estie told herself. Impossible. Nobody begrudged babies their parents. "I should call Alice," she told Owen. "Tell her we're home."

"It's the weekend."

Estie shrugged. "So? She's probably at work." She angled her body away from Owen and pulled out her phone. "I'm home," she said when Alice picked up. "I have a baby."

"Wow," Alice said. "That was fast."

"They don't believe in convalescence," Estie said. "Or else they just really underestimate it." She felt a twinge of pride at using such a lovely, old-fashioned term as *convalescence*—a term that evoked seaside retreats and healthful air and not the evil nurse coming back on shift and complaining that Estie had lost the baby's hospital-assigned hat. "You're making this so hard for me," the evil nurse had said, and then she'd paged housekeeping to come clean up the blood Estie had tracked all over the bathroom. So much blood. How was it possible Estie had any left?

"So anyway," Estie said, but before she could work herself up to asking Alice about the diapers, Alice jumped in: "I have some news too," she said. "Guess who came up on my Tinder last night?" She paused dramatically. "Dan."

It took Estie a moment to register what she was saying. First, she'd had no idea Alice even used dating apps. And second, Dan. "*Dan* Dan?"

"Yes," Alice said. "Can you believe it?"

Estie didn't answer. She couldn't.

"He's in town for a conference," Alice continued. "We're going to have drinks."

"Huh," Estie managed with great effort.

"Want me to say hi from you?"

"I guess."

"Okay," Alice said. "I will." Then, apparently because it was time to introduce yet another topic, she said, "Anything else to report?"

"You mean other than the baby?"

Alice hesitated. "You're right," she said apologetically. "Of course there's nothing other than the baby."

"And Dan," Estie wanted to add, but she wasn't sure she could keep the hysteria out of her voice. For Dan to reemerge after all these years, and on Tinder, of all places—well, none of it made sense. Wasn't Tinder a hookup app? Alice hated hookups, and she rarely dated, or at least she rarely mentioned dating to Estie.

"Are you crying?" Alice asked.

"No," Estie said. She touched her face. "Maybe. I'm being so hormonal."

"You have to stop saying that," Alice said. Thinking like that, she'd explained to Estie over and over again throughout Estie's pregnancy and even before, during especially bad bouts of PMS, was the reason why nobody wanted a woman president and why there were so few women CEOs. "You never hear men blaming their actions on hormones," she said now.

"That's because they blame their penises."

"Fine," Alice said. "Then at least blame it on your vagina and not on your hormones."

"Fine," Estie said right back. "I'm being so vaginal."

Alice was quiet for a moment. "I see your point."

"This whole baby thing is freaking me out."

"It's only been a day," Alice said. "It's too early to freak out." Then she said, "I'd better get back to work."

"But it's Saturday."

"I know," Alice said. "I'm the only one here. It's wonderful."

After they hung up, Estie checked the time. Three hours and thirty-seven minutes. She was sore and worn out and terrified by the truth that had been slowly sinking in ever since they'd left the hospital: Giving birth was nowhere near the end of the story. Now they were supposed to actually keep the baby alive. "Dear Rita," she imagined writing the childbirth instructor, "what the fuck?" She groaned and hoisted herself up off the couch, then made her way to the laundry room only to discover that Owen had put the sheets in the washer but forgotten to actually run it. She added soap and pressed start. Three hours and thirty-nine minutes. She used the bathroom, which also meant cleaning it afterward, then pulled up her shirt and stared at her loose belly in the mirror. Three hours and forty-six minutes. She made her way to the kitchen, where Owen was staring glassy-eyed at the screen of his laptop. "You awake?" she whispered.

Owen started. "What? Yes. You okay?"

She nodded, but suddenly she was crying again. "Maybe we could ask your parents to come?" But she already knew they couldn't, that Maine was too far and flights were too expensive. "God," she said, "we're so alone."

Owen smiled indulgently, or tried to—the result was more of a grimace. "But we're not alone," he said, and Estie could tell he was doing his best not to sound impatient. "We also have the baby."

7

MAYBE THEY HAD THE BABY, but the baby was a girl, and Owen was fired, and now Alice was meeting Dan for drinks. Even though she was exhausted, Estie lay awake, heart pounding, while everyone else slept: Owen next to her, the cat between her knees, the baby in her little bedside bassinet. Or at least Estie *thought* the baby was sleeping. She sat up and used the light from her phone's screen to check for the rise and fall of the baby's chest, then lay back down, relieved but not exactly relieved, since the fact that the baby was breathing now didn't necessarily mean that she'd still be breathing later, and wouldn't that—a small, ambivalent part of Estie piped up—be a kind of relief as well? Estie felt herself stiffen, and so, apparently, did Herbert, because he clamped down on her left foot, not hard, just enough of a warning that she could feel it, a disbelieving *Really?* as if the cat were disgusted that Estie was already imagining the baby dead. God, Estie thought, by the time the baby turned eighteen, she'd be fifty, and Alice and Dan would be married. It was what happened in all shows when couples who had barely missed out on dating each other in college ran into each other years later, the man now finally ready to commit, the woman now more willing to compromise, with a special brief appearance by Estie, the married-and-newly-postpartum best friend, there only to provide a baby for Alice to hold and thereby illustrate that she'd make not only a fabulous wife but also a perfect mother.

Estie had met Dan in the fall of her sophomore year in college, when he was still a football-playing freshman—fresh *person*, she corrected herself—who sometimes watched *Star Trek: The Next Generation* reruns in the TV lounge of her dorm. He usually came with his girlfriend, who was tall and muscular, the kind of person who ran five miles each morning when she wasn't busy practicing the bassoon. For a few weeks, she and Dan sat together in the back of the room, holding hands, the would-be Homecoming King and Queen of Planet Earth, but by November, the football team was 0-8, and Dan was showing up alone and sitting up front with Estie and Alice, smelling clean and tart, like Granny Smith apples and soap.

Alice sighed. "He's so cute. Even if he is a jock."

"You think so?" Estie said, even though she thought so too and spent minutes, if not hours, wondering whether his thigh was pressed against hers because all guys liked sitting spread-legged, or if all that touching meant something more.

"Have you seen his biceps?" Alice said. "Regular guys don't have biceps like that."

Estie took a deep breath, then asked because somebody had to, "Do you like him?"

"He's nice," Alice said. "For a jock."

"Yes, but do you *like* him like him?"

"He's a *jock*," Alice said again.

But Dan wasn't just a jock, or even though he was a jock, he was nice, and smart, and funny, and made fabulous pancakes. College Estie couldn't believe her good fortune, and so she'd thrown her virginity at him with a decisive fierceness that still surprised her when she thought about it. He and Estie had dated for three and a half years, and then he'd moved to Boston for grad school while Estie stayed behind at Big Earth because you didn't give up a job with benefits and move halfway across the country to work at a coffee shop while your boyfriend made something of himself. "You're only twenty-two," Estie's mother pointed out. "I married my first serious boyfriend, and look how that turned out." And thank God Estie had listened to her advice, because Dan had moved to Boston and pretty much disappeared, never to be heard from again.

Until now. If Dan matching with Alice on Tinder wasn't fate, then Estie didn't know what was. Even if they didn't end up getting married, they'd have sex for sure. Surely Alice must have lost her virginity by *now* even if she'd never quite managed to do so in college. And even if Alice were somehow still a virgin despite living in Chicago for nearly a decade, she certainly wouldn't remain one for long, not with Dan and his biceps and his pancakes back in the picture.

Stupid, Estie told herself. Why was she worrying about other people's sex lives when, in the bassinet, the baby had startled herself into wakefulness and was now issuing various demands? Estie carried her over to the living room so that Owen could keep sleeping, then spent who knows how long trying to get her to latch. Outside, everything was silent, the street bathed in the cold, sterile light of the LED streetlamps the city had installed earlier that summer, and between the baby's screams and Estie's own throbbing headache, she felt like she was the only survivor of a disaster she didn't quite understand. Once the baby was finally nursing, Estie watched the reflection of the morning sun on the darkened TV as it worked its way through the blinds. Slowly, the couch and coffee table came into focus on the screen, then Estie and the small bundle she was holding, which was, of course, the baby, her reflected face small and ghostly and blank. It might not have been an apocalypse, but it certainly felt like one.

"Hold the baby," Estie told Owen when he finally got up at around 7:30. "I'm going to bed." This time, she fell asleep almost instantly, waking up with a start some unspecified amount of time later to the squishy sound of toilet brush against porcelain and the smell of Clorox. God, how she loved Owen for thinking to clean up the little drips of blood she couldn't help but leave all over the bathroom. Why had no one warned her in advance that all the periods you got to skip when you were pregnant would arrive back-to-back once you finally gave birth, along with each of those missed period's missed cramps? She gingerly raised herself into a standing position, which was when she saw that it wasn't Owen scrubbing away in the bathroom but Penny, hunched over the toilet in cigarette pants and a flowy tee, clearly on her way to work.

"Oh God," Estie cried, horrified. "You don't have to do that!"

Penny waved her off. "Already done." She flushed the toilet and put the brush back into its stand, then washed her hands.

The blood on the floor, Estie couldn't help but notice, was gone. "The baby is beautiful," Penny said, drying her hands on a towel. "And I brought cinnamon rolls."

"They're really good!" Owen, that eavesdropper, called from the kitchen.

"Come on," Penny said. "I've got half an hour before I have to be at work. Tell me everything."

And Estie did tell her everything, except for the part about Owen lying, and soon she was feeling cheerful enough to show Penny some of the lovely parting gifts she'd received from the hospital. For the baby, there was a onesie that read "Help prevent SIDS" on the front and "If you can read this, turn me over" on the back. For Estie, there was an inflatable plastic donut for sitting on and a plastic potty—a "sitz bath," the nurse called it—that came with a squeezable bottle that the nurse called a "perineal irrigator" that Estie was supposed to use every time she went to the bathroom. And if that weren't mortifying enough in itself, she was given sanitary pads so large she could've used them to swaddle the baby, as well as horrid panties made of nylon mesh that were supposed to hold the pads in place.

Penny looked suitably horrified. "You're kidding."

"No," Estie assured her gleefully, and later, after Penny left, she marveled at the speed with which she'd joined the ranks of women who enjoyed scaring mothers-to-be. She also couldn't help but note that, already, Penny had spent more time with the baby than Estie's own mother. *Whatever*, she thought grimly and turned to Owen. "What were you thinking, letting Penny clean the bathroom like that?"

Owen looked surprised. "She said she needed to pee."

"Fine," Estie snapped. "Next time, make sure it's clean first." And when her mother texted her a moment later wanting to know how the first night at home had gone, she deleted the message without answering.

8

OWEN'S SEMESTER STARTED THE NEXT day, and in preparation, Herbert spent the night zooming from couch to table to kitchen counter, knocking over silverware and shattering a saltshaker at around two a.m. "I'm sorry," Estie apologized. "It must be all the stress."

Owen didn't say anything. Bleary-eyed, he stood in the middle of the living room, checking his bag for his laptop, the charging cord, the textbooks he used in class. In honor of the first day of class, he was wearing a polo shirt and wrinkled khakis, and he'd shaved, although not well. For a moment, Estie contemplated not saying anything about the spit-up stain on his shoulder and the patch of stubble on one cheek, but then she thought better of it—you dressed for the job you wanted, not the one you had. "You missed a spot." She rubbed a finger across the offending bristles. "And there's something on the corner of your mouth."

"There better not be any traffic," Owen said, checking his watch, but he shaved and washed his face and changed his shirt so that by the time he left the duplex, he looked more or less respectable. And then it was just Estie and the baby, and the baby and Estie, and Estie and the baby and Herbert, who left the room, indignant, every time the baby cried. If time had moved slowly during those first forty-eight hours at home, well, now that Owen was gone, it stopped moving entirely, and still Estie couldn't find time to shower or do anything other than feed the baby and change the baby and hold the baby while she slept, afraid that if she moved, the baby would wake up and the whole cycle would start over again.

At around eleven, Owen's parents called. "So?" Owen's mother said. "Your first day alone! How's it going?"

"Good," Estie said automatically, before adding, "I'm tired."

Owen's father laughed. "Welcome to parenting. Get used to it, hon."

"I'm just so surprised Owen didn't get any parental leave," Owen's mother said. "I would have thought a place like Norton would have *something*."

"It does."

"Then why—" Owen's mother started. "Owen said—"

With a start, Estie realized that Owen's mother didn't know what had happened. "I mean," she said before his mother could continue, "they *used* to have parental leave, but they've been having financial problems." She was surprised at how easily the words came to her, how genuine they sounded. She knew it wasn't her job to tell Owen's parents that he'd been fired, but Owen spoke with them every Sunday, so how was it possible that they didn't know? Then again, Estie wouldn't have known either if she hadn't run into Cathy, and she certainly wouldn't have grasped the extent of Owen's deception if it hadn't been for Alice. For a moment, she wanted to shake her fist ruefully at the sky—why hadn't Alice left well enough alone?—but didn't Estie herself consult Google on all matters, large and small? If Alice hadn't found the newspaper article about Owen, Estie would have run across it eventually, or worse, the baby, by then an internet-savvy tween, would have googled Owen for some class project and been endlessly traumatized by his lies, thus embarking on a downward spiral of sex and drugs.

"Why is my husband lying to his parents?" Estie asked Google after hanging up, but Google didn't seem to understand the question, instead offering answers to "Why would a husband lie about his wife?" and "How to tell if your husband is cheating." She tried again: "Why is my husband lying about his job?" This time, Google presented page after page of explanations. Apparently, men lied about their jobs all the time, mainly to impress their friends and lovers. Estie knew she ought to find this comforting, the idea of Owen as a hapless victim of capitalism and the stringent standards of masculinity, but wasn't this also what people said about men who randomly opened fire in public places?

Maybe this was the reason for what Estie did next, which was to google Dan. Or maybe that wasn't exactly why she googled Dan right then, but she figured that, surely, Dan's reappearance demanded some assistance from Google. In fact, Estie told herself as she typed Dan's name into her phone's browser, it was probably a failing on her part that she hadn't googled Dan years ago: Wasn't the internet specifically invented so people could stalk their exes?

It took her a while to find him—there were quite a few Dans out there with his same last name—but then she did. He was living in Indiana, about an hour outside of Chicago, it turned out, working in financial aid at Erasmus, a small college Estie had never heard of, where, it seemed, he spent a part of every day meticulously documenting his lunches in a blog he called, appropriately, "Dan's Lunch." "Diet Coke," that day's entry read. "Leftover turkey chili. Three sticks of Juicy Fruit." The previous day's read, "Diet Coke. Leftover turkey chili." She had to go back three more days to find a lunch that didn't include chili: "Diet Coke. Tuna salad on seedless rye: soggy. Leftover salad: romaine, carrots, tomatoes, balsamic." And it took a full week of lunches to find a leftover-free meal: "Diet Coke. Whopper: onion, no lettuce. 12 French fries: cold, undercooked." The whole endeavor struck Estie as quaint—Who even kept blogs anymore? And why lunch, of all meals?—but finding the blog was infinitely better than having to track down his social media and friend him more publicly.

She clicked back to Dan's official photo on the Erasmus College website: his hair, longish when they were together, had been replaced by the faintest outline of stubble. He was wearing a regulation green-and-gold polo and standing in front one of those swirly blue backgrounds people used in school photos. The smile on his face was professional, practiced, and very, very white, the smile of a man so staid and mature that you knew he must have recently divorced his meek, well-coiffed wife, a man who woke up one morning and realized that he had an average sex life and a riding mower and then immediately created a dating profile for himself. In other words, Dan had turned out ordinary, like Estie had, even if he did appear to be a bit obsessed with what he ate. Estie felt relieved. *Quit while you're ahead,* she told herself. There wasn't anything else she needed to know.

Still, even after she'd closed her browser app and erased her search history, she couldn't stop thinking about him, about the timing of his reappearance, which felt especially portentous compared to the randomness of their first getting together all those years ago. Back in college, if someone had asked Estie to bet whether she or Alice would be the one to end up with a husband and a baby, Estie would have bet on Alice without hesitation, and now she found herself wondering what would have happened if Estie had gotten the flu that day instead of Alice and ended up missing that evening's *Star Trek* rerun. Would Dan have gotten together with Alice rather than Estie? Would she and Alice still have been friends? Would Estie still be living in Briarwood? There was no way. Still, even though she didn't *really* believe in predestination, Estie couldn't help but wonder if maybe Dan's return was a kind of cosmic course correction, and, if so, for whom? Just asking the question filled her with a longing so intense she had to close her eyes. *Please, God,* she prayed, even though she didn't really believe in prayer. *Please, God. Please let it be for me.*

Owen came home stubbly and smelling faintly of fries, exhausted from the drive and from talking to students about the importance of actually doing the reading. "What a day," he said, flopping down on the couch next to Estie and the baby. "How were things here?"

"Your mom called," Estie told him. "She asked about your parental leave."

Owen sat up with a sigh. "What'd you tell her?"

"Financial difficulties." Estie considered leaving it there—what else needed saying?—but still she kept going. "You haven't told them?"

Owen eased back and resumed his slouching. "Not yet," he said, his voice low. "I just can't. Not right now."

"Why?"

"Because." Owen crossed his arms over his chest. "I don't know. I want to tell them in person."

"When? At Christmas?"

Owen shrugged.

"But I hate lying to them," Estie said.

"You aren't," Owen said. "Not really. Not if you don't actually say anything."

"A lie of omission is still a lie."

"Okay," Owen said, "but what are you omitting? What important part are you leaving out?"

"The part about faking your Ph.D.," Estie said. "The part about losing your job."

Owen didn't even blink. "But why would it even come up?" Estie opened her mouth to answer, but he cut her off at the pass: "It's not like anything is all that different. I'm still teaching."

"At three different schools," Estie said. "Without tenure. Without parental leave."

"Look," Owen said, "the fundamental truth of what I do hasn't changed. The rest is just details."

He seemed so certain, so confident that he was right, that Estie suddenly wasn't sure whether she was making a big deal out of nothing, or at least whether any of it was really her business. She tried to think it through and found that she didn't have the energy, and anyway they still needed to figure something out for dinner, except . . . "If it isn't a big deal," she asked, "why can't you just tell them?"

Finally Owen had the decency to look a little guilty. "Why would I?" he asked. "So they can resent me like you do?"

Estie felt her breath catch. She thought she'd been doing a decent job of being supportive, that she'd managed to hide her resentment that Owen was the one who decided to bring forth a child but somehow—well, yes, Estie did know how—Estie was the one solely responsible for the baby's survival, the prime earner, and, once Owen's students turned in that first set of papers, the cook and cleaning lady too. And yet despite all her efforts at pretending everything was fine, Owen had still sensed the dark, tight ball of anger and disappointment she couldn't seem to get rid of no matter how hard she tamped it down. "I'm sorry," she said, because she really was. "I'm still getting used to all of it, I guess."

"I know," Owen said. "I'm sorry too." He held out his arms and Estie carefully began the delicate procedure of transferring the sleeping baby to him, but apparently she wasn't careful enough. The baby's eyes opened, and, after a moment of deliberation, her chin began to tremble. "Shh . . ." Estie whispered, "you're okay." But the baby wasn't okay. She wanted to nurse. Or she wanted somebody to change her diaper. Or she wanted to stay with Estie. Or she wanted nothing at all. Whatever it was she wanted, though, she wanted it right then.

9

AT SOME POINT DURING THOSE first few weeks with the baby, Estie asked Google, "How long does it take to get used to being a mother?" and Google answered, "Four months and twenty-three days," a number so specific it had to be true. She flipped over to the calendar app and counted off the twenty or so weeks until January 23, the day she'd magically wake up feeling competent. "I can make it," she told Herbert, who was supervising her from his perch on the kitchen counter. Or at least she hoped she could. In the meantime, though, her life was a blur of feedings and diaper changes, baby spit-up and cat vomit. On the days that she managed to make it outside, she took the baby to County Park, where she studied the other mothers pushing strollers along the paved fitness trail, scanning them for signs that they were struggling too: puffy eyes, greasy hair, pants crusted with dried milk and baby drool. Usually, though, she came up empty. The other moms seemed happy, speed walking vigorously in yoga pants while their babies napped adorably or gnawed on squeaky toys. Not one of them, Estie noted, had panty lines. How did they manage? She was too embarrassed to ask Alice, so she asked

Penny, who immediately answered, "Thongs," like it was a no-brainer. But Estie couldn't imagine wearing a thong, maybe because she *could* imagine quite clearly her cellulitic ass hanging out on either side. Motherhood—or, at least, the public-facing side of motherhood—was like high school all over again, except now it wasn't just Estie sitting clueless in her room, mooning over some boy she couldn't have, there was also the baby to think of, the baby who would one day need to pick out appropriate undergarments and attract lovers of her own while managing not to get raped or pregnant. "God, Penny," Estie wanted to wail, "how am I going to raise this baby?" Instead, she forced herself to inquire as to how Penny's pregnancy was going so that she wouldn't come across as self-absorbed, or at least as *too* self-absorbed, although, really, what she was feeling was the opposite of self-absorption, as if she'd ceased to exist apart from the baby, that black hole of neediness and manipulation. What was it about the baby's trembling chin and tearless crying that forced Estie to drop everything and pick her up? Stupid oxytocin. Stupid uterine cramping.

Or maybe independent Estie hadn't ceased to exist entirely, because in addition to the part of her that spent entire days cooing, "What? What's wrong?" at the baby, there was a part that insisted on checking her phone multiple times a day, which actually meant refreshing Dan's blog obsessively, especially around lunchtime. "Diet Coke," it read. "Leftover spaghetti: disturbingly crunchy." Or "Juice box: apple. Open-faced turkey sandwich: top slice moldy." *Why?* Estie wondered. Why was the top slice moldy? Why hadn't Dan noticed the mold when he was making his lunch? Why hadn't he finished the bread before it spoiled? The answers didn't matter, of course: there was no way he and

Alice weren't going to get together, if they hadn't already, which they must have. Not that Alice was volunteering any information. "Have mtg in 5," she'd text back whenever Estie tried to check in. To be fair, Estie always happened to call Alice during working hours, because privacy, but still, it seemed odd that Alice had so many meetings, all of them five minutes away. "Why can't she leave me alone?" she imagined Alice texting Dan whenever Estie's name popped up on her screen, to which Dan would respond almost instantly with one of those eye-rolling emojis, along with a bunch of eggplants and peaches and hearts.

At least Estie's mother was always there to put things in their proper perspective. According to her mother, Estie had been a difficult, colicky baby who constantly demanded to be held. "And, unlike with you, my own mom had just passed," Estie's mother liked to remind her. "I was all on my own."

"Except for Dad," Estie wanted to point out but didn't, despite her father's gleeful stories of washing out cloth diapers "by hand. You have no idea how easy you have it." She pictured her father with dark circles like Owen's under his eyes. Had her father also repeatedly forgotten to turn off stovetop burners, as if he were unconsciously trying to off them all? "I'll get Rosie tonight," Owen would tell Estie. "You need your rest." But then he'd sleep so heavily that Estie had trouble waking him up. And sometimes, when he did wake up, he wouldn't return to bed, and Estie would find him asleep on the living room floor, a stack of student papers under his head, the baby on her back next to him, wriggling in that slow-motion way babies had, as if they were flailing underwater. Mostly, though, he seemed to exist in an orbit of his own, whooshing in and out of the duplex, worn down and miserable, full of complaints about the drive to work, the reams of bad student writing, the McDonald's where he was forced to meet with students because adjuncts didn't get their own offices. "Everything I own smells like fries," he'd say. "Or like cat." Then he'd sneeze into his elbow, the very same elbow, Estie couldn't help but notice, where he liked to nestle the baby, thus freeing up his other hand for grading and shoving the cat off his lap. "I swear," Estie would sometimes hear him hiss, his words followed by the thud of the cat landing on the kitchen floor and the feline grunt of Herbert immediately leaping back into Owen's lap, eyes wide, fur standing on end, as if to say, *Shove me one more time, asshole.* "I hate your cat," Owen told Estie while he dug through the junk drawer, looking for Band-Aids, and again, later, when he stepped barefoot on a hairball the cat had hacked up, and again, even later, when the baby peed all over the changing pad, which hadn't even been Herbert's fault. "So what?" Owen said when Estie pointed this out. "I still hate him. I need to hate something." No. If someone as easygoing as Owen was having this much trouble handling new parenthood, there was no way Estie's dad, who expected his dinners at six and *Wheel of Fortune* at seven, could have been much help to her mother.

But Estie's mother didn't believe in wallowing. She believed in orderliness and sticking to a schedule. Now that the baby had arrived, she came by frequently—almost always without warning, Estie couldn't help but notice—wedging her visits between yoga classes and whatever else it was she did all day: manicures, reflexology, trips to the mall. "Establishing a routine is important," she told Estie, holding her arms out for the baby. "I'm sure you'd feel better if you made the bed."

"I never make the bed."

"Then you should start."

Estie gritted her teeth. There was no point in arguing, and yet she couldn't help it: "It's fine not to make the bed when you have a newborn. All the books say so."

"Well," her mother declared in a dignified voice, "*I* say that you'd feel better if you did." It was the same voice she used when she warned Estie that babies who didn't wear hats caught pneumonia, and babies who didn't wear tiny mittens to protect them from their own razor-sharp fingernails were more likely to self-harm as teens. "Don't forget that those neural pathways are forming," she reminded Estie about matters large and small. That, and "You can't hide anything from a baby." Not that this prevented her mother from playing a round of baby peekaboo and then asking, "Are you sure you're sure that much acne is normal?"

After her mother's visits, Estie wanted to howl with rage. Instead, she cried quietly, clutching the baby in her arms. She was so, so tired, and here was the baby, watching her with her big blue eyes as if thinking, *One day I'll feel about you the way you feel about your mom.* Which was what? Estie didn't even know. She stared distastefully at the bag of groceries her mother had left behind: frozen lasagna with meat sauce, frozen lasagna with spinach, a sleeve of low-fat imitation Oreos. "Fuck that," she told the baby, who was surely too young to start picking up profanity. "I'd rather fucking starve."

"I take it your mom stopped by," Owen observed diplomatically when he came home and found Estie's mother's lasagnas in the trash along with the empty cookie wrapper. He washed his hands, then took the baby onto his lap so that Estie could stand up straight, stretch luxuriously, and then head into the kitchen and stare at the freezer, where all she found was two more frozen lasagnas. She shuffled back to the living room where Owen was now flipping through the hundreds of channels on their TV, his bag of papers beside him.

"I'm done with lasagna."

"Me too," Owen said. He picked up the baby and deposited her in a sling he looped around his neck and shoulder, then reached for Estie's hand. "I really miss you," he said, his voice low and tender.

Estie swallowed. "I miss you too."

"We could get some Chinese."

"Yes," Estie said. "Chinese."

It was nice to eat Kung Pao chicken and drink wine together while the baby sighed and slept, cocooned against Owen. Estie had forgotten how alcohol warmed her up, how it made her eyeballs feel as if they were radiating heat. She felt relaxed, mellow, able finally to exhale deeply without her breath catching on the lump of anxiety at the base of her throat. "Now this," she told Owen, "is why people become alcoholics."

"Yes," Owen agreed. "Contentment is a leading cause of alcoholism."

"Owen?" Estie lowered her voice into a whisper, leaning forward gingerly so that the baby wouldn't wake up. "I'm not sure I like being a mom."

"I know," Owen whispered back.

As if on cue, the baby began to squirm, and all that pleasant heat drained out of Estie's body: the baby was waking up, and she was going to want to eat, and here was Estie, buzzed and talking shit about her. Estie glanced at the wine bottle, startled to see that it was already half empty. "Shit," she said, her voice rising. "Shit. Shit. Shit."

"What?" Owen said, alarmed.

"I'm drunk," she said. "And the baby's hungry." Owen looked blank, as if he didn't know what she was talking about, as if he hadn't read all the parenting books right along with her. "Owen," she said, "I can't nurse her when I'm drunk. Alcohol isn't good for babies."

"Oh, sweetie," Owen said in a gentle, pitying voice. "Oh, sweetie. A little metabolized alcohol never hurt anybody."

Estie could feel herself flushing in shame. Or maybe it was anger. "Don't condescend," she snapped, but it was too late. She was crying, again—all she seemed to be able to do lately was cry. She started crying harder. "I'm a terrible mother," she sobbed. "She'll get fetal alcohol syndrome! Her growth will be stunted forever!"

"Oh, sweetie," Owen said again, more firmly, "she can't get fetal alcohol syndrome. She's a *baby*, not a fetus."

By now, the baby was crying too, tentatively, but Estie could tell that she was warming up for a full-on crisis. "Shh . . ." Owen said, jiggling the baby up and down gently like they'd learned to do in their parenting class. "Shh . . ." But the baby was in no mood to be shushed. She started crying louder, and, as if in response, Estie could feel the fabric of her bra stick to her nipples—she was leaking.

"I'm sorry," she told the baby. "I'm so sorry." But the baby wasn't interested in apologies. She wrinkled her brow, opened her mouth, and started screaming full-throated, red-faced baby screams. "What do we do?" she asked Owen. "Use formula?" Formula, she'd been taught, was evil, but not as evil as alcohol: it poisoned your baby more slowly.

"We don't have formula."

Normally—prebaby—Estie would have taken the time to look at him incredulously and perhaps roll her eyes in derision, but the baby's cries made everything feel urgent, rushed, as if there were no time for explanations or for clueless husbands to stand around dumbly trying to put it all together. "Then go get some," she hissed. "God."

And still, Owen refused to be moved. He handed Estie the howling baby, then disappeared into the bedroom, returning a minute later with the laptop. "Look," he said, turning the screen toward her, "less than two percent of the alcohol you consume makes it to breast milk. And you've consumed hardly any."

"Fine," Estie said. "Fine. If you don't care, I don't either." Still, she couldn't stop crying. She cried, and cried, and—just to prove Owen wrong—she went ahead and fed her baby tainted breast milk, thus ensuring that the baby would grow up to lead a life addled by drugs and crime, and then she cried some more. She was going to be scarred for life, this baby, and it was all Owen's fault, and Estie's fault too because all she did around the baby was cry.

For a while, the only sounds were Estie's sobs and the baby's noisy sucks and hiccups. "Oh, Estie," Owen said. "I'm sorry. I had no idea you were *this* tired." He handed Estie a Kleenex, looking so worried that Estie felt all her anger draining away. She breathed in, and out, and in again. Once she was sure she could speak without her voice cracking, she said, "Stupid hormones."

"Tonight for real," Owen said. "I'll watch the baby. You go to sleep."

10

DRAINED FROM HER BRUSH WITH starvation, the baby slept for a good five and half hours, and so did Estie. When she woke up, her breasts were as full and hard as soccer balls, but *my God*, she felt lovely, like a new woman—a woman whose face was covered with dried snot and streaks of tears, but still new nonetheless. She nursed the baby, who clutched Estie's thumb as if still unable to quite register her good fortune, then put her back in her crib and went digging around in the kitchen for some kind of breakfast to make Owen. They were out of milk and they had no eggs, so she had to settle on stale Cheerios that they'd have to eat dry.

"On the bright side, Cheerios do last forever," she told Owen with the enthusiasm of the newly well-rested when he stumbled into the kitchen.

"Actually, that's only true for Twinkies," Owen said. He smiled, but the smile seemed forced, worn out. His eyes were puffy, and he was doing that annoying clicking thing where he ran his thumbnail under the nail of his middle finger, then snapped it loose. *Clearly*, Estie thought, *he was just no good without sleep*. Maybe women really did have a higher threshold for pain.

Owen cleared his throat, then hitched up his pajama bottoms as if he were some kind of old-timey sheriff who meant business. "Listen," he said. "Last night kind of freaked me out." *Click click* went Owen's thumbnail. He cleared his throat again. "It just wasn't like you, all the crying, and I guess I'm wondering if maybe . . . you're a little depressed."

Estie breathed in and out, and in again, feeling a flicker of rage. The baby wasn't even a month old. She dumped the stale Cheerios out of her bowl and back into the cereal box. "I'm not depressed," she said. "I'm exhausted."

"I know," Owen said quickly. "But I'm exhausted too, and—"

"What?" Estie interrupted him. "What did you say? You're exhausted?" She stood up. "*You're* exhausted? You're *exhausted*?"

Click click. "See," Owen said. "Listen to yourself. This isn't you."

"Yes, it is," Estie said. "Who else could it be?"

Owen shrugged. "You didn't used to be like this."

Estie looked up at him sharply. "You didn't used to be like this either."

"What's that supposed to mean?"

But there was no point in beginning that conversation, at least not right then, when Owen had to go to work. Still, Estie had to have the last word: "I don't know," she said. "I mean, haven't you heard? We're parents now."

Owen left for school, and Estie nursed the baby, and changed the baby, and wiped the baby's spit-up, and changed the baby again, all of it while watching a movie in which a blind woman fought off a stalker using little more than her sensitive hearing and a paring knife. At ten, though, her mother called and announced cheerfully, "Owen told me about your little freak-out."

That bastard, Estie thought. *How could he?* "It wasn't a freak-out."

"Crying over wine for three hours is a freak-out."

"It wasn't three hours," Estie snapped. "And it wasn't over wine."

"Whatever," her mother said. "It was still a freak-out. It certainly *freaked* Owen out."

"Whatever," Estie said right back. "I'm fine."

"Because I can come over if you aren't."

"No," Estie said. "I'm fine. I'm going for a walk." She hung up. She didn't really want to go for a walk, but now she had to follow through on the off chance that her mother decided to check up on her. She swapped her pajama pants for sweats, wriggled into a bra without removing the stained Norton College T-shirt she was wearing, buckled the baby up in her bucket, and double-checked the diaper bag, the whole process taking so long that it was nearly eleven by the time she made it out to County Park.

Already breathless, she unloaded the baby and the stroller, then headed out on the paved fitness trail toward the exercise stations. At the chin-up station, she stopped and sat down on a bench, then focused on inhaling through her nose and exhaling through her mouth until she felt calmer. The baby had nodded off, and Estie positioned the stroller so she could watch her make faces in her sleep, little half smiles Estie knew were really grimaces or gas, although at least the baby was beginning to look a bit less like an alien, filling out her onesies and developing an extra chin. *God*, Estie thought, *please don't let her grow up to be fat*, and then immediately felt ashamed for thinking it. God, though, apparently approved, because just then the sun came out from behind a cloud and warmed her scalp and the back of her neck. She sighed, leaned back, and pulled out her phone to check Dan's blog even though it was too early for lunch. It was Friday, and so she texted Alice, "Any exciting weekend plans?" and Alice texted back, "Work." Had Alice always worked this much? Estie didn't think so. She composed a second text—"You going to see Dan?"—then deleted it. The last time she'd asked about him, Alice had gone radio silent for a good two days and only resumed responding after Estie had sent her a photo of Herbert curled up in a half-empty diaper box, because if nothing else, they still had Herbert in common.

According to Estie's calculations, this weekend would be Dan and Alice's third weekend together. Even if they hadn't had sex yet, surely it would happen this time around: they were adults, after all. Still, just thinking about them doing it made Estie want to cry, although she couldn't put her finger on why exactly. And now that she was swallowing back tears, she absolutely had to know. She opened her browser and searched for Dan's email. "Ran across your blog," she wrote, "so wanted to say hi. Hope you're well and enjoying your many lunches." She hit send before she could lose her nerve. It was a perfectly respectable email—she was absolutely certain—so she didn't know why her heart was hammering against her chest.

Owen came home that evening with bags of cold McDonald's, a can of formula, and a plan that he'd written out on the back of a handout about similes and metaphors. "Okay," he announced, "I've made a sleep schedule. Sleep is very important to new mothers."

"Have you been getting medical advice on the internet again?" Estie asked. She'd spent the afternoon madly refreshing her email, but so far nothing, even though Dan had updated his blog at around two p.m.: "Instant microwave mac and cheese and two graham crackers, stale."

"Yes," Owen said. "We both have cancer. That's the real reason we're so tired."

"Are you trying to jinx us?" Estie said. For a moment, she imagined the baby in her bucket, alone and crying, a dead Owen and Estie sprawled on the floor at her feet. "We should make a will," she said. "And take out life insurance policies."

"Sheesh," Owen said. "Rough day?" He unwrapped a burger, put it on a plate along with some fries, put the plate in the microwave, and assumed his superhero stance: he would, it seemed, brook no dissent. "Anyway," he continued, "I'm taking over night duty—you're not getting enough sleep." There was something about his tone that made Estie bristle: she wanted to be asked, not told. Then again, sleep sounded lovely. The microwave beeped and Owen pulled out the food, which now looked sad and oversteamed. He cleared his throat. "So," he said, "are *you* okay?"

"I'm fine," she said. "I'm not going to drown the baby in the bathtub or anything."

Owen blanched. "Don't even joke about it."

"Oh my God," Estie said. "You just joked about cancer."

"It's not the same thing."

As usual, he was right. Even so, Estie could see the whole thing playing out in her mind. She skipped over the drowning part—she wasn't a *monster*, after all—and lingered instead on the aftermath, on Owen finding Estie curled up in some corner of the house, weeping and muttering, "I had to do it. The voices told me to." Or fast asleep, finally able to relax now that the baby was gone. Then there would be Owen's horror, his recoil, Estie's time in jail, the media circus, the sentencing, the Movie of the Week based on her life, the early parole for good behavior, the envious way she'd look at other moms, other children, and think things like *The baby could be learning to add, learning to braid her hair, learning to drive.* Owen, in the meantime, would have divorced her, and even after he married the doctor—who had been there to comfort him even as others accused him of being blind to Estie's distress, to her needs—and had three children, he would be prone to dark spells when he'd lock himself up in his study and watch old videos of the baby without the sound, because he couldn't stand hearing Estie's voice in the background, his crazy wife, his mistake.

It took Estie maybe three seconds to imagine all this, and the whole thing made her feel sick to her stomach. Maybe she didn't love the baby quite yet, but she certainly didn't wish her harm. Yes, she was dragging a little bit, and maybe she was a little too preoccupied with her phone, but there was no comparison between her behavior and that of the truly depressed, sometimes-psychotic new moms—both celebrity and otherwise—featured in the magazines lining the grocery store checkout aisle: she didn't spend most of her time out-and-out sobbing or staring listlessly out the window; the kitchen appliances weren't sending her secret messages; she didn't want to die. No. Estie fed the baby. She changed her diapers. She held her for hours on end and made sure she was clean and comfortable. She was fine. She really was.

"Don't worry," she told Owen. "I'm just tired. It'll be good to get some sleep."

At around ten p.m. there was still no email from Dan, so Estie nursed the baby one last time, and then Owen gathered his pillows and a blanket and tucked Estie in. "Sweet dreams," he whispered, and she felt weak with gratitude for the sacrifice he was about to make.

She was lying there, eyes closed, wondering if she should check her phone again, maybe even drifting off for a second, when somewhere in the bowels of the duplex, the baby began crying. And kept crying, and crying, and crying, until Estie couldn't stand it, she couldn't. What was Owen doing? Didn't he know the baby was hungry? She got up and shuffled to the living room, where she found the baby all alone, buckled into her bouncy seat, her face red and contorted as if her abandonment were too great a betrayal to bear.

"Shh." Estie picked up the baby. "Shh . . . I'm here."

The baby took a couple of big gulping breaths, then turned her face to Estie's chest. "That's right," Estie told her, lifting up her T-shirt. "Moo."

"Hey," Owen said, returning to the living room, "this wasn't our deal." He held up a bottle. "I was just mixing up some formula."

"But she was crying," Estie said.

"She's a baby. That's what she does." He sat down next to her on the couch. "Okay," he said, "you win this time, but no more getting up tonight." Then he squeezed her fingers and promptly fell asleep, the bottle of formula slowly leaking onto his lap. This couldn't be easy for him either, Estie reflected. She lowered the now-sleeping baby back into her bouncy seat, thinking she'd head back to bed, except that before she could, the pile of dirty onesies next to the washing machine called out to her, and so she had to start a load of laundry. She did. Just like she had to sweep the floor.

By then it was almost two a.m., and Herbert was doing his nightly sprint-and-yowl combination. Owen slept on, and still no email. "U up?" Estie texted Alice, and when she didn't get an answer, she called, but the call went straight to voicemail. She knew it was unlikely that Alice and Dan were having sex right at that very moment, but she still couldn't help hoping they weren't.

―――

The next morning, when Owen discovered the swept floor and clean dishes, he was angry rather than pleased. "I can't believe you folded laundry," he told Estie. "I'm not staying up with the baby so you can do housework."

"Well," Estie said, "someone has to do it." What she didn't say was, "You're not staying up with the baby at all."

"No," Owen said, "no one has to do it," and Estie was too tired to argue. Instead, she checked her email and Dan's blog. Nothing. Not that she was surprised: lunch was still four hours away. But then it was two hours away, and then one, and then Estie ate more Cheerios because anything else was too hard. "Three deviled eggs: left over," read that day's entry. "Two chicken satay skewers: left over, dry. Three mini eclairs: left over, squashed." Clearly, Dan was going to parties or else hosting them. Or maybe ordering tapas at a dark, romantic Chicago restaurant. *Good for him,* Estie told herself, but she didn't mean it. *Let it be anyone but Alice,* she thought. Anyone but Alice. Although of course it was Alice. It had to be.

And then, at 3:43 p.m., she refreshed her email again and there it was. "Guessing you heard I ran into Alice!" Dan wrote. "It's really good to hear from you! The three of us should have a mini reunion one of these days!" When she read that last part, Estie froze. Was Dan being polite or did he actually want to get together? She read the email a second time, and a third. So many exclamation marks! No, she decided. Dan was being perfunctory, issuing one of those rhetorical Michigan invites all the way from Indiana. She couldn't believe that she'd allowed herself to get so worked up. She could feel herself flushing with embarrassment even though nobody except the baby was there to see her, and the baby didn't know how to read. Still, she was irritable, too ready to jump down Owen's throat when he came home from Target with six five-packs of shrink-wrapped underwear for him and Estie and five six-packs of onesies, all of them on tiny plastic hangers.

"See?" he said. "Now we don't have to do laundry for a month."

Estie fingered the onesies, which were plain white and sized 12 months. "They're too big," she said.

"She'll grow into them."

"Yes," Estie said, "in a year." She didn't say anything about how the underwear he'd bought her was too small, how it would have been too small even before she'd gotten pregnant, and didn't he pay attention to anything that mattered?

They didn't talk after that, not before Owen went back to Target to get some 0–3M onesies, leaving Estie alone with the baby yet *again*, or after he came home the second time, or while he sat in the kitchen grading papers and Estie stood at the counter, shoveling even more cereal into her mouth so they wouldn't have to talk about dinner. It was embarrassing, really, what a hard time they were having while, halfway across the world, peasants with babies strapped to their backs were doing all that thatching.

"Exactly which peasants are you talking about?" Owen asked once they were finally talking again. "The ones dealing with unsanitary water and malaria? Or the ones trying to survive civil war?"

"See," Estie said, "we have no problems."

"That's not what I meant," Owen said, then yawned. He could talk a good game—he delivered lectures for a living, after all—but when it came to actually keeping his eyes open, he had no willpower. When Estie told him to go to bed, he only objected halfheartedly. He was asleep before Estie could cover him with a blanket.

"So what do you think?" Estie asked the baby, who was sitting, bright-eyed, in her bouncy seat. "Are men less resilient than women?"

The baby gazed at her for a moment, as if considering, then pooped so spectacularly that Estie had no choice but to give her a bath.

11

AND THEN ALICE AND DAN met for drinks. "I thought I told you," Alice said. "That was, like, two weeks ago."

Estie wanted to throttle Alice. "No," she said. "It's been weeks since we've talked. You haven't been returning my calls."

On her end of the line, Alice sighed. "Yes, I have. It's just that there's so many of them."

"Not that many."

Alice didn't respond, and anyway, the last time Alice had complained about the frequency of Estie's calls, which had been back at the beginning of her pregnancy, she'd gone as far as to send Estie a screenshot of her missed-calls summary, in which Estie's name was followed by some ungodly number like twenty-two. That had been humiliating enough. "Anyway," Estie said, clearing her throat, "tell me everything."

"It was good," Alice said, her voice neutral. "He's the same, only older."

"The same how?" Estie asked.

"You know," Alice said. "The same. Running marathons. Maybe a little lonely."

"Huh," Estie said. "I guess that explains Tinder."

"I guess," Alice agreed.

"Is he still cute?"

Estie could practically see Alice shrug. "I guess."

"Are you going to see him again?"

"I don't know. Maybe."

"Maybe?"

"Anyway," Alice said, "I have to go. I have a meeting in five minutes."

How was it possible that this was the same woman who, back in college, panicked every time a guy asked her out? "All he wanted was sex," Alice would report, teary-eyed, after each date. "We were kissing and then he was groping my boobs."

Estie, who, thanks to the early prom ministerings of Joseph Van Vranken, was already an expert in all things booby, tried and failed to muster up some outrage. "So?"

"You'd think he'd wait until a second date. Or ask. Or something."

Even back then, Estie had wondered how someone so beautiful could also be so naïve. It didn't make sense. At least on paper, Alice, with her golden hair and perfect nose, should have been leading a perfect life, replete with husbands and cotillions and horses. Instead, someone, somewhere—probably Alice's parents, because it was always the parents—had messed up big, had allowed Alice to stay in her room and read while other girls played soccer and did each other's makeup. And in so doing, they'd allowed Alice the kind of upbringing that was all mind, no body, and now, it was as if Alice had no idea what to do with her long legs, her flawless skin.

"I mean," Estie remembered asking Dan shortly after they'd started dating, "isn't she more your type than I am?" But Dan had merely rolled his eyes: "A," he said, "I like the way *you* look. And B, listen to yourself. Maybe *you're* the one who should be having sex with Alice."

The truth was, though, that when Estie tried to imagine sex with Alice, she couldn't get past the fact of their bodies, of her body, of Alice looking at her body. Everyone knew that guys were easily distracted, easily blinded by the sight of a breast. But women, especially women like Alice, knew better, were more discerning, more particular. Estie simply couldn't imagine Alice standing naked in front of her, appraising, taking in the stray hairs around Estie's nipples, her stubbled legs, the cellulite on the backs of her thighs.

Dan had laughed at the expression on Estie's face. "It's fine if you don't want to have sex with Alice," he said, which at the time had made Estie suspicious. "You wouldn't do a threesome?" she'd asked, and Dan answered, "How could we have a threesome with you passed out on the floor?"

At the time, she'd felt so relieved, so chosen: no one she had gone to high school with, including Estie herself, would have ever suspected that she'd end up with a football player, even one from a perpetually losing Division III team. Even now, the story of how they'd gotten together filled her with pride—she'd been so brave, so awesome, inviting Dan into her room under the guise of showing him her Deanna Troi action figure with its creepy bendable arms and legs, and then, once he was sitting next to her, his thigh once again pressed against hers, saying, "I really think you should kiss me." In the morning, when she glanced in the mirror in the women's bathroom, she couldn't help but admire her puffy lips, the stubble burn around her mouth and down her neck, the way that the Estie reflected back at her had known what she wanted and had no qualms about taking it, frizzy hair and social awkwardness be damned. No doubt about it: a girl like that deserved a big, swooning love from someone who would sleepily pull her back to bed in the morning, who *knew* she was awesome, who wasn't merely making do.

And for a while, it seemed as if she'd been right. She and Dan stayed together for three and a half years, Estie driving back and forth from Briarwood while she waited for him to graduate, first from college and then from his accounting program, or at least that had been the plan until Dan moved to Boston to get his CPA and pretty much vanished from Estie's life.

For maybe the millionth time, Estie found herself thinking about an image she'd seen making the rounds on social media: a handsome, muscular man and his roly-poly wife on a beach in bathing suits, grinning as they squinted into the sun. It was a feel-good photo, the caption declared, proof that love was blind. It was clear from the picture, though, that only the man needed blinders. Estie didn't know how the wife could stand it, knowing that thousands—or maybe millions—of people were lauding her husband for loving someone who looked like she did. "Don't you feel bad for her?" Estie had asked Alice when she first saw the image, and Alice had said, "I guess." Then, sensing a question behind the question, Alice had added, "Don't worry. You're nothing like her. She must weigh at least three hundred pounds." She'd meant well, Estie knew, but she ended up feeling even worse. She couldn't imagine anyone ever saying something like that to Alice, just like she couldn't imagine Joseph Van Vranken ever daring to touch Alice's boobs, to sully someone so blond and pure, so clearly Madonna rather than Whore. Alice, it seemed, was the beautiful Protestant version of Estie, the version without the Jew and without the fat, without the very traits that made the body an obstacle impossible to ignore. Yes, the world was clearly optimized for white, virginal women, their bodies somehow both visible and invisible at once, but didn't Alice's awkwardness, her loneliness, serve as proof that the physical wasn't everything? That there were other things that mattered more?

Except now Dan was back, and he was dating Alice, which meant that Alice's looks trumped her awkwardness after all, and that Estie had greatly overestimated her own importance to either of them, because who wouldn't choose Alice over Estie? Or—worse—*Dan* over Estie? Estie shuddered. No doubt about it, she was going to lose Alice, was already losing her, in fact, because people like Alice and people like Estie didn't belong together. If only surfaces mattered, then Dan and Alice deserved a happily ever after, and Estie deserved Owen, never mind his steady supply of snot rags and his excuses and his fake degree. She was married and a mother, and right now, her baby was sleeping, so maybe, if she was lucky, she had time to empty the dishwasher.

"Please tell me you still like red Kool-Aid," Penny told Estie when she came over that weekend. "I got it special to cheer you up." She was at the charley-horse stage of pregnancy, and Jack was traveling for work, and she liked holding the baby, Penny insisted, liked sitting on the couch with the baby and admiring her rosebud mouth and long lashes. To hear Penny tell it, the baby was beautiful, and while Penny was there, Estie could see it too—the baby's sweet little fingers, her perfect pink ears.

"I do still like Kool-Aid," Estie said. In the kitchen, Owen was sitting in front of a giant pile of student papers, snot rag in one hand, phone in the other. "Uh huh," he was saying to the person on the other end of the line. "Uh huh." *"My mom,"* he mouthed to Estie when she came in to look for a pitcher, then put the phone down so he could blow his nose. "No, Ma," he said, adjusting his grip, "it's just allergies." Estie turned on the tap and filled the pitcher, then emptied the Kool-Aid packet into it. "It's been a little hard," he went on, "but we're managing." Then he said, "Well, the endowment took a hit during the housing crash," and Estie understood that he still hadn't told his parents about Norton. She clanged the spoon she was using against the side of the pitcher to signal that she'd heard, and Owen made a face at her. "Oh, that," he told his mother, "that's just Estie cooking."

In the living room, the baby was back to being just a baby. Estie felt deflated. Here it was, her life: only three miles from the house where she'd grown up, still hanging out with her only childhood friend, except that instead of going to school, she was on unpaid maternity leave from a job whose wages couldn't support a family of three. Meanwhile, Penny was killing it with her giant accountant husband and flattering wardrobe, with her job as a speech therapist who actually helped people. Penny's life, it seemed to Estie, was unfolding like a fairy tale, the ugly duckling transforming into a swan. In another year or so, it would be time for their fifteenth high school reunion, where Penny would finally have the opportunity to wipe the floor with the likes of Joseph Van Vranken while all the now-matronly former cheerleaders looked on.

"Oh Estie," Penny said, reaching over to squeeze Estie's knee. "Are you crying?"

"No," Estie said. "Maybe." Her eyes were watering, she knew that much, but God, if this was her life, why couldn't she appreciate it? It was shameful, really, her insistence that there was more out there, that she deserved more—she was like the child who, when her parents insist she only eat three Oreos, dreams that one day her true parents, the king and queen of some small European principality, would come and whisk her away to assume her rightful, Oreo-laden place on the throne.

"Estie?" Penny said, her voice gentle.

Estie swallowed. The last thing she needed was to bare her true selfish self to Penny, and yet she had to say something. "I have no parenting instincts," she said finally, blinking back tears. "I hate changing diapers." Maybe that wasn't the real reason she was crying, but at least it was part of the truth.

"Oh, sweetie," Penny said, almost perfunctorily, "everybody does."

"I hate giving baths."

"Then make Owen do it."

"I don't like wearing thongs."

Penny arched an eyebrow. "Then don't wear them."

"You don't understand," Estie told her. "You grow up surrounded by parents—hundreds of parents—and you read books and see movies and watch *A Baby Story* and all those videos in childbirth class, and you still end up completely unprepared, and nobody cares, and you're still expected to raise this little baby into adulthood, which is eighteen years away. And don't tell me everyone goes through this when they become parents. I know they do."

For a few moments, Penny didn't say anything and just sat there with Estie's baby pressed against the baby inside her. Then she said in a low voice, "You seem really down. Are you sure you're okay?"

"I'm fine," Estie said. Suddenly, she couldn't wait for Penny's visit to be over. She took a deep breath. "Sorry I'm being so hormonal," she said in as calm a voice as she could muster. "I think I just need more sleep."

Penny nodded, but she didn't look convinced. "I'm sorry it's so hard."

"It'll get better," Estie recited flatly. "It has to."

"I know," Penny said, but she didn't know. How could she? Her baby was still safely ensconced in her belly, requiring no more than what her body already knew how to give.

After Penny left, Estie refreshed Dan's blog and then her email. Nothing. She checked on the baby, who had fallen asleep in Penny's arms and was now napping in her bouncy seat, and Owen, who was also napping, using his stack of papers as a pillow, and Herbert, who was sitting on the windowsill staring mournfully at the birch on the front lawn, which was quickly losing its leaves. Once everyone was accounted for, she opened her email again and reread the message from Dan—"The three of us should have a mini reunion one of these days!"—and quickly composed another email. "So listen," she wrote, "I'm going to be in the area next week. Want to have lunch?" Her heart was pounding again, but she ignored it, just like she ignored the churning in her stomach. What, exactly, did she think she was doing? *Nothing*, she told herself, and then clicked on Send. Seeing old friends. Airing herself out.

This time, Dan wrote back almost immediately: "Lunch sounds great! Let me know!" Beneath that, he started a new paragraph: "Weird timing, btw! I had a dream last night that I went to the credit union and you were one of the tellers!"

It wasn't a sex dream or anything, but at least he was thinking about her, and if he was thinking about her, maybe he wasn't thinking about Alice. Either way, she would see him, and she would know, or if she didn't know, she would ask him. For one brief second, she allowed herself to imagine Dan touching the hem of her jacket, then her hair, then her skin, and saying something like "I've never stopped loving you," but that was beside the point. She didn't necessarily want to sleep with him, or to beat Alice to sleeping with him—what she wanted was certainty, and maybe, as a kind of added bonus, a chance to feel beautiful and competent and awesome the way she used to back in college. She googled the distance of the drive—just under two hours. She could go, have lunch, and be back well before Owen got home from school. She wouldn't even have to tell him she was going, although she definitely would. Unlike him, she had no reason to lie.

12

IN THE END, ESTIE DECIDED she'd drive down to see Dan that Wednesday, which left her enough time on the front end to worry about what she was going to wear, and enough time on the back end to recover before the weekend, when it was harder to keep up appearances. Also, on Wednesdays, Owen had a late afternoon class.

Monday afternoon, Estie's mother stopped by with a baby-sized witch hat even though Halloween wasn't for another month. "Baby's first costume," she said. "Also, your brother called. He's getting a divorce." She blinked, and for a moment Estie was afraid her mother would start crying and Estie would be called upon to comfort her, which was something she'd never been good at doing. Her mother, though, didn't fall apart, saying instead, "You really can't tell about other people's marriages."

"No," Estie agreed. "You can't." She'd lived with her parents her entire life and she'd still been completely blindsided by their divorce, which they'd announced the day after she'd turned sixteen because, her father explained, they didn't want to ruin her birthday. "Plus, now that you have your license," he'd said, "you can drive Sammy to soccer."

"But where are you going to be?" Estie had asked, and Sammy, who had watched the whole thing unfold, said, "I'll just quit soccer. I don't mind."

Estie's father shook his head. "This isn't about soccer."

"Then what's it about?"

Her parents exchanged glances. "Damned if I know," Estie's father said.

And now, more than fifteen years later, Sammy seemed as equally mystified by his own divorce as Estie's father had been about his: "I just don't know what happened. I really thought everything was fine."

Estie thought back to the last time she'd seen Sammy and his wife, a week or so before Owen's summer term ended. They'd seemed so pleasant, so content, Sammy grilling hamburgers in their mother's backyard, his wife playing Chutes and Ladders with the children. The littler one was just finishing preschool, and Estie's mother baked him a graduation cake complete with a rolled-up fondant diploma. "I saw it on YouTube," she said modestly in a gorgeous imitation of a real grandmother. "I watch it every night before bed."

Later, after Sammy's kids had gone to sleep, Owen had asked Sammy's wife what she planned to do once both of them were in grade school—"All that free time," he'd said without a drop of irony. "I envy you"—and Sammy's wife had smiled and shrugged, because what else could she say? Researching alimony? Finding a lawyer?

"I know exactly what happened," Alice declared gleefully when Estie called to tell her Sammy's news. She had a theory, she explained, that between the stress of having babies and the general cluelessness of most men, many couples ended up falling out of love once they had kids. "And by couples," she said, "I mean the women who get stuck with the brunt of the work." But because raising children required so much effort, and because nobody was really having sex anyway, women frequently decided to bide their time until the children were finally old enough for one parent to manage. "And this is why," Alice concluded, "so many people end up getting divorced once their kids are in preschool."

"That's the most depressing thing I've ever heard," Estie said.

"Then tell me it isn't true."

"It isn't."

"Well," Alice said, "I'll bet you real money that that's exactly what happened with Sammy. It's certainly what happened with Dan." She stopped short, though, of saying, "And it's definitely what's going to happen with you and Owen," although Estie heard it anyway and felt herself flush, not because she couldn't imagine her life without Owen, but because she couldn't imagine her life alone with the baby, and wasn't that exactly Alice's point?

"Anyway," she said, changing the subject, "Dan has kids? How old?"

"One kid. Three or four," Alice said. "Didn't I tell you?"

"I didn't even know he was married, let alone divorced."

"His ex is a dental hygienist or something. He says he still flosses after every meal."

"His gums must be sore all the time." Estie flossed once a day, or at least she used to, before the baby. Now just brushing teeth seemed a huge accomplishment. Suddenly, though, she saw her opening. "I bet that interferes with kissing."

Alice didn't take the bait. "Hmm," she said noncommittally. "I guess."

Estie wanted to stomp her feet in frustration. Alice was impossible. The whole thing was impossible.

"Maybe I'll send him a SmartSonic Pro," Alice continued. "It eliminates the need for floss."

After hanging up with Alice, Estie asked Google, "Do kids cause divorce?" and Google answered, "Divorce is more common among couples without children," which was really neither here nor there. Then again, hadn't Estie's parents' divorce been due, at least in part, to her mother's endless list of chores, the majority of which involved Estie and Sammy? Every evening during Estie's childhood, her mother spent a good half hour grimly updating the calendar she kept on the refrigerator, then briefing everyone on the next day's itinerary: "Sammy has piano lessons at four and Estie has the orthodontist at 5:30. Then I'm going to pick up some chicken for dinner. Then Estie and Sammy will do homework, and Dad will mow the lawn, and I'll fry. Eat at 7:15. Estie works on her history paper. Watch TV for an hour at 10. Brush teeth. Bed at 11."

"Sir, yes, sir!" Estie would salute her smartly.

But then her mother would forget to bring a cooler for the chicken, and the orthodontist would be running late, and the parked car would get too hot, and what about salmonella? And instead of doing their homework as scheduled, Estie and Sammy would fight over the remote, Estie usually winning because she was the taller one and could hold it just out of Sammy's reach. And then, instead of working on her history paper, Estie would watch back-to-back reruns of *The Real World* on MTV or *Little House on the Prairie* on TBS.

"Oh, Estie, really," her mother would say. "Do we have to cancel our cable?"

And so they'd end up eating McDonald's, and then Estie's mother would sit next to Estie and Sammy to make sure they actually did their homework, and Estie's father would flit in and out of the room wondering whether Estie's mother had had a chance to get the dry cleaning and if she knew where his nail clippers had gotten to.

"For heaven's sake," Estie's mother would snap at Estie if she dared put down her pencil. "You really think I want to sit here and watch you do this crap? I have much better things to do with my time."

"Like what?"

"I don't know," her mother said. "Clean out the tile grout with a toothbrush. Pick my nose."

Those kinds of statements never seemed to bother Sammy, but they made Estie crazy. "Ha ha, Mom," she would say. "You need to stop living vicariously through me."

"Right." Her mother didn't miss a beat. "Because what I want to be more than anything is an unpopular, insecure high school student. Once just wasn't enough for me."

Then Sammy would hoot and Estie would storm off, and after the requisite apologies, her mother would fetch the calendar and begin reworking the next day's schedule, looking for a way to make up the forty-five minutes they'd just spent fighting and the hour Estie had wasted earlier. "At this rate," she'd mutter, "we're going to be up until one for the rest of the week."

"You don't have to do this," Estie told her again and again. "I can manage my own time." And her mother would say, "Oh, really? Then show me." And later she would lock herself in the bathroom—she was always locking herself in the bathroom—and stay there until Estie knocked dutifully on the bathroom door, saying something like "I'm sorry" or "I need to brush my teeth" or "I need help with calculus." If none of those worked, she'd send in Sammy, who was generally better at getting her mother's attention because he was younger and cuter and willing to say things like "Mom, come out. I think I have a suspicious mole."

"Just give me a minute," her mother would tell him, and Estie would retreat to her perch in front of the television until the next set of commercials when, if her mother still wasn't out, Estie would head back to the bathroom: "Are you okay? You need me to call Dad?"

Her father, somehow, seemed to exist outside all the drama, a cheerful figure who showed up just in time for dinner and spent the evenings hunched over piles of financial documents. Sometimes Estie would interrupt him and say, "I think Mom's upset," and her father would sit back in his chair, take off his glasses and rub the bridge of his nose, and sigh. "Yes," he'd say, "she's always upset about something."

Except that gradually her mother no longer was, and if Estie had to pull an all-nighter to complete this or that paper, instead of staying up to help her, her mother would just shrug, say something about natural consequences, and go watch TV.

"Do you think she's having an affair?" Penny had asked Estie. They were doing homework in Estie's bedroom, and they could hear Estie's mother in the kitchen humming along to the radio. "I mean, it's not that she seems happy, exactly, but she seems as if she *could* be."

"That's disgusting," Estie snapped. "And why wouldn't she be happy?" It was okay if *she* talked about her mother's unhappiness, but she'd be damned if she'd listen to anyone else do it, especially Penny, whose parents still made out on the living room couch. And even if Estie's mother wasn't happy, exactly, at least she'd arrived at a kind of happy busyness. She gave up cooking and started buying frozen lasagnas. She took up jogging and joined a book group and a knitting club. She dyed her hair and began using words like *self-care* and talking like the host of a daytime talk show: "I hear what you're saying," and "I respect where you're coming from," and "Your father is in the bathroom somatizing."

"Somatizing? What's that?"

"Instead of allowing himself to feel actual emotions, he gets diarrhea."

"God, Mom," Estie said. "Gross."

And then, one morning, while Estie was looking for Band-Aids, she discovered the reason for her mother's newfound composure: a vial of Prozac with her mother's name on it. This discovery finally proved what Estie had always suspected: Her mother wasn't normal. She was crazy—crazy enough to be medicated *for her own good*, like all those miserable fifties housewives who popped valiums just to get through the day. After the conversation with Alice, though, new-mom Estie wondered whether she'd misunderstood the situation, and her mother's improvement hadn't been evidence of resignation, of her need to numb herself just to get through the day, but rather a sign that her mother had decided, finally, at long last, to put herself first, to cede control of Estie's and Sammy's lives so she could reclaim her own and leave their father. After all, once Estie and Sammy could manage without her, surely she'd be free to go.

And Estie *had* managed without her mother's hovering, her schedules, her frozen lasagna. On the days Sammy stayed after school for soccer, she'd loved coming home to an empty house, sitting in front of the television with her secret stash of Hershey's Kisses, watching movie after made-for-TV movie about teenage girls nobody noticed right up until they did. During the summers, when she and Sammy went down to Florida to see their father and her mother stayed in Michigan by herself, Estie liked imagining that her mother did the same, sat in front of the TV with her legs up on the coffee table, eating ice cream straight out of the container, then skipping dinner to make up for it. God, Estie had been so naïve, so optimistic, mistaking binging for freedom. These days, sure, adult Estie could eat whatever she wanted, watch whatever she wanted, but none of that changed the fact that everything began and ended with the baby, even those things that had nothing to do with being a mom. Alice was right, Estie couldn't go it alone, she was too weak, too tired. Not that she wanted to walk away from her life or Owen or anything—at least, not exactly—but she wanted to know that it was an option. She wanted to know that at least she could.

It took Estie until Tuesday night to work up the courage to tell Owen about the lunch. She told him during dinner, which that night was eggs scrambled with pieces of hot dogs, a dish that filled Owen with nostalgia for his childhood, for his mom, who liked to make everything in a skillet. "It's even better with sausage," he told Estie as he spooned the mixture onto his and Estie's plates. "Or ham. Mmm . . . ham."

"Shouldn't have married a Jew, then," Estie said matter-of-factly, and then blurted out the part about Dan, kind of: all she managed to get out was a choked "Oh, and I'm meeting a friend for lunch tomorrow."

"Oh yeah?" Owen asked, looking interested. "Who?"

"A friend from college," she said. She speared a slice of hot dog with her fork. "Dan."

"Dan?"

"You know," Estie said, keeping her voice light. "*Dan* Dan."

"Oh," Owen said, understanding. He chewed in silence for a few minutes—had he always been such a loud chewer?—then said, "He's coming to town?"

Estie patted her lap, inviting Herbert into it so she would have somewhere to look other than Owen's face. "I'm going to drive to Indiana. He's working at a college near South Bend."

"Oh," Owen said. He chewed some more, then took off his glasses, wiped them with the hem of his T-shirt, and slid them back on. "Can I ask why?"

Estie swallowed hard. "I need somewhere to go," she said, her voice shaking, "and South Bend is closer than Chicago."

"I can go with you."

"How?" Estie said. "When?" She pointed at the stack of papers piled up in the chair next to Owen's.

"On the weekend. We could drive to the dunes. Spend the night."

"How?" Estie said again. "With what money? I'll go, I'll take the baby, I'll be back in time for dinner."

"I don't understand," Owen said.

"Me neither," Estie wanted to say. Instead she said, "It's like a mini reunion. Alice might be there too." It wasn't so hard to lie to your spouse after all, it turned out. Or, apparently, to lie to yourself.

That was the end of *that* conversation, although later, while Estie was trying to transfer the baby, who had fallen asleep on the boob, into the crib, Owen came and stood in the doorway, his expression inscrutable, and watched as she set the baby down on the mattress. The baby moaned, and she froze. "Come on, baby," she whispered. "Sleep." The baby sighed, and her eyelids fluttered, but she didn't wake up, and after a moment Estie tiptoed out of the room. In the hallway, she held out the palm of her right hand so that Owen could high-five her. He didn't. Instead he rubbed his eyes with his fists.

"Why don't you ever use Rosie's name?" he asked. "She has a name, you know. A good one." Then he said, "This is so hard. Why is this so hard?"

"I don't know," Estie said. "Hormones?"

Owen took her hands in his and pressed them against his chest. "Tell me I'm the love of your life," he said quietly.

"I married you, didn't I?"

Owen didn't let go of her hands. "That isn't the same thing."

"Sure it is."

"Tell me."

Estie forced herself to look directly into Owen's eyes, which were red, the skin under them a faded purple. "You are," she heard herself say. "Of course you are. It's going to be all right." She wrapped her arms around him and patted his back soothingly, just like she was supposed to. "We're going to be all right," she said, which maybe was kind of a lie as well, but it was the best she could do right then, and she hoped it would be enough.

13

IT WAS DIFFICULT NOT TO spend the entire morning rushing to the bathroom to ponder the ravages of age, the blemishes and dark spots and gray hairs that liked to stand up straight and gleam under fluorescent lights. Estie did her best to resist, to focus instead on keeping her hands steady and precise. She had worn her favorite maternity jeans and her favorite blouse, a gray linen shift that she imagined made her look billowy and mysterious, but now, upon further inspection, she worried that the jeans emphasized her postpartum belly, that the shirt screamed out "matronly." Owen was always saying that men had it easier when it came to clothes, and really, he was right. All he had to do was put on ironed khakis and a polo shirt to look crisp and fresh and intelligent, like the kind of man you hoped your kid would turn out to be.

Out on the highway, the sky was gray and bleak, the road brimming with semis. At times, trucks' trailers rose around Estie like walls, "Wash me" and "Jesus saves" finger-scribbled into the grit on their sides. At first, all that driving felt exhilarating, just Estie and the baby—Rosie—and the wide-open highway—but less than an hour into the drive, traffic slowed down, then slowed down some more, finally settling into an agonizing, on-and-off crawl. It took another mile—a good thirty minutes—before Estie could make out the flashing lights of emergency vehicles and plumes of black, oily smoke. After a few hundred more feet of stops and starts, Estie saw two cop cars, a fire engine, and an ambulance, its bay doors wide open. The smoke, she realized, was coming from a hatchback going up in bright orange flames in the left lane. The fire was so intense there was no way anyone in the car could have survived—was that a shadow in the driver's seat? Just the thought made her sick to her stomach. She glanced away, and for a moment, she ended up locking eyes with a pimply, teenaged boy driving a rusty sedan whose rear window was a sheet of plastic held in place by duct tape. Estie felt her face grow hot, but the boy's expression remained impassive, as if he were merely taking in one more cow by the side of the road. His vacant glance untethered her, and even though she could see herself in the rearview mirror, she had to reach up and touch her face to verify that the reflection was actually hers, that she hadn't disappeared entirely. She must have lifted her foot off the brake then, because she heard the sound of metal against metal and an unseen force seemed to jerk her forward. In the back of the car, the baby made a weird, strangled gasp, then started crying. It took Estie a minute to understand what had happened, but then she did: she'd rammed into the car ahead of her. "You're okay, baby," she told the baby—Rosie—then tried to twist around to see whether she really was okay. Rosie began crying louder.

By then, the cars behind her were honking and the driver of the car Estie had rear-ended had pulled over onto the shoulder of the highway. Estie straightened herself out and turned on her signal, catching another glimpse of the boy in the car next to hers. His hand was covering his mouth, and his shoulders were shaking. Was he *laughing*? Estie couldn't believe it. *"Fuck you,"* she mouthed, then pulled over behind the car she'd hit. She turned off the engine, got out of the car, then opened the rear passenger door and scooped Rosie out of her bucket seat, cradling her tightly against her chest. "You're okay," she said again, and apparently the baby believed her, because she stopped crying almost immediately and started hiccupping. "That's right," Estie said. "You're fine." She waited patiently, the baby a warm, steadying weight in her arms, as the other driver, an elderly man in a beret, worked his way out of the driver's seat of his LeBaron. He was wearing a cannula that led to a black shoulder bag.

"I'm so sorry," Estie told him once he'd freed himself from the car. "I'm so, so sorry. Are you okay?"

"I'm seventy-nine," the man told her. "I don't need this crap." Slowly, slowly, he shuffled all the way around his car, examining it. "At least nobody's hurt," he conceded finally. "And you're the one with all the damage."

Estie shrugged, but the man was right, although it was only after they took photos of the cars and of each other's licenses and registration, and after the old man squeezed his way back onto the highway, that she realized that she had, in fact, managed to mangle the car so badly that the steering wheel seemed loose, disconnected from the whatever it was that enabled the wheels to turn.

By then, one of the cop cars from the accident had made its way over. "Everyone all right? Baby okay?" the cop—a woman whose red hair was shaved on the sides—asked her. "Need me to call a tow truck?"

Estie nodded. She felt humiliated, weak, even though she towered over the cop.

"Need me to call anyone else?"

"No, thank you," Estie said.

"Okay," the cop said. "Just be sure to stay away from that mess up ahead."

Once it was clear that no tow truck would be coming until the police cleared away the other accident, Estie called Penny because Owen was teaching and a good hour out on the other side of Briarwood. At least that's how she explained matters to Penny. She wasn't sure how she was going to explain the whole thing to Owen, her distraction and endangering the baby, not that Rosie had been in any real danger: rear-facing infant seat, five-mile-an-hour collision, emergency vehicles nearby. And then there was the part about money—thinking about the money made Estie woozy. How much would repairing the car even cost?

At least Penny didn't ask any questions. "Sure," she told Estie almost immediately. "It'll be an excuse to skip out on our staff meeting. Give me five minutes and then I'll head out."

Estie pulled the stroller out of the trunk and lowered the baby back into her bucket. She recalled seeing a sign for an exit not long before she had reached the accident, so once she had the baby locked and loaded and had tucked the car seat base into the stroller basket, that was the direction she headed. She could feel her skin prickling under the gaze of the cars inching past—were they judging her, out with a one-month-old baby, walking toward a burning car that was emitting God-knows-what chemicals? And what about those people who rolled down their passenger-side windows and asked if she needed help, as if this weren't the setup for some slasher film? What did they think when she said no, she was fine, a friend was coming to get her?

It took her maybe five minutes to reach the site of the burning car, and she used those five minutes to pray for no dead bodies with an earnestness she didn't know she had in her. Once she got close enough, she saw that a woman was sitting in the back of the ambulance, an oxygen mask over her smudged face, her hair sticking to her cheeks and forehead in sweaty tangles. She was rocking back and forth while a paramedic wrapped a blood pressure cuff around her right arm. Estie exhaled in relief: that had to be the driver. The woman looked up right then, her eyes unfocused, so Estie kept on moving, nodding obediently when one of the cops, a man, this time, with a thick caterpillar mustache, intercepted her and said, "So you're the one we're getting all those calls about?"

"My car broke down, and a friend is meeting me at the exit."

The cop leaned over to peek at Rosie. "Cute baby," he said thoughtfully, and suddenly Estie had a vision of him declaring her unfit and calling Child Protective Services. She felt herself starting to sweat. The cop gave her a searching look. "It's another quarter mile," he said finally. "If you wait a few minutes, we can have someone drive you."

"That's okay," Estie said. "I'm almost there."

The cop shrugged. "Suit yourself. Next time, though—" and then he stopped. "Oh, who am I kidding?" he said. "What are the odds of a next time?"

Once she was off the highway, Estie didn't have to wait long for Penny. "Tell me that isn't your car," Penny said, indicating the dark plume of smoke. Estie shook her head no, then busied herself trying to install the car seat base in Penny's back seat. "We probably don't even need it," she told Penny, cribbing from the mustached cop. "I mean, what are the odds of getting in two accidents on the same afternoon?"

Penny shrugged. "Ask that man who took the train from Hiroshima to Nagasaki and ended up getting bombed a second time."

"Ugh," Estie said. "Really?"

Penny nodded. "I heard about him on a podcast."

They drove on the service road parallel to the highway, then got back on once it was clear they were past the accident. After the noise of the traffic and the fire, the car seemed quiet, a cocoon of silence gliding along I-94 while large trucks rattled by. Estie felt a lump in her throat. "I can't believe you came all this way to get me."

"You'd have done it for me."

But Estie wasn't sure that she would have. "I don't know," she said.

"Sure you would have," Penny said. "That's just what friends do."

"You're wrong," Estie said. "Remember that time we went to Taco Bell, and you didn't have any money, and I ordered two tacos and ate them both? It never even occurred to me to share."

"Well," Penny said, "do you remember that sparkly gold pen you had in ninth grade? You didn't lose it. I just took it for myself."

"What did you do with it?"

Penny shrugged. "I don't know. Hid it under my bed and forgot about it."

"I loved that pen," Estie said. She looked out at the side of the highway, blinking back tears.

"Oh no," Penny said. "I didn't know it meant so much to you." Estie glanced at her to see if she was joking, but Penny looked sincere. "I thought it was just a pen."

"It's not the pen," Estie said, crying even harder. "It's this whole thing with Owen's job. I just wish he was still at Norton."

Penny reached over and squeezed Estie's hand. "I'm so sorry," she said. "There are tissues in the glove compartment."

Naturally, the glove compartment was pristine: just tissues and the driver's manual. Estie blew her nose, then tucked the tissue into her pants pocket. "I'm sorry I'm so hormonal."

"You keep saying that," Penny said. "But what if you're not?"

Estie sighed impatiently. "Have you been talking to Owen? Are you also going to tell me I'm depressed?"

"No," Penny said, "but I am going to tell you that it's okay to be actually upset if something's actually upsetting you. Like Owen losing his job."

For a moment, Estie considered telling her all of it, the part about the Ph.D., the part about the newspaper article, the part about Owen's parents not knowing, but wasn't it enough that Alice pitied her? Did Penny need to pity her too? "Nothing's upsetting me," she said. "Except for the car. I just don't know what we're going to do about the car."

"You look tired," Owen said when he came home from work. "How'd the lunch go? Is it true that first love never dies?"

"I didn't make it," Estie said. "I wrecked the car out near Jackson."

"You're not serious."

"I am."

Owen closed his eyes for a long moment, then opened them again. "I knew you weren't in shape to drive." He picked up Rosie, holding her out at arm's length, inspecting her carefully for any damage. "I guess she looks fine."

"Because she is fine."

"Are you fine?" Owen asked the baby. She didn't answer. He turned to Estie. "Are *you* fine?"

Estie nodded. She knew she was at fault—even the law said so—but Owen's disbelief irritated her. "And you don't have to worry," she said, "Dan's dating Alice."

Owen stared at her uncomprehendingly. "What?"

"Dan's dating Alice," Estie repeated, "so it's not like I'm going to leave you for him." She felt like an idiot the moment the words were out of her mouth. Like leaving Owen for Dan was even an option. And anyway, it wasn't as if Dan seemed all that heartbroken that she hadn't made it: "Thanks for letting me know," he'd written in response to her email canceling their lunch. "Maybe another time." She may as well have been a business acquaintance.

"Well, fuck," Owen said. "I can't believe you wrecked the car."

The aborted road trip had apparently worn Rosie out: the next morning she woke up irritable and insistent on being held, her chin trembling every time Estie put her down. And on top of that, they were dangerously low on diapers. On the way home in Penny's SUV the previous afternoon, Estie had managed to convince herself that not having transportation while her car was being fixed wouldn't matter, but now she saw that she'd been overly optimistic—Target was four miles away and Owen was in class. This was her penance for being so careless, for obsessing over Alice, for wanting to see Dan. She picked up the phone and forced herself to call her mother, who said, "I don't understand. Why were you even out on the highway?"

"Because I was," Estie said with as much finality as she could muster.

"I don't understand it," her mother said again. "What were you thinking?"

Penance, Estie reminded herself. *Penance.*

"Fine," her mother continued. "I'll get you some diapers. But I have yoga at eleven." Then she said, "Why is that baby still crying? Is she hungry?"

Rosie *was* hungry—ravenous, in fact. According to Google, this was the dreaded six-week growth spurt. "Just hang in there," Google advised, "It'll be over in two or three days." Easy for Google to say—it wasn't the one with no milk and cracked nipples—just like it was easy for her mother to advise "She's probably cold" when she arrived with the diapers. She rooted through her purse, triumphantly producing a long-sleeved shirt that read "Grandma's Favorite Gal." Estie watched her mother struggle to fish Rosie's small fists out of the sleeves of the new shirt but didn't offer to help. Rosie kept on crying.

"Huh," her mother said, handing Rosie back to Estie, then staring as Estie bared a breast and tried to ignore her mother's eyes on her body, on her gigantic areolas and flabby belly. Estie steeled herself for a comment about her weight, but instead her mother resumed complaining about Sammy's soon-to-be ex, which was her new favorite thing to do: "She made Sammy do all the grocery shopping. And she didn't even wash the outside of bowls." Rosie, finally calm, started hiccupping, and Estie's mother laughed. "Look how she's watching you," she said. "I remember you looking at me like that."

Estie looked down and caught Rosie gazing up at her as if she were marvelous and precious and rare. The intensity of her gaze made Estie uncomfortable—nobody else looked at her so intently. What was Rosie seeing? And how did a person go from that kind of adoration to ambivalence or something worse? No, thank you. If Rosie ever ended up feeling about Estie the way Estie felt about her mother, she'd be bound to . . . do what? Kill herself? Run away? "You'd be better off without me," Estie would tell Rosie and any other future children, her voice calm with resolve, and then she'd get on the next plane to wherever, where she'd start over as a single woman, a woman on whom no one depended, who disappointed no one.

She was shaken out of her reverie by Herbert, who'd decided that this was the perfect time to sharpen his claws on the corner of the couch.

"I can't believe you let him do that," Estie's mother said. "He'd be out of my house so fast . . ."

"He's a *cat*," Estie said.

"You could at least declaw him."

"Because that's humane," Estie agreed.

"Okay," her mother said. "Fine. I see you're in a mood."

"I'm not in a *mood*!"

Her mother sighed in exasperation. "See what I mean? This parenting thing never ends. And now I'm late." She stood up to go. "On the bright side," she added as an afterthought, "eventually you get more sleep. I swear, I barely slept until you were in high school."

"That wasn't my fault," Estie wanted to snap. "You just needed some meds."

"One day you'll understand," Estie's mother continued, a little gleefully. "And when that happens—"

"—you'll remind me that you told me so," Estie interrupted. Had her mother forgotten how deeply unhappy she used to be? And if she hadn't forgotten, why would she wish something similar on Estie? On Rosie? She held her breath until she heard her mother's car start up outside, and then she exhaled in relief. *Penance.* She set Rosie down in her bouncy seat and got up to grab a stack of Oreos from the kitchen. By the time she was back, Rosie was crying again. Estie picked her up and nestled her in her arms. God, she thought, please let Rosie stay quiet long enough that Estie could eat her cookies slowly, twisted open, one half at a time. Rosie, though, was apparently in cahoots with Estie's mother. Already, she was squirming, mouth working, head twisted toward Estie's chest. How was it possible that she was hungry again already? And then the phone rang: it was Estie's father.

"Hang on to your hat," he said. "I'm coming to meet my granddaughter. And you can't say no because I already have tickets."

"You do?" Estie asked over the sound of Rosie's intensifying wails. "For when?"

Her father paused dramatically. "For tomorrow," he said, triumphant, as if announcing some kind of prize. "And I'm bringing Mara with me."

Estie could barely hear him over Rosie's indignant crying. "Mara?"

Her father raised his voice. "My lady friend." Then he said, "My goodness, I swear, what on earth is all that ruckus?"

14

ESTIE'S FATHER'S VISIT—OR, MORE ACCURATELY, Mara's visit—was a kind of epiphany. Not at first—at first Estie was just angry. You were supposed to give moms of newborns some warning, not drop in on them at 10:30 a.m. on a Friday wearing a T-shirt that read "Are you looking at my putt?" At least Mara was dressed normally in a cardigan over one of those strappy tank tops only flat-chested women could pull off. She was slim and tan, and she wore her silver hair in an angled bob. She smelled, just faintly, of coconut.

But what really won Estie over to Mara's side was her calm, the way she walked into the kitchen, where Estie was frantically trying to sweep the floor, and said, "I'll do that. You look exhausted." Her voice was firm, the voice of a nurse or a teacher who refused to be argued with. She put her thin fingers around Estie's wrist and gently guided her down the hallway to her bedroom. "We've got this," she said again. "Don't worry. Sleep." This was, Estie reflected, why women were far superior to men. Why couldn't it be Owen who guided her to her room, and then, while she slept, folded laundry without first composing a lengthy treatise on why cleaning was pointless? Instead, it was Owen who came home after all the work was done, the cleaning rags laundered and neatly folded, and thanked Mara so profusely that Estie felt embarrassed. Not that this prevented her from lording Mara over her mother. "And then I woke up," she reported, "and everything was clean. And there were muffins baking in the oven."

"What kind?" her mother asked. And then, more petulantly: "I could have helped clean if you'd asked me to. I didn't want to overstep any boundaries."

"Boundaries?" Estie repeated, incredulous. "What boundaries?"

"You know," her mother said. "Boundaries."

But there weren't any boundaries, at least not when it came to Estie's mother: twenty minutes later, she showed up at the duplex door carrying a bouquet of pineapple and melon slices cut to look like flowers. And she'd dressed up, too: instead of her regular yoga pants, she was wearing a knee-length purple skirt and matching sandals. "Hello there, Thomas," she said, setting the bouquet down on the coffee table with a small thunk. "How are you?"

It was just like old times, really, if you ignored Owen eavesdropping from the bedroom, where he'd retreated to grade, and the fact of the baby's and Mara's presence: Estie's mother tense and uncomfortable, her voice a little shrill; Estie's father oblivious, standing up to—of all things—hug her, and saying, "You look well, Olivia. You look very well!"

"I'll go get us some plates," Estie said once the greetings were over, and her mother said, "I'll help," by which she'd meant she'd supervise. "She's very tall," she noted with disapproval while Estie gathered plates and spoons. "Definitely taller than your father."

"She's nice," Estie said. "I like her. She's super helpful."

Her mother lowered her voice. "I bring you lasagnas," she said, counting out napkins. "I buy you diapers. I bring you *fruit arrangements*."

"Just the one," Estie said. "And you didn't have to."

"Of course I had to," her mother said. "I'm not losing this contest without a fight."

"What contest?"

"The one you've set up between me and *her*."

"You're being ridiculous."

"Right," her mom said. "*I'm* being ridiculous. Well, let me give you a tip, Estie. A mother isn't the same thing as a maid. And don't think I haven't noticed that you haven't said a word about your father's helpfulness." She turned to glare at Herbert, who had come in to check on them and was now perched atop the kitchen table. "I can't believe you let that cat walk around on *food surfaces*." When Estie didn't answer, her mother inhaled deeply, as if bracing herself for a dive into cold water, and returned to the living room.

Finally alone for a second, Estie picked up her phone and checked Dan's blog—"Eggroll from Thai Too," it read. "Leftover panang curry"—then opened the browser. First she checked if Thai Too was in Chicago—and exhaled in relief when it wasn't—and then she asked Google, "What is difference between mother and maid?"

"You can't (and shouldn't) have sex with your maid," Google answered. If Owen hadn't been hiding, he would have no doubt added, "Or with your mother either."

As things stood, what Owen ended up saying—later, after Estie's mother had left—was, "Wow. Your mother has balls, showing up to meet her ex-husband's girlfriend."

But Estie thought it wasn't so much bravery as curiosity, the desire to see by whom, exactly, her mother had been replaced. And clearly, the visit had backfired. Could anyone doubt that Mara represented an upgrade, a move toward the kind of life that involved very little weeping and no locked doors?

For dinner, Mara assembled a quiche out of the groceries Estie and Owen happened to have on hand, although she might as well have conjured it from thin air. "Are you going to marry her?" Estie asked her father when Mara got up to use the bathroom. "Please tell me you're going to marry her."

"I wish," her father said, "but she's not interested. She lives in this fabulous house on a private lake, with a lanai and a pool and a dock. And she has this roommate, Carol. They've been living together maybe thirty years." He shook his head ruefully and pretended to whisper, "I'm just her side piece."

"You are not," Mara said, startling them both. She smiled at Estie and sat back down. "Carol is my oldest, dearest friend. And I could never leave the menagerie."

It turned out that between them, Carol and Mara had five cats, three dogs, an African gray parrot, and a wandering tortoise.

"When we got the parrot, we swore neither one of us would leave until he died. They're really sensitive, and he was a rescue, so it took him forever to settle in." She pulled out her phone and showed Estie a photo of the African gray wearing a pair of sunglasses and another of her tortoise sitting on a green velvet couch. "That's Maurice. He's *such* a good boy."

"African grays can live up to sixty years," Estie's father pointed out.

"Even married couples don't stay together for sixty years," Estie said. And because she had no self-control, she added, "Some don't even stay together for twenty."

"Touché," said Estie's father, and Mara said, "My point exactly."

Estie tried to imagine it, taking such pleasure from a creature so cold-blooded and leathery. What would she have done if Owen had shown up with a tortoise in a pillowcase like Mara had way back when? She certainly wouldn't have been as calm about it as Carol, who, according to Mara, wasn't even remotely what you'd consider an animal lover but was willing to make exceptions. Unlike Carol, Estie knew, she herself would have put her foot down—maybe even stomped it—and demanded that Owen take the tortoise back to whatever gully it had come from. Then again, hadn't Estie taken in Herbert way back when just because Alice had assumed she would? And if Alice had asked her to take in a tortoise along with the cat, she probably would have said yes to that too. It was easier to adopt an animal than to lose a friend, although apparently the same wasn't true for husbands.

That night, Estie nursed the baby in the clean, dark nursery feeling more relaxed than she had since Rosie'd been born. There was just something about being able to walk around barefoot without collecting crumbs. The baby was warm and heavy in her arms, her right hand strumming Estie's bra strap absently while she nursed and snuffled and nursed some more. What was it like to be her, Estie wondered, to wake up every three or four hours certain that she was neglected and starving, only to be rescued again and again? She could feel the baby gradually leaning into her with the realization of her good fortune, her breath hot and regular on Estie's skin. It seemed impossible that Rosie had once been inside her, that Estie had made her and grew her and that now she was snoring little baby snores, smelling of baby shampoo and milk. Motherhood, Estie thought, was there anything more strange, more mysterious?

She set Rosie down in her crib and headed to the kitchen for a glass of water, but when she switched on the light, she startled Herbert, who was standing on the counter—another *food surface*—and lapping up what remained of the quiche. Mara must have left it on the counter, and Owen hadn't put it away, and now there would be no leftovers. "Goddamn motherfucker," she hissed, although she wasn't quite sure who she meant. She loved Owen, and she loved the cat, but God, was there no end to what was expected of her?

She scraped the quiche into the trash, then filled the pan with hot, soapy water. At some point, she must have started crying, because when Owen came to find her, he said, "Oh, sweetie. I'm sorry," and "It was just a quiche," which only made everything worse. He dug through his pockets for a snot rag, then thought better of it and fetched some toilet paper from the bathroom: "By the way, we're out of Kleenex."

Estie stared at him, at his red-rimmed eyes and the chapped skin around his nostrils. It was unbearable. As if on cue, the baby stirred in her crib, and both Estie and Owen froze, the night stretching out in front of them—although really in front of her—dark and quiche-less and full of interruptions. And then, as if commiserating, the baby began to cry.

The next morning, Mara and Estie's father showed up bearing thawed doughy bagels and little packets of cream cheese they had stolen from the motel's breakfast buffet along with half a dozen tiny Danishes. "Dad," Estie told him as she watched him lay the spread out on the kitchen table, "you don't have to steal food. We have plenty." She was bleary-eyed with fatigue. "Eh," her father said, "it's free." He proceeded to toast one of the bagels and smear it with cream cheese. "There's no food like free food," he proclaimed, taking a bite, and Mara said gently, because apparently she did everything gently, "Isn't breakfast included in the price of the room?"

"What can I say?" Estie's father told Estie. "I like them mouthy." Which was a lie, Estie thought, as evidenced by the divorce. Really, there was no doubt that Mara could do better than a man like him. Estie tried to imagine herself older and Owen-less. Would she ever really be so desperate as to date a man who hoarded single packs of instant coffee and left his dirty dishes and socks to the women in his life, first to Estie's mother, then to Estie, then to the Indonesian maid who came by his condo twice a week?

For the millionth time, Estie found herself wondering how differently she'd have turned out if she'd had the kind of father who cooked and took you to soccer practice, and—if you believed Alice, whose own dad was reportedly perfect—taught you to French braid your hair. The one time Estie had visited Alice at her parents' house, Alice's father had asked Estie such deep, insightful questions over dinner that for days after she'd returned home, all her conversations seemed stale. Not that Alice had been sympathetic. Yes, she agreed with Estie, her parents were lovely, her childhood exceptional, but perfection came with its own set of challenges. "All I want is the fairy tale," Alice said. "Don't tell me it doesn't exist."

But maybe the thing about not very engaged fathers like Estie's was that they taught you the subtle art of attracting others, of orbiting around them, of faking an interest in their interests, anything to get and keep their attention. By the time Estie had met Owen, she knew to hand over the remote without hesitation, to set her car radio to his favorite station so that his favorite tunes became her favorites too.

She even found herself waiting eagerly for the next installment of the *Amazing X-Men*, although she'd never liked superheroes. And she'd done all this with the same ease with which her nineteen-year-old self had worked her way through the oeuvre of Jane Austen for Alice's sake and learned to like NPR. Estie's strategy for making friends and influencing people was to go into her relationships so open-minded as to be blank.

After breakfast, while the baby was down for her morning nap, Estie's father sat her down and began grilling her: "Have you made a will? Have you started saving for college?" He pulled out a checkbook and wrote out a check for $1800—he always gave gifts in multiples of eighteen. "Baby's first savings," he said, handing it over to Estie. Estie nodded. It was more than a month's rent. Was there anything more pathetic than borrowing money from a six-week-old?

Later, he and Mara took Rosie for a walk, leaving Estie and Owen alone in the apartment for the first time since Rosie had been born. Owen must have realized this too, because suddenly, there he was, pressing up against Estie and whispering, "Aren't you wearing too many clothes?"

"Oh God," Estie said. Even though the doctor had given her the all clear, she wasn't sure she was ready, but was there any cliché worse than the one about how parents never had sex, except maybe the one about men who turned to other women because their wives wouldn't put out? Even so, looking down at Owen kissing her newly gigantic breasts, the whole situation seemed so perverse that it was all she could do not to cringe or start laughing. What could she have possibly found sexy about a mouth on her nipples in the past? And was there any way not to see Owen as a stubbled, overgrown man-baby who, more than thirty years after being weaned, still couldn't quite let breasts go? Still, she lay down and dutifully ran her fingernails up and down Owen's back in just the way he liked it, worrying a little that it would hurt when he entered her, but then, when it didn't, not really, she focused on imagining herself in some distant future, all that birthing and nursing behind her, when she'd hopefully, hopefully—God willing—finally get her body back and resume being fully and truly herself.

Maybe it was the sex that had been the final straw. Or maybe it was the sex, followed by her father handing her—*her*, not Owen—the baby for yet another diaper change. Or maybe it was the sex and the sight of Mara and her father sitting side by side on the couch, doing the Sunday crossword, while somewhere in Florida, Carol babysat Mara's parrot and Mara's tortoise confident in the knowledge that Mara was coming back, and somewhere in Chicago, Alice and Dan were holding hands and not even thinking of Estie. Or maybe it was the sex combined with the understanding that this was now her life: picking up socks and taking in animals and spreading her legs and allowing grown men and babies to suckle at her teats because that was what women like her—Grade B women—did, and nobody noticed, and nobody cared, and nobody made TV movies about their personal triumphs because nobody regarded them as triumphs: Today, I kept my baby alive. Today, I didn't yell at my mother. Today, I had sex even though I didn't want to.

Suddenly, Estie felt frantic. If only the car accident had been more serious, she could have still been in a hospital bed, sleeping off a concussion, and not here, watching her father gaze lovingly at Mara while saying things like "Try Oleo. It's always Oleo." She needed to do something, but what? She imagined calling Alice and saying, "You were right about all of it," but she wasn't sure what *it* was, and anyway the phone would make it too easy for Alice to dismiss her, to conclude that Estie was overwhelmed by new motherhood, or worse, that Estie was blinded by jealousy, unable to deal with the fact that Dan had chosen Alice, that he would have chosen Alice way back in college if only Estie hadn't jumped the line. But even if Estie wasn't quite sure *why* she was so fixated on the idea of Dan and Alice dating, of them making out and fucking and soaking together in bubble baths, they were a scab that needed picking so that Estie could see what was under it: the raw edges of peeled-back skin, the beads of blood still working their way to the surface. Or maybe she just needed to see Alice, to stand in front of her and say, "Fine, marry Dan, but don't forget I'm your Carol." Or "Don't forget you're my Carol"—she wasn't sure which. Or maybe she'd say nothing, just stand in front of Alice and wait for the lightning bolt—a flash of insight; a set of divine instructions—that would finally, at long last, reveal how she was supposed to move forward.

When Estie's dad and Mara stopped by on their way out of town, Mara hugged Estie so closely that she could feel Mara's chunky necklace pressing into her own collarbone. "Poor you," Mara murmured. Really, Estie thought, her mother was right. Could her father have had it any easier, alone in Florida with Mara? Why did *he* get to land on his feet? What had he done to deserve such joy?

"Don't go," Estie blurted in spite of herself. "Stay."

"You're sweet," Mara said, cupping Estie's face in both her hands and kissing her on the forehead. "Things are hard now," she said, "but Rosie won't be a baby forever." And then she left anyway. After Estie's father's rental car had turned out of sight, Estie found herself trying to imagine Mara back in Florida, walking into the house she shared with Carol and their tortoise, parrot, three dogs, and five cats. "I missed you," she'd say, rushing into Carol's open arms. "I missed you. I'm so glad to be home."

15

NOW THAT MARA WAS GONE, Estie was so restless, so *bored*, that everything filled her with despair: the sight of her greasy hair in the mirror and the work of soaping herself in the shower; the dirty dish pile in the sink and the clean dishes that needed to be put away. "I think I'm in love with my dad's girlfriend," she texted Alice. "She lives with her BFF. They have three dogs and five cats and a parakeet and a tortoise."

Alice ignored the BFF part but commented on the rest: "Ugh . . . Her house must reek."

But it wasn't the animals that Estie wanted: she was barely able to take care of Rosie, let alone the cat, and there was only one of each of them. Maybe if it had been just a matter of feeding Herbert and cleaning out his litter, she could have managed, but Herbert, for his part, wanted more: to eat from Estie's plate, to tear down the stuffies that hung from Rosie's baby gym, to clamp down on Estie's ankles in the middle of the night. And then there was Owen, who was always too worn out and full of mucus to do anything but grade or sleep, and wasn't that also Herbert's fault, kind of? What had Alice been thinking, burdening Estie with a pet that could easily live another decade and required her to pony up hundreds of dollars each year in Meow Mix and vet bills? Mara might have brought home a parrot with PTSD, but she'd also stuck around to take care of it instead of leaving Carol to do all the work. Not that Estie could say any of that to Alice, not over text, and certainly not over the phone, so instead she emailed Dan, who she knew wouldn't say "I told you" so because he hadn't, in fact, told her anything: "I had a baby. Did Alice tell you?"

"Congratulations!" Dan emailed back. "It's a brave new world!"

Estie tried again: "My brother is getting a divorce. Alice thinks having children destroys marriages."

This time Dan wrote back, "Parenting is hard, but SO worth it!"

Estie rolled her eyes. Why did he refuse to mention Alice? Why did Alice refuse to mention him? "Did Alice tell you that she gifted me a cat?" she emailed, but by then Dan had stopped responding. Not that Estie could blame him. Who had the time to answer so many emails? Estie wasn't even *reading* the emails she kept getting from Big Earth: a new design announcement, a request that folks stop leaving dishes in the lunchroom sink, professional photos of Jillian's baby dressed as an angel, each of his blond ringlets aglow with heavenly light (subject line: "Could he be any cuter???").

On Tuesdays and Thursdays, Owen generally made it home by 3:45. "Here," Estie said, handing him Rosie. "Maybe I'll go get ice cream with Penny." She held out her hand for the car keys; her car was still in the shop. It turned out, though, that normal people were still at work at 3:45 p.m., because apparently other people's lives hadn't stopped just because Estie's had, so instead

Estie headed to Big Earth. She had three more weeks of leave, which seemed both like forever and like no time at all. God, she thought as she turned into the parking lot, at least at work she'd be responsible only to herself and to Sylvia, her boss, and Sylvia already knew how to feed and toilet herself. She couldn't imagine it, couldn't imagine dropping Rosie off at Miss Matilda's Darling Daycare, which was where she and Owen had already paid the equivalent of first and last month's rent to reserve a spot. If Estie, who was supposedly chemically bonded to Rosie, couldn't handle being with her all day, how would someone else manage all that neediness, someone who felt nothing for Rosie, who owed her nothing, who might ignore her tearless wails and poopy diapers? Really, it was a miracle most babies made it to adulthood: if their parents didn't accidentally leave them in an overheating car, their day care providers shook them senseless because they refused to stop crying, and how would Estie ever live with the guilt?

At Big Earth, Estie parked in her usual spot, at the far end of the lot, in the section that backed onto the service road for I-94. She was almost to the building—had just stepped onto the sidewalk, in fact—when, casual as anything, a buck emerged from between two of the arborvitae that lined the path to the entrance. When he saw Estie, he froze, foreleg poised midair, and raised his head as if trying to catch her scent. Estie gasped. She'd forgotten all about the sick doe, and even if she hadn't, this buck was sicker: the flesh of his neck and chest looked as if it had boiled over and bubbled, then spilled down his front in a dark, bloody froth.

Estie could feel her skin crawling. "Shoo," she said. "Shoo!" She clapped her hands loudly, but the buck just kept gazing at her. Or maybe he wasn't gazing at her, maybe the massive lumps over his eyes were making it hard for him to see exactly what was going on. Estie clapped again, and the buck took a tentative step in her direction. Estie felt the blood drain from her face. This was another omen. She knew it. What horrible hidden truth would now be revealed? Her knees weak with dread, she began to back away even though there was no way she could outrun a deer. When the buck took another step, she turned and sprinted back to her car. It wasn't far, of course, but suddenly something slammed into her and she felt a pain in her side so intense that, for a few seconds, she was certain that the buck had caught up to her and gored her. She twisted away and began to run even faster, and it was only once she was in her car that she looked back and saw that the buck hadn't even really moved, that he was still by the path watching her with a bemused and haughty expression. *Maybe I'm ugly, lady*, he seemed to be thinking, *but I still have my dignity.* Even so, the throbbing in Estie's side was real, and when she lifted up her shirt, she could see that the right side of her rib cage was already beginning to swell and turn purple, its shape not of teeth or antlers but of a car's side mirror. She must have accidentally smacked into one at full speed. *Perfect*, Estie thought, pressing her hand into the tender area. She leaned back in her seat, wondering what to do next and thanking God that Big Earth's windows didn't face the parking lot.

After some internal back-and-forthing, she dialed Big Earth's front desk and asked Jillian for help. A few seconds later, Jillian emerged from the front door, waving her arms and stomping her feet. The buck trotted for a couple steps, then slowed down and casually ambled away, as if to say, "Relax. I was just planning on going."

"That was a bad one," Jillian said once they were both safe inside. "I guess the snipers haven't gotten all of them yet."

"What snipers?"

"DNR brought in snipers to cull the herd. I guess it's only warts, which aren't contagious or anything, but the drivers on the highway keep freaking out every time they see them. Last week someone jumped the median and almost died." Jillian made what Estie could only think of as a frowny face. "On the bright side," Jillian said, "Sylvia has to let us go early because the snipers come at sundown. That's when the deer are most active." She shrugged, then gave Estie an appraising look. "I can't believe you didn't bring the baby. Did you at least bring pictures?" She pulled out her phone and unlocked it. "I'll show you mine if you show me yours?"

Estie felt herself start to blush. The truth was, it rarely occurred to her to take pictures of Rosie. She had way more photos of Herbert on her phone than she did of the baby. "Oh my God," she said, changing the subject. "Snipers? Really?"

Still, despite the risk of stray bullets, Big Earth seemed like heaven with its bluish fluorescent lighting and its scent of damp clay. From where Estie was standing, she could see Ben and Ryan discussing something earnestly while they unloaded bisque from one of the kilns. She wandered over to the shelves where they kept their stock and picked up a tile etched with two fish swimming in a circle, running her fingers over the raised ridges that outlined their bodies.

"Have you seen the new design?" she heard someone behind

her say. It was Sylvia, looking more tired than Estie had ever seen her, dark smudges under her eyes. She pointed at a tile featuring a doe and stag standing in profile, snouts touching as if they were kissing, the space between their necks forming a heart. "Because of the deer."

"Nice," Estie said.

"You didn't bring the baby?" Sylvia asked, but at least she didn't ask for pictures. As far as Estie knew, Sylvia didn't have any children of her own. "Anyway, there are donuts in the lunchroom."

Estie nodded, then looked around wistfully and said, "I can't wait to come back." It was the truth, she realized, with the added bonus that once she returned, she'd be the primary wage earner, the responsibility for Rosie would fall to Owen, and he would finally understand the mind-numbing boredom of caring for an infant, the sheer impossibility of getting anything meaningful done. "Oh, Estie," she imagined him saying, "I had no idea," and Estie would reply, "I tried to tell you, didn't I?"

"We miss you too," Sylvia said absently. She hesitated as if unsure what to say next, and Estie realized she wasn't exhausted, she was sad.

"Is everything okay?"

Sylvia gave her a searching look. "Do you have a couple minutes? Let's go into my office."

Estie felt her heart sink. Nothing good happened in people's offices, especially not on days you saw sick deer. She followed Sylvia back past Jillian, who took this as an opportunity to announce gleefully, "Did Estie tell you she was practically attacked by a buck on the way in?"

Sylvia motioned Estie into her office. "Was it bad?"

"No," Estie said. "Just gross."

Sylvia sighed, closing the door behind her. "Have a seat," she said, then pulled up a chair beside her and switched to a low voice. "I need to tell you something, and I need you to keep it quiet until I'm ready to tell everyone else." She glanced at the closed door, then turned back to Estie. "The truth is, I'm thinking of selling."

"What?" Estie crossed her arms across her chest, pressing one hand against the bruise. It throbbed. She wasn't dreaming.

"I know," Sylvia said. "But this thing with the deer just feels like a sign"—"*Right?*" Estie wanted to exclaim—"and I have an offer. The thing is, the buyer wants to move production to China and automate most of it."

"You're moving to China?"

Sylvia shook her head. "I'd switch to just doing design. That was always my favorite part anyway." She put a hand on Estie's shoulder. "I'm sorry. I'm waiting to let everyone know until everything is finalized, and either way, nothing is going to happen before January, but since you're on maternity leave . . ." She trailed off. "I'm just glad I could tell you in person."

Estie drove home the long way, slowly. Stupid deer, she thought. No wonder people liked to hunt them. Back at the duplex, she sat in the car, hands on the steering wheel, unsure what to do next. This, she thought, was the real reason Owen hadn't told her about losing his job right away—all of it seemed too impossible, walking inside, saying hello, sharing the news. And then what? It was going to be her, not Owen, working the drive-thru window at Taco Bell, doing her part as the member of the first downwardly mobile generation in America, except that even the drive-thru window would be beyond their reach because minimum-wage jobs couldn't cover day care. Estie could feel herself blanch: instead of eight weeks at home with Rosie, she was looking at five years—babies didn't stop needing you on the weekends or at night, and neither did toddlers. She pulled out her phone. "How long until kids can stay alone at home?" she asked Google, and Google answered, "Age ten in Michigan, age six in Nebraska." As if. Estie might not love mothering, but there was no way she was moving to another state and leaving six-year-old Rosie to fend for herself.

She breathed in through her nose and out through her mouth like Rita, the childbirth instructor, had taught them. She couldn't face Owen. Not yet. And it wasn't as if him knowing would change anything. He'd still have to finish out the school year. Estie would still have to stay home. They'd still have five months on their lease before they could move to a less expensive neighborhood on the other side of the highway. The only difference would be that now Owen would be watching her, judging her for buying name-brand cereal, for insisting on fancy diapers that turned blue when wet, in the same way that she was already judging him for ordering Big Macs instead of hamburgers, for stopping at Starbucks on his way to work. These next few weeks, she realized, were likely to be her last chance at anything resembling freedom, anything resembling privacy. Her pulse pounded in her ears, and her breath caught in her throat. She needed air. She needed a cool shower.

But first she needed to feed Rosie, who started wailing the moment she heard Estie's voice. As if in answer, Estie felt milk seeping into the nursing pads she'd tucked into her bra. She scooped Rosie up and retreated to the bedroom, one breast already bare by the time she sat down on the mattress. Rosie latched on, and for a few minutes, Estie just watched her nurse: she was gasping between gulps, tears still streaming down her scrunched-up face. And then, slowly, Rosie began to relax, her shoulders and back losing some of their rigidity, fists opening like flowers.

"See?" Estie told her. "No big deal. You're fine." She'd been sitting hunched over, back against the headboard, but now she adjusted her position so that both she and Rosie were lying on their sides. If she fed Rosie this way all the time, she thought, she could stay in bed for hours, Rosie clutching her index finger with that firm grip of hers. Estie must have dozed off after that because she woke up to Owen leaning over her, prying Rosie out of her arms. "You know that's not safe," he scolded. "You could have smothered her."

That evening, Estie checked Dan's blog, more out of habit than anything. "Giordano's sausage and mushroom pizza," Dan had written. "Food coma!" It was, she thought, yet another bad sign—wasn't Giordano's a Chicago chain? What was he doing in Chicago? She handed Rosie to Owen and retreated to the bedroom to call Alice, not that Alice would tell her anything, at least not of her own volition. "So," she said when Alice picked up, "what have *you* been up to?"

"Just work," Alice said. "I was just about to head home."

"While it's still daylight?"

"It happens."

Estie could hear the smile in Alice's voice. "You should mark the occasion," she said, careful not to sound eager or pointed. "Order some pizza. Drink some wine."

"Maybe," Alice agreed.

In for a penny, Estie told herself. To Alice she said, maybe a tad too dramatically, "What I wouldn't give for some deep dish!"

"Blech. No, thank you," Alice said. "You know I hate soggy crusts."

It was true. Alice did hate soggy crusts. She hated all soggy bread products—buttered toast, sweaty bagels, ice cream-soaked sugar cones. How had Estie forgotten? If Dan was in Chicago eating Chicago-style pizza, he had to be eating it with someone else. Estie felt lightheaded with relief, awash with fondness for Alice who maybe wasn't seeing Dan after all, for Dan who maybe wasn't seeing Alice. "God," she said, "I miss you so much. We haven't seen each other in ages."

"Well," Alice said, "you've been busy."

"And I wrecked the car."

"What?" Alice sounded suitably horrified, so Estie told her the whole story, kind of, careful to omit the part about how she'd been on her way to see Dan, the part where she'd sent him email after email, the part where she was probably going to lose her job. "So anyway," she concluded, "maybe you could come visit me instead?" Even before she was done asking the question, she felt pathetic. "I just really miss you."

Alice sighed, but she didn't say "I miss you" back. "Maybe after Christmas. I'm so swamped."

"Yeah," Estie said. "I figured." She could hear Rosie cooing in the next room, and Owen saying to her, "You think so? Really? You don't say!" It was the kind of moment meant for Hallmark commercials, the gruff father, preferably shirtless and six-packed, holding a baby against his bare, hairless chest, while the mom, all misty-eyed, looked on—except that after Estie hung up with Alice and peeked into the living room, what she found was Owen slouched on the couch, scrolling through his phone, and Rosie on the floor, kicking her legs and gazing adoringly at a little black-and-white kitten that was hanging from her little baby gym. Here it was, the rest of her life, day after day after day of it. She didn't mean to, but she started to cry.

"What?" Owen said, looking startled. He put down his phone. "What is it?"

"I don't know," Estie said, but then she did. "I'm just stir-crazy. I need some time to myself. I need to go somewhere. I need to see Alice."

Between the mechanic and the body shop, Estie's car would be out of commission for another ten days. It was too long to wait, would provide Estie with too much time to obsess and worry and online shop for I-swear-I'm-not-fat postpregnancy outfits she could wear out in public without cringing, except that she already knew no such outfits existed and that she'd end up cringing anyway, then hiding them in the back of her closet. Better to skip the whole cycle and just wear the clothes she already hated. "So I'll leave Friday after you get home from work," she told Owen, "and be back by Sunday afternoon."

Owen shook his head. "We can't afford another accident." Because he was sitting down, instead of assuming his superhero stance, he tilted his head and looked her straight in the eye, every inch the disapproving father. "You're not in shape to drive and that's all there is to it."

"You can't talk to me that way," Estie told him. "I'm not a child."

"I can," Owen said, "and I will." He said it with such finality that Estie couldn't think of a response, even though, at the very minimum, this trip was something she'd earned after making an entire human out of two cells and then nursing that human between seven and twelve times each day, and changing that human's diapers at least as often, and supporting Owen even though he'd lied and then lied about lying, and accidentally rear-ending someone on the highway, which *wasn't even really her fault*, never mind the legal technicalities that dictated it was. People made mistakes and/or had accidents all the time without being placed on what was, essentially, house arrest, or at least small-town arrest.

"You don't understand," Estie tried again, then stopped to wait for Owen to finish blowing his nose into a snot rag he pulled out from between the couch cushions.

"Ugh," Owen said, sniffling. "This sucks." It wasn't until later, though, when they were both lying in bed, Owen flat on his back and snoring so noisily that even Herbert was glaring at him, fur bristling, that the solution came to Estie. She shook Owen awake. "I could take the cat back to Alice. If I go to Chicago." She could already see the whole thing playing out in her head: Alice opening the door to discover Estie with a cat carrier in her arms: "Surprise!"

Owen sat up and cleared his throat noisily, bolting to the bathroom to spit all that phlegm into the sink. He coughed a couple more times and then ran the water for a few seconds. When he came back into the bedroom, he said, "You're not serious."

"You have to stop saying that," Estie snapped because, really, how much incredulity was she supposed to tolerate? "I wouldn't joke about something like this."

For a moment, Owen looked hopeful, awake, a lost hiker finally spotting a trail marker, but then he thought better of it. "It won't make the drive any shorter."

"What won't?"

"Taking the cat." He exhaled morosely. "Fine," he said. "I'll drive you. But it'll have to wait until the end of the semester."

"But this is *urgent*," Estie wanted to say. "And *private*." Instead she rolled her eyes, which Owen must have somehow heard or imagined.

"Fine," he said. "Then get your mom to drive you." He switched on the bedside lamp, then propped himself up on one elbow so he could—yet again, Estie couldn't help but notice—gaze down upon her from on high. "Okay," he said. "Let's say we both go—"

"We can't *both* go," Estie pointed out.

Owen ignored her. "So just you go. What do you think will

happen? I mean, how do you see this playing out? Like, you walk in, you say hello, she says hello, and then what?"

"Do we really have to do this?"

"Yes," Owen said. "We do. I'll be Alice," and here he launched into a little skit. "Oh, Estie," he said in his best impression of an upper-crust New England housewife, "it's lovely to see you, but I'm going to spend the afternoon being better than you, more sophisticated and worldly, quoting *The New Yorker*, and making obscure literary allusions, and baking bread from scratch, and implying your husband is a loser, all of which, I might add, aren't particularly useful skills—except maybe the husband thing—but they'll still make you feel shit." He turned slightly to signal that he was now being Estie. "Oh, Alice! I was hoping you'd confirm my worst fears about myself. Thank you!"

"It's not like that," Estie said, because it wasn't. She didn't need Alice to make her feel like shit—she was perfectly capable of doing that all on her own. She needed Alice to make her feel good, feel competent—and Alice needed her too. When they were apart, they were awkward and ordinary and unathletic, their bodies fleshy machines that kept them alive. Together, though, they grounded each other: they were still awkward, yes, but whole and embodied, verging on brave. So what if Alice was afraid of heights, and Estie was afraid of bugs, and neither of them could run a mile in under ten minutes? Together, they were able to go rappelling in Wisconsin, drive down to Indiana for the emergence of Brood X cicadas, run the International Half-Marathon in Detroit in two-and-a-half hours. Or at least they'd been able to before Estie got married and had to use her vacation days to visit Owen's parents in Maine.

Estie rolled away from Owen so she was facing the wall. Somewhere, a clock was ticking, and time was moving forward as it always had, but she could no longer see it. Having a baby had transformed time into something elastic, like chewing gum, that could be stretched out, torn, snapped and wadded up, rubbery and glistening and flavorless. If she didn't do something soon, didn't force herself to start moving, she would suffocate. "I have to see Alice," she told Owen. "And it has to be this weekend."

"I can't," Owen said. "If you won't ask your mom, maybe ask Penny?"

And just like that, Estie knew she'd be able to go. Penny would say yes, or else Estie would convince her to say yes. Penny liked rescuing people, or at least she liked rescuing Estie. In high school, she'd let Estie come sleep over on nights Estie's parents were particularly sad; in college, she'd driven all the way back to Briarwood because Estie was home for the weekend; and then there was the way she'd cleaned the bathroom and helped Estie after the car accident. People changed, but they didn't change that much.

~~~~~~

"I'm seven months pregnant," Penny said when Estie asked her about Chicago. "All I want to do is look at baby furniture."

They were walking in County Park, Estie pushing the stroller in which Rosie, in a pair of baby sunglasses, was gnawing on her fist. The sunglasses had been another gift from her mother, a hedge against future cataracts and retina damage and *cancer*, but even Estie had to admit that there was something unbearably adorable about a baby in shades. "She's already cooler than I've ever been," Estie told Penny, and Penny agreed because, well, it was the truth.

"You know where they have nice baby furniture?" Estie asked. "Chicago. It could be a girls' weekend. We could get massages, and a pedicure, and drink Sazerac in some dark bar."

"I'm pregnant," Penny reminded her.

"Then we'll drink Shirley Temples."

It was finally starting to feel like fall, leaves turning but still on the trees. The sky was very blue, and it was easy to feel optimistic, Estie thought, especially now that she was taking control, resurrecting her teetering friendship with Alice by playing Mara to Alice's Carol, a first step toward a future in which she and Alice, and maybe Penny, would be living, if not in a house on a small Florida lake, then across the hall from each other at some senior-citizen complex, their cats wandering back and forth between their apartments in a kind of shared custody arrangement. It would be like one of those sitcoms where a group of older women ended up living in Miami, sunning themselves on chaise longues. One of them would be divorced, another widowed, the third one promiscuous and busty. The pool boy, cute and shirtless, wouldn't have a fighting chance.

"I'll pay for gas," Estie told Penny. "I'll pay for a hotel. You can pick the movies on pay-per-view."

Penny laughed. "Okay. When you put it like that . . ."

And so for about five minutes, the trip was a go, kind of, right up until Owen pulled up their account balance and pointed out that they were in no shape to bankroll a girls' weekend in

Briarwood, let alone in Chicago. "You're not thinking straight," he told Estie, which frankly was infuriating, especially coming from someone who had tried—and failed—to make a living in the highly remunerative field of English literature.

"God," she said, or maybe yelled, "can you just stop? Just, please, stop?"

Owen gaped at her—lately he always seemed to be gaping at her.

"And don't look at me like that," Estie added. "You did this. We were fine until you—*lost*—your job." Even before the words were out of her mouth, she could feel herself flushing. Hadn't she lost her job too, for all practical purposes? Then again, in her case, it wasn't her fault, and nothing was happening until January, and losing her job wouldn't even be a big deal if Owen hadn't also lost his, except that of course it was, because everything was a big deal when you had a baby.

Owen stood up and assumed his superhero stance. "I didn't lose my job on purpose," he said, his voice quiet.

"Then what did you think would happen?"

"Not this." For a moment, they stared at each other, and then Owen said, "I can't think. I'm going for a walk."

"See?" Estie said. "You get to storm out but I'm stuck here with Rosie—I'm always stuck here with Rosie."

"Fine." Owen threw his arms up in the air. "You go for a walk."

"How?" Estie said. "She's going to need to nurse soon."

"I'll give her a bottle."

"Don't you get it?" Estie said. "Don't you see? I can't just not feed her—my boobs already weigh like fifty pounds. Each."

"You could pump."

"When?" Estie said. "Outside? On my *walk*?" God, how she hated the pump, which had been yet another gift from Estie's mother, ostensibly in preparation for Estie going back to work, although Estie suspected it was more about humiliation. When the pump was on—Estie was trying to stock their freezer with milk in case some tragic accident befell her or her boobs—the suction stretched her nipples in ways that shouldn't have been possible, a reminder that this was the same technology farmers used to milk cows. Humans may have invented ribeye steaks and well-done burgers, toilets and TVs and microwave technology, but ultimately, none of it mattered: they still peed and shat and copulated, gave birth and made milk. Yes, the pump came in a fashionable leather carrying case, the irony of which wasn't lost on Estie, but it was still a pump, a tether to the animal self she was supposed to perfume and wipe out of existence.

"Look," she tried again, calmer this time. "I need a break. I need to see Alice. I won't spend a lot of money. I promise."

Owen snapped his thumbnail against the nail of his middle finger—*click*—then snapped it again. He seemed to be losing air, shoulders drooping, fists unclenching, spine loosening into a sag. "Okay," he said finally. "Okay." And then he put on his shoes and went for a walk anyway.

16

"WHAT'S ALL THIS?" PENNY ASKED Friday afternoon when she came to pick up Estie and Owen came out of the duplex with the cat carrier in one hand and Rosie in her bucket in the other.

Owen turned to Estie, incredulous. "You didn't tell her?" and even Estie could hear the whine in her voice when she said, "I thought I did." She didn't *think* she was lying, at least not about taking Herbert, but bringing Rosie was a last-minute decision, prompted by a sudden fear that Owen would put his grading first and Rosie would spend the weekend wriggling alone on the floor, wriggling alone in her bouncy seat, wriggling alone in her crib. Here it was, that fabled mother-baby connection inconveniently rearing its ugly head. She looked pleadingly at Penny, who muttered something about pregnancy brain, and then helped Estie install the car seat and watched without comment as Owen loaded bag after bag of supplies into the back of her SUV: a box of diapers, a folding playpen, a bag for the baby, a bag for Estie, the litter box (empty), a box of litter (full), a box of cat toys and cat dishes.

"Okay," Estie said. "That's everything."

They headed west on I-94, retracing the first part of Estie's drive out to Dan's college. Because Estie wasn't the one driving, she noticed things she'd missed the first time through: a statue of the Virgin Mary on the edge of a field, a barn painted to look like the American flag, a giant leafless tree dotted with vultures. "Real Men Love Babies," a billboard announced. "Heartbeat at 18 days."

"God," Estie said. "Can you believe we live here?"

Penny glanced over at her. She'd kept silent since they hit the road, but now she said, "Do we?"

"What?"

Penny waved vaguely in the direction of the back seat. "Are you leaving Owen?"

"No," Estie said. "Of course not. He just has so much grading he can't parent full-time. And the cat is for Alice."

"Alice?"

"You know, my friend from college. She lives in Chicago."

"Okay," Penny said. It wasn't quite Estie's mother's skeptical *Oka-ay* with the upward lilt on the third syllable, but it was close enough. "I guess I just wish you'd told me what you were really doing instead of all that girls' weekend crap."

"We can still do all that."

"How?" Penny wanted to know. "With the baby?"

Penny was right, Estie realized: there would be no spa visits and no darkened bars, not if they had to bring Rosie along. How had this not even occurred to her? She tried to think of something to say, something that would explain the trip, the cat, and the baby all in one fell swoop. "I'm sorry," she said finally. "We haven't even started, and I've already ruined the trip."

"Don't kid yourself," Penny said. "There's plenty left to ruin."

Estie glanced at Penny's profile, at that hooked nose and mess of curls, but she couldn't tell if Penny was joking.

"Relax," Penny said. "There are gummy bears in the glove compartment."

Estie twisted around to check on Rosie, but she could only make out the top of her head—stupid rear-facing car seat. She could, however, see straight into the carrier, to Herbert, shivering, wide-eyed, and silent. What *did* she think she was doing? Why *had* she brought him along? She turned back to face forward. The road, she noted, was lined with dead skunks and possums, crows pulling at their skin and cartilage. "Remember that sparrow in the parking lot?" she asked Penny. She hadn't thought of it in years, the sparrow she and Penny had seen dragging itself in circles, its left wing extended and limp, in the snow outside of a movie theater. Because they hadn't known what to do, Estie had crouched down and scooped it up, and in her mittened hands, the sparrow's weight had felt insubstantial, as if Estie were carrying a handful of air. She and Penny had headed toward the theater entrance, walking briskly, even though Estie wasn't sure what they'd do with the sparrow once they got inside, and that's when it happened: Estie tripped. One moment, she was fine, and the next she was flying forward, trying to twist around and avoid using her hands. Not that it mattered: the sparrow fluttered to the ground, and Estie had landed on it, a small, crushed lump beneath her hip.

"Ugh," Penny said now, shuddering. "What made you think of that?"

"I don't know." Just on the other side of the yellow line marking the shoulder, a doe lay contorted, one leg up in the air as if it were raising its hoof. A few hundred yards later, they passed another on its side, its mouth wide open. All that carnage, all that spilled blood. A little past Kalamazoo, only a few miles from the exit Estie would have taken to go see Dan if she hadn't gotten into that accident, they passed something that looked like a golden retriever.

The sun was setting by the time they crossed into Indiana. They stopped at a rest area near a nuclear power plant, Penny pumping gas while Estie nursed Rosie in the back seat. "I need to close my eyes for a minute," Penny said when she got back in the car. "This pregnancy is wiping me out."

"No worries," Estie said. They switched seats, and Estie drove the section on the Indiana Toll Road, an ugly, flat stretch of I-90, while Penny slept. She drove carefully, hands on ten and two, making sure to always signal before changing lanes—this time the accident wouldn't be her fault. After they crossed into Illinois, she pulled over. She checked the time and tried to decide—should they go to Alice's office or directly to her condo? Where was Alice most likely to be? *At a restaurant with Dan*, a voice inside Estie whispered. It was Friday night, after all.

"This isn't Chicago," Penny said.

"You're awake."

"Where are we?"

"On the Chicago Skyway." Estie turned right into the parking lot of a squat office building and turned off the ignition. "I just need to figure out where we're going." After that, there was no avoiding the rest of the truth: "I thought we'd surprise Alice."

"She doesn't know we're coming?"

Estie shook her head.

Penny gave her an incredulous look. "Then maybe we should go to the hotel first."

"That's just it," Estie said. "I figured we'd stay with Alice." She picked up her phone. "I'll just text her quick to make sure she's home." As she typed, she was aware that Penny was still staring at her, but she was too nervous to meet her gaze head-on. In the back seat, Herbert stirred in his carrier and Rosie squealed. *Come on*, Estie thought. *See my text*. She waited breathlessly for the gray bubbles that would have indicated that Alice was writing a response, but all that happened was that Herbert started meowing. "Huh," she said, because she had to say something. "That's weird. She's not answering."

By then, Rosie was making restless, snuffling grunts, and Penny was typing furiously into her own phone, no doubt filling Jack in on Estie's bait and switch. Estie's stomach churned. "Are you there?" she texted Alice. "This is urgent." Then, because it *was* urgent, she actually called, but her call went straight to voicemail. She could feel herself starting to sweat. Alice was ignoring her. Behind her, Herbert's meows escalated into a wail.

Penny stopped typing. "Okay," she said, ignoring the racket from the back. "I got us a room at the Palmer House Hilton."

Estie cleared her throat: "Isn't that pretty fancy?"

Penny shrugged. "We'll split it."

They switched seats again, Penny taking over the driving. In the back seat, Rosie began full on crying. "She's hungry," Estie said.

"It's only another twenty minutes."

Estie gritted her teeth. Twenty minutes was fucking forever. In the back seat, Herbert continued wailing.

———

Just the parking for the Palmer House Hilton cost $50 a day, but Estie was too desperate to argue. As soon as Penny stopped the car, she climbed into the back seat and tore at Rosie's car seat buckles, anything to get her to be quiet. "You go ahead," she told Penny between Herbert's wails, then helped Rosie latch on. Once Penny was out of sight, though, Estie smacked Herbert's carrier as hard as she could. "Shut up," she hissed. "Shut up, shut up, shut up!" Herbert yowled.

By the time she made it out of the parking ramp, she was done. Her ears were ringing, Rosie had spit up on her shirt, and God, why had she brought so many things? The thought of having to face Penny, to share a room with her, the cat, and Rosie, made her want to weep. She stood in line at the front desk, blinking back tears. She didn't care how much it cost, she needed her own space, except that once she was presented with the bill, she came to her senses. For that much money, both she and Penny could suck it up, and even then she'd probably have to borrow from Rosie's nascent college fund. Slowly, she made her way to the elevators, feeling as if she'd walked onto a movie set: the columns, the gilt, the ceiling murals and candelabras. In one corner of the lobby, middle-aged men and women in suits were holding drinks and laughing.

The hotel room itself was plain by comparison—once upon a time, it must have been two tiny separate rooms, each with its own bathroom. She set both cat and baby in their various containers on the floor, then headed back to the ramp to get the supplies, which required two trips all on their own. Once everything was stacked in one corner of the room, she collapsed, breathless and sweaty, onto one of the double beds. Penny was already lying on the other bed, her swollen feet elevated. "We need to talk about this," she told Estie, "but not right now."

Estie nodded. She busied herself unfolding the Pack'n'Play and setting up the litter box, then released Rosie from her bucket and opened the door to Herbert's carrier. She placed Rosie in the Pack'n'Play so that she could kick and wriggle to her heart's content and did her best to ignore Herbert's accusatory glare. Then she picked up her phone and texted Alice, "Where are you????" Nothing. The silence in the room was oppressive. "Do you mind watching Rosie while I shower?" she asked Penny, then retreated into the bathroom on her side of the room, where she sat down on the edge of the tub, her head in her hands. There had to be something she could do to make this better. She turned on the water.

By the time she was done, Alice had finally texted back. "What's going on?" she asked. "Did something happen?"

"Guess what?" Estie wrote, teary with relief. "I'm at the Palmer House Hilton," then changed the period to three exclamation marks: "I'm at the Palmer House Hilton!!!"

"You are?"

"When can I see you??"

It took Alice a few minutes to answer, although that could have also been the spotty cell service. "Lunch tomorrow?" read the text when it finally arrived. "Meet you in the lobby?"

"It might be easier to come to you," Estie offered. "Rosie's with me."

"I'll come to you," Alice replied. "See you at noon."

No exclamation mark, Estie noted. She imagined Alice kissing a half-naked Dan goodbye before leaving to meet Estie: "Back in a jiff." She glanced over at Penny, who by then was flipping through the on-demand movie catalog, her face blank. "Want to get room service?" She was already spending so much money that what did a little more matter?

Because desperate times called for desperate measures, or at least comfort food, they ordered a cheese plate and warm, marinated olives, a basket of artisanal French fries and stuffed mushroom caps, a raspberry white-chocolate cheesecake and a homemade brownie with vanilla ice cream. They spread a sheet on the carpet and put on a movie about a thirty-year-old woman sent back to high school. "So it's horror?" Estie asked, and Penny said, "Ha."

They took turns holding Rosie and trying to coax Herbert out from under the bed. When the movie was over, Penny went down to the lobby to call Jack, and Estie thought about calling Owen but texted him instead: "We're here. All is well!" As she did all these things, she also tried to come up with an explanation for the trip, for not being honest with Penny from the get-go, but everything she came up with felt both too obvious and batshit crazy—she couldn't decide which. In the end, she settled for a mere apology. The rest would have to wait. "I'm sorry," she blurted when Penny returned from making her phone call. "I should have told you. I don't know why I didn't."

"You didn't tell Alice either," Penny pointed out.

Estie felt herself bristle. Penny and Alice had only met each other once, but they'd liked each other immediately. Really liked each other, in fact, and really immediately. This had been during their first year in college, when Estie brought Alice home for a visit. Estie hadn't meant to invite her—she and Alice had still been at the wooing stages of early friendship—but Alice had said, "If I have to eat any more dining hall pizza, I'm going to die," and Estie's mom was a pretty good cook. Also, that weekend had been the annual Safer Sex Fest, which was rumored to include drunken orgies and drunken group showers, and so Estie had been glad for an excuse to leave campus: nobody could boot you out of their drunken orgy or shower if you weren't actually present, let alone boot you while welcoming your much-prettier soon-to-be best friend who would no doubt realize that there was much more fun to be had in college without you weighing her down.

The thing was, though, that once Alice was in Briarwood, Estie wasn't sure what to do with her—What if Alice thought her family's dinner conversation boring? What if she found Estie's mother's use of paper napkins unconscionable?—and so she'd called up Penny, who was only an hour away from Briarwood, at Michigan State, and invited her too. She'd thought it would be fun, the three of them eating popcorn and watching reruns of *Star Trek: The Next Generation*, but then Penny had introduced herself to Alice as "the Best Friend," and Estie had felt herself recoil. Not true, she'd wanted to tell Alice, the position of Best

Friend was still wide open and wouldn't Alice look fabulous in it, not that Estie could say that, and anyway, by then, Alice was already admiring the glitter on Penny's nails, the way her hair curled into Jew-girl ringlets, and Penny was raking her fingers through Alice's long blond hair and twisting it into a French braid, the loose strands seeming to glint and spark in her hands. "Your hair could have its own TV show," Penny had told Alice, and watching her, Estie had been overwhelmed by a hot wave of jealousy: What if Alice ended up liking Penny more than she liked Estie? And so, just to be safe, once *Star Trek* was over, she'd told Penny that she and Alice were leaving first thing in the morning, then promised herself never to bring them together again, which turned out to be easy because she lost touch with Penny soon after.

Of course, the three of them were older now, and yet as Estie watched Penny dig through her overnight bag for a toothbrush and pajama pants, she was dismayed to discover that nearly fifteen years after the fact, the idea of Penny and Alice teaming up against her still made her queasy. "She ambushed you too?" Estie imagined Alice saying, and Penny responding, "It's like she's still back in high school. Pathetic." Just the thought made Estie's eyes burn and her nose start running. "I'm sorry," she said again. Pathetically. She turned to look for Herbert, because weren't animals supposed to lower blood pressure in times of stress?—but Herbert just continued glaring at her from under the bed.

"Does she even know you're bringing her a cat?" Penny waited for Estie to answer, and when Estie didn't, her eyes grew wide. "She doesn't *know?*"

Estie shook her head no, then blurted out, "It was her cat first." She couldn't look at Penny, so she stared down at her hands. "And Owen's allergic. And I just can't."

"Jesus, Estie," Penny said, and Estie was pretty sure that Penny was tugging on her curls in frustration, although she was still too scared to look at her directly. "What are you trying to do?" This time, when Estie didn't answer, Penny disappeared into the bathroom.

"Come here, you fucking idiot," Estie whispered to Herbert. "Please." She was pretty sure she was crying, and even more sure she had to stop crying before Penny returned, but Herbert turned away from her and began grooming his paws. In the Pack'n'Play, Rosie sighed softly in her sleep. Estie pulled up the hem of her T-shirt and dried her eyes.

"Is it Alice?" Penny asked when she came back. "Is this whole thing something about Alice? Or about me? Because last time . . ."

Was it possible to die of shame? Estie wasn't sure. She hadn't realized that Penny also remembered that weekend long ago, remembered the way the panicked Estie had lied about her and Alice leaving town. And it would have been a perfectly good lie too, except that the next afternoon she and Alice ran into Penny at the movie theater concession stand where they were seeing, of all things, the ten-year-celebration screening of *Fatal Attraction*. "Turns out we could stay after all," Estie had spluttered, but Penny wasn't an idiot, and with more dignity than Estie could ever hope to muster, she'd said, "Plans change. Enjoy the show." And that had pretty much been the end of their friendship. "I'll call you," Estie had said before Penny walked off, but she hadn't called Penny, and Penny hadn't called her, and then the two of them *had drifted apart*, which was to be expected when you went to different colleges. Or when one of you lied and only owned up to it under duress many years later. "It's definitely not you," Estie said. "It's me."

Penny arched an eyebrow. "That's the best you can do?"

Estie covered her face with her hands. "God, Penny," she wailed. "Why are you even friends with me?"

Penny neatly folded the clothes she'd worn all day and stacked them into a pile. "Because this isn't you. Or it isn't you most of the time. Or at least it didn't used to be."

But Penny was wrong. This *was* Estie, the real one. What was wrong with her? Why was she like this? It was one thing to half-ass a friendship in high school, another thing entirely to do it as an adult and assume that Penny wouldn't notice. And what was it about motherhood that made it all worse? "I'm sorry," she told Penny. "I'm so, so sorry," but Penny didn't say anything, didn't even look at her, just crawled into bed and turned her face to the wall.

"I'm sorry," Estie said again. She felt exhausted and too full from dinner—she was never going to lose the baby weight, just like her mother had warned she wouldn't—and when Penny still didn't respond, she pulled the covers up over her head, checked Dan's lunch ("Hot dogs: poppyseed bun; no relish; lots of peppers"—weren't those Chicago-style dogs?) and googled the services offered by the hotel's spa because sometimes, when regular apologies failed, you could still buy your way to forgiveness, and surely a prenatal massage would be worth a try.

It was maybe midnight when Estie was startled awake by the sound of Penny vomiting. She lay there for a minute, trying to decide what to do, then got up and knocked on the bathroom door before carefully cracking it open. "You okay?"

Penny was on her knees next to the toilet, disheveled and sweaty. "The baby doesn't like olives."

Estie found a glass and filled it with water, then handed it to Penny.

"I don't think I can," she said, retching.

"Then just swish."

"Oh Jesus." Penny leaned over the toilet and vomited again.

Here, at last, was something Estie knew how to do. She moistened a washcloth and placed it on the back of Penny's neck and found a hair tie to keep her curls out of the way. She knelt down next to her and rubbed her damp back. Together, they waited it out until Penny spat one final time and said, "I think I'm finally done."

"Okay," Estie said. She helped Penny stand up and walk back to her bed, then found the empty ice bucket and placed it on the nightstand beside her in case she woke up nauseous. She checked the time—2:30 a.m.—Rosie would be waking up soon for her middle-of-the-night feeding. She sat down to wait, trying to quash the despair she was feeling. Maybe, she told herself, this was the dark night of woe that, in movies at least, spurred the main character to pull it together and open a little bookstore/bakery/coffee shop. Or maybe Alice or Owen or Dan or someone would show up at her hotel room door at 6 a.m. and offer to whisk her away from all her troubles. *Please*, she thought, or maybe prayed, her hands clasped, her eyes squeezed shut. *Please. Please let this be the low point. Please don't let things get worse.*

17

SOMEHOW THE NIGHT PASSED, THE gray morning light leaking in through the gaps in the chintz curtains. Herbert had traded the space under the bed for the space between Estie's knees, nudging her awake at 4 a.m. so he could burrow under her covers. Rosie slept all the way until 6:30 and, after nursing, was content to lie next to Estie and wriggle. Across the room, Penny was asleep on her side, hands tucked under her neck.

Estie had figured they'd stay in the hotel until the time came to meet Alice, but now that she was awake, she couldn't shake the certainty that waiting for Alice to come to her was a mistake, that lunch at a restaurant just wasn't the same as being at someone's house. She got up slowly and crept into the bathroom, where she examined herself in the mirror. There were dark circles under her eyes, and her hair was matted flat on one side. She ran a wet brush through it and pulled it back into a ponytail, then decided that pulling back her hair made her look too jowly. She had no choice—she needed to shower, which she managed to do in under three minutes, before Rosie could start complaining.

Once she was dressed, she tucked Rosie into a sling and ambushed Herbert. "Went for a walk," she texted Penny, then snuck out, carrier in one hand, litter box in the other. It was 7:30 a.m. Whatever. She asked the concierge to call her a cab.

It was after eight by the time the cab dropped her off outside Alice's building, a massive red-brick place with a coffee shop and a dry cleaner on the ground floor. She stopped to buy some croissants and then headed inside, where a doorman stopped her and insisted on calling ahead. "Fifteenth floor," he said, nodding in the direction of the elevator. In the sling, Rosie started to squirm.

Upstairs, Alice was waiting for her in the doorway to her condo. She looked good, well rested, in black leggings and a purple hoodie with her company's logo, her hair in a loose braid down her back. For a moment, Estie felt a stab of dread. She'd never been able to pull off leggings, not in front of other people—what if Rosie couldn't either? And what if she could? Estie recalled sticky Saturday afternoons in a fitting-room stall with her mother, the sharp scent of her mom's sweat, the way her mother had to suck in her gut when it was time to zip up a pair of pants. *See*, the dressing-room mirrors seemed to say, *this is what you're going to look like one day.* Would it be worse or better if Rosie turned out to be beautiful?

"I thought we were meeting later," Alice said. "I thought I was coming to you."

"I know," Estie said. "I couldn't wait." She held out the box of croissants as a peace offering. "I brought breakfast. And Herbert."

Alice eyed the carrier with suspicion. "You brought the cat?"

Estie nodded.

"Why?"

"Long story."

"Okay," Alice said, waving Estie inside.

The condo hadn't changed much since the last time Estie had visited, which had been a few months before she'd gotten married. That time, she and Alice had gone to the Brookfield Zoo and spent an hour in the fruit bat exhibit, a darkened room where the bats flew freely. Although the signs promised that the bats stayed away from the visitors, it was one thing to understand that logically, another to stand facing the exhibit walls, which were alive with movement, without your skin crawling. Estie and Alice had stood there, tightly gripping each other, for nearly an hour, watching the bats argue over pieces of orange and swoop from one end of the room to the other. "Wow," Alice said once they'd emerged, blinking, into the sunlight. "I am so creeped out," and then, eyes shining, she turned to Estie and added, "I'm so glad we did that." The next morning, they'd also rearranged Alice's living-room furniture, which at that point had still been from IKEA, repositioning the coffee table and armchairs four times before Estie declared, "This is it." And she'd apparently been right, at least about that, because although Alice now owned actual furniture from an actual furniture store—her couch was the kind of pristine white that clearly signaled a home without children or pets—the overall layout hadn't changed except for the vase of tulips on the kitchen counter and the laptop sitting open on the coffee table.

"Were you working?"

Alice nodded. "I wanted to get some stuff done before coming to see you."

"I couldn't wait," Estie said again. She began untangling Rosie from the sling. She felt like a person on an awkward first date: if only she could say the right thing, if only she could figure out what that right thing was, then there would be a second date, and a third, and then a shared home with cats and a tortoise and a lanai. Instead, she had to content herself with saying, "I really wanted you to meet Rosie."

"Oh my goodness," Alice said. "A baby." She leaned in to take a closer look, and Estie, observing Rosie through Alice's eyes, was pleased to note that at least in that moment, the baby was clean and bright-eyed, pink-cheeked, happy to suck on the fingers of her right hand.

"You can hold her."

Alice took a step back. "I'm not a baby person."

"Yeah," Estie said. "Me neither. Can I use your bathroom?" She started to set Rosie down on the couch, then thought better of it and laid her down on the carpet, a beige number with sprinkles of sparkly white. "I'll be quick," she said. "You don't have to touch her or anything."

In the bathroom, there was no sign of a lover either, no second toothbrush or bath towel, no shaver on the counter or dark hair in the drain. Estie felt strangely deflated. She considered looking in the medicine cabinet—was it going too far? Not as far as Briarwood to Chicago, she concluded and gently pried the door open: Q-tips, aspirin, some extra toothpaste, and two bottles of facial cleanser. *I don't believe you*, she told her reflection. *You disgust me.*

"So what's with the cat?" Alice asked when Estie returned from the bathroom, stopping briefly to peek into the master bedroom: lumpy white comforter on the bed, no clothes on the floor.

"I thought . . ." What was it Alice had said when she showed up with Herbert all those years ago? "I thought maybe you could use a cat?"

Alice gaped at her. "You're giving me Herbert?"

Estie nodded.

"But I don't want a pet."

"I didn't want a pet either," Estie said, "but then I got used to him."

"That was different," Alice said. "You were twenty-four and sad. And you never told me you didn't want him."

"Well," Estie said, "now I'm thirty-two and sad. And I didn't want to hurt your feelings."

Alice knelt down and peeked into the carrier, recoiling when Herbert swiped at her through the bars of the door. "I don't want to hurt your feelings either," she said quietly, "but I can't take him. I'm not home enough."

"Cats are pretty independent."

"No," Alice said. "I'm sorry."

It hadn't occurred to Estie that Alice would refuse to play Carol to her Mara, or maybe it had occurred to her and she'd wanted Alice to prove her wrong, wanted Herbert to be the gift horse into whose mouth Alice would refuse to look for the sake of their friendship. She felt stung—not stung, slapped. For a moment, she imagined scooping up Rosie and bolting, leaving Herbert and all his belongings behind, but she knew Alice would catch her before she reached the elevator. "Please," she said. "Owen's allergic."

Alice pursed her lips. "I knew it." She stood up and headed

to the kitchen area, where she pulled a couple of plates out of one of the cabinets.

"I don't get it," Estie asked, "why don't you like Owen?"

"Because he doesn't like me."

"Sure he does," Estie said. "He likes you fine."

Alice opened the box of croissants and placed one on each plate. "Want something to drink?"

Estie shook her head no.

Alice carried the plates out to the coffee table. "Okay," she said, after a moment's consideration. "It's not that Owen doesn't like me, although he definitely doesn't. It's that he isn't good for you."

Estie stared at her. She could feel a little flicker of outrage deep inside her, but something else too, a thrill, a small, hopeful voice saying, *Here we go.* "Meaning what?"

Alice hesitated, and Estie could see her thinking through and dismissing various responses. "Look," she said finally, "I'm not saying that Owen isn't a nice guy, just that you've never seemed all that passionate about him. It's more like you—well—met him and purposely decided that he was the one."

"I'm passionate about Owen," Estie objected.

Alice bit her lip. "I know you. I've seen you happy. You know that. And with Owen, with all his I'm-top-of-the-middle shit—it's like you . . ."

"Decided . . ." Estie filled in for her.

Alice nodded. "*Purposely* decided that it was time to get married. And then you got married. And now here we are." She picked up a croissant and took a small bite, curling her lips back to avoid getting crumbs on her face.

"That's how it's supposed to happen."

The croissant was apparently too flaky, because Alice stood up and got a knife and fork: "Do you want any silverware?"

Estie ignored her. "I mean, isn't that how marriage is supposed to happen?"

"You tell me." Alice began cutting her croissant into bite-size pieces that she speared before eating.

Estie watched her in fascination. Back in college, when she and Alice and Dan all ate together, she and Dan would exchange glances behind Alice's back while Alice, hunched over, carefully sliced spaghetti into half-inch strands or cut a hamburger, bun and all, into small squares. All that fastidiousness just so Alice would never be caught with marinara sauce on her chin or a drip of ketchup on the front of her shirt.

"You know," Estie heard herself say, "Dan had this theory that if you'd been teased more as a child, you wouldn't do that."

"Do what?"

"Chop your food into small pieces."

She wasn't sure how she'd expected Alice to react to this— Would she laugh? Would she flinch at the mention of Dan's name?—but she definitely hadn't expected Alice to look hurt.

"Why would he even say something like that?" Alice said, setting her fork down. "And what makes him think that I wasn't teased?" She shook her head and picked her fork back up, then changed her mind and set it down again. "You think I *choose* to be this way?"

"I'm sorry," Estie said, and she really was. "I didn't know." Then the other part of her took back over: "Be what way?"

"Introverted," Alice said. "Meticulous. This is why I'm never getting roommates again if I can help it."

"Not even me?" Estie wanted to ask, but she couldn't, so instead she said, "Not even a . . ." Here she paused to find the right word, because *lover* seemed too intimate, *boyfriend* too presumptive. ". . . a partner?"

"No," Alice said. "Or a cat. I like my space. I like my things my way."

After that, both of them were silent, Estie racking her brain for something to say, because who was she to judge Alice for living the way she wanted to, no apologies, no excuses? Then again—although Estie wouldn't think of this until after she returned to the hotel—didn't Estie deserve the same courtesy, the same assumption that she'd deliberately chosen her own life—Owen, Rosie, Briarwood, Big Earth—and was prepared to face the consequences? And wasn't there something laudable about the constant compromise that marriage and motherhood required, about always putting your baby and your husband first? There were, after all, entire movies dedicated to this very notion, movies in which women like Alice went home for Christmas and discovered that their fabulous careers paled in comparison to sex with brawny men who volunteered at soup kitchens. Later, back in her hotel room, Estie would even fantasize about providing Alice with a carefully curated watch list, but by then the two of them would no longer be friends, and anyway, Alice didn't watch TV, or at least she didn't watch television for women.

All that would come later, though, and right then, in

Alice's apartment, watching Alice eat her croissant so neatly, Estie felt she had no choice but to go there: "So, um, are you seeing anybody?"

She watched Alice carefully to see how she'd respond, but all Alice did was look surprised: "That came out of nowhere." She pushed the plate with her bits of croissant toward Estie. "This is too much food."

God, Estie thought, if she never heard another woman complain about something being too much food, it would be too soon. How was it even possible for a single croissant to be too much food? She picked up one of the pieces between thumb and forefinger and popped it into her mouth. "What I mean is," she tried again, "are you seeing Dan?" She imagined adding, "What I mean is, I know you are," but suddenly she didn't have it in her. She thought back to that first time she'd seen Alice in the cafeteria, to that deep sense of recognition she'd felt, that certainty that they were meant to be friends. Even more than ten years later, that was still the closest Estie had ever gotten to feeling the kind of love at first sight that she saw in movies. And then she'd fallen in love. And gotten married. And then she'd gotten pregnant, which felt like breaking through a membrane so fine and translucent that she'd never even noticed it was there, a membrane Alice didn't believe existed. Now, watching Alice wiping invisible crumbs off the table, Estie caught another glimpse of the membrane rising up between the two of them, shimmering like those rainbows you sometimes saw on the surface of oil slicks, so fragile that it seemed that all Estie needed to do was reach out and brush it aside, which of course she couldn't.

Alice didn't answer her question. Instead, she got up and put her dishes in the sink, then glanced at her watch. "I need to tell you something."

Estie felt her skin prickle. "You and Dan are getting married?"

Alice didn't even smile. "Let me get through this. Please." She took a moment to compose herself, squaring her shoulders. "I've tried to be there for you. I really have. And I know things haven't been easy, that you're overwhelmed and depressed. But I can't give you what you want, at least not right now. It's just too much."

"But—" Estie began, but Alice interrupted her: "I'm not done." Her face was pink, and she swiped at her eyes. "I mean this in the nicest possible way, Estie, but sometimes—lately—all the texts and phone calls—you showing up like this—this *neediness*—it's just too much." Estie must have looked stunned, because Alice immediately added, "It's not that I don't want to be friends. We've been friends a long time. I just need some space."

Was this what Estie had been expecting all along? She didn't know. "It's just—" she started to say, but that wasn't right, so she tried again: "You see, the baby—"

Alice rolled her eyes in impatience. "Ugh. The baby," she snapped. "I *know* you had a baby, okay? But billions of people have babies and do just fine. You don't have to let it change you. It doesn't have to take over your *life*."

It sounded so reasonable, coming from Alice, except that Alice was wrong. Babies did take over your life, at least if your life was war- and hunger- and illness-free. Yes, Estie hadn't had to give birth in a field, without medical assistance, and she hadn't had to immediately resume thatching her roof with a baby swaddled on her back. But so what? Even when everything was peachy, babies liked to screw up their faces and demand to be fed, or held, or fed and held at the same time. Even worse, they never seemed grateful, even on nights when you rushed to their side at 1:30 a.m., 2:00, 2:15, 3:00, 3:30. Stupid, selfish babies. They always wanted more than you could give, even when you gave them everything you had.

"You're wrong," Estie said. "You're so wrong. I mean, you'll see. Just wait until you have babies of your own."

For a moment, the words lingered in the hushed quiet of Alice's condo, with no way around them, no way of taking them back. Had this been Estie's plan all along, to blow up their friendship? Estie wasn't sure. She was sure, however, that you weren't supposed to assume all women wanted to be mothers, let alone wives, and you weren't supposed to lord the fact that you had both a baby and a husband over your soon-to-be-ex-best friend. What further proof could Alice have needed to know their friendship was over? And what further proof could Estie have needed that, despite all her kicking and screaming, she'd finally become a full-fledged member of Mommy World?

It was Alice who spoke first. "You've changed, and so have I, and we've both moved on. It happens to everybody." She didn't sound angry, just resigned. "I really do hope things start going better for you, Estie."

"Did you and Dan have sex?" Estie hadn't expected to actually ask the question, especially not right then, but apparently breaking the friendship wasn't enough—she wanted to shatter it beyond repair.

She watched Alice's face go from pink, to white, to pink again. "Fuck you, Estie," she said, even though she never swore. "I think you should leave." And then she stood around and watched, hawkeyed, as Estie gathered her belongings and slid the baby back into the sling. "Don't forget the cat," she said, holding the door open for Estie. "Maybe I'll see you around."

18

ESTIE WAS BACK AT THE Palmer House Hilton by 9:30, terrified that Penny's anger would now expand to include not just "You made me drive to Chicago under false pretenses" and "You gave me food poisoning" but also "You didn't even get rid of the damn cat." But all Penny said was, "My stomach hurts. I know you're supposed to meet Alice for lunch, but I think I just need to go home." Her voice was hoarse, and she certainly looked crappy, her eyes sunken, her skin pale.

"Okay," Estie said. "Of course."

For a moment, she considered allowing Penny to think she was canceling lunch out of the goodness of her heart, that the weekend had turned out to require sacrifices on both their parts, Penny for Estie, Estie for Penny, and therefore Estie deserved forgiveness, except that there was no goodness and there was no sacrifice, and it seemed important that Penny know this. Estie cleared her throat. "Anyway, I just got back from seeing Alice."

"And?"

"She wouldn't take Herbert."

"Oh," Penny said, her voice neutral. And then she turned away from Estie and started to pack.

At least it was Saturday, so there wasn't much traffic. Penny adjusted the passenger seat so she could lean back, and while Estie drove, Penny closed her eyes, which was just as well because Estie discovered that she couldn't stop crying even though she was careful not to lean into it, not to contort her face or sob or sniffle—she was, it seemed, leaking tears, which were dripping down her neck and soaking the collar of her T-shirt. When she caught glimpses of herself in the rearview mirror, her eyes were red, her lashes clumpy and wet. "Are you awake?" she whispered to Penny as they drove by Gary, then again as they passed Michigan City, Indiana, but Penny slept on. This was probably just as well too, because the last thing Estie needed was confirmation that she'd lost Penny's friendship on top of everything else. If she hadn't lost Penny's friendship already. And if *that* weren't enough, she was going to lose her job too, the job she'd lucked into right after college, the job she'd insisted on holding on to while she waited for the stars to magically align so she could begin living the life she was promised, the one with the minivan and the husband who did his share of the chores and the rewarding career that she would seamlessly transition into once everything else fell into place. *What rewarding career?* Estie wondered. *What share of the chores?* Here was something you never saw on TV: a story that was all middle, all ordinary trips to the grocery store and oil changes every three thousand miles, no flashes of insight, no redemption, no larger plan or secret signs from God. Just a middle that kept going and going. And then your children left home. And then you died.

Estie glanced at Penny, still pale and sleeping, one hand resting on her belly. "Do you mind if I put on some music?" she asked softly. Penny didn't answer, not that Estie was expecting her to. "I'll take that as a no." She switched on the radio and started flipping through stations. Even something like Christian talk radio would be better than hearing herself think.

A short while after crossing back into Michigan, Estie pulled into the parking lot of a McDonald's: Rosie was going to need to nurse soon, and she and Penny hadn't really had anything to eat, if you ignored the three croissants Estie had scarfed at Alice's. Plus, all of Penny's sleeping was starting to weird her out.

"Hey," she said, "hey. Penny?" She raised her voice. "Penny?" She reached over and squeezed Penny's hand, which, she discovered, was uncomfortably hot and dry. "Penny?"

Penny grunted and blinked herself awake. "Are we home?" She reached up and pressed her hands against her temples. "Wow, do I have a headache."

"I need to feed Rosie," Estie told her. "First, though, I'm going to get you some water, okay?"

Penny nodded hesitantly. She looked around. "Where are we? This isn't Briarwood."

"We just left Indiana," Estie said. She'd initially thought that she'd go into the dining room to order, but now she decided to go through the drive-thru while Penny got her bearings. "So water, yes?" she asked Penny. "And what else? What sounds good?"

"I'm not hungry," Penny said. She closed her eyes and resumed rubbing her temples.

"You need to eat something."

Penny grunted and opened her eyes. "Where are we? Are we home?"

"No," Estie said. "We still have a couple of hours." She offered Penny her water, but Penny couldn't seem to get a grip on the cup. "I'll get it," Estie said, holding the straw up to Penny's mouth, but Penny shook her head no and closed her eyes, then opened them: "Where are we again?"

"Just two more hours," Estie said again. She parked the car and moved into the back seat, where she changed Rosie's diaper in record time and pulled her to her chest so she could nurse. Once Rosie was latched on, Estie opened the browser on her phone and searched on "pregnant," "vomiting," and "confusion." She felt her heart sink. Yes, Google tended toward dire, often fatal, diagnoses, but then again, who was Estie to determine whether she was looking at hyperemesis gravidarum or preeclampsia or some kind of horrible cancer, and whether whatever it was could wait the two hours until they got back to Briarwood. *Shit*, she thought. *Shit*. And then she googled "Emergency rooms near me."

They ended up at a small hospital about twenty minutes away, a sprawling brick box with dark glass windows located across the street from a Tony's Pizza and a cluster of mobile homes. Once Estie had made up her mind to go, she'd rudely pried Rosie off her breast because a pissed-off, hungry baby was better than a lost pregnancy, then did her best to ignore Rosie's screams while she sped along according to the GPS's instructions.

"Slow down," Penny moaned. "I'm going to be sick."

"Okay," Estie said, "but it's your car." Just in case, though, she emptied the McDonald's bag over her shoulder into the back seat and handed it to Penny. *So long, fries*, she thought. Strapped into her little bucket, Rosie screamed and screamed. "Just a few more minutes, baby," Estie hollered in Rosie's direction, or maybe in Penny's. "Hang on. We're almost there!"

She pulled into the patient drop-off lane in front of the emergency department's sliding doors, then waved over a guy in a blue uniform who looked barely old enough to be out of high school. "It's my friend," she told him. "She's sick."

"This is silly," Penny protested. "I just have a headache."

The guy nodded and helped Penny wobble out of the car and into a wheelchair. "You can park over there," he told Estie, directing her into the adjacent lot. She parked, then unbuckled Rosie, hesitating. Her breasts ached, and Rosie was apoplectic with rage, but the thought of sitting in the car to nurse while God knows what was happening with Penny felt unbearable. She scooped up the baby and grabbed the diaper bag, then headed to the sliding doors, had almost reached them, in fact, when she remembered Herbert and ran back to the SUV to roll down the windows—it wasn't a particularly warm day, the temperature somewhere in the fifties, but you never knew.

By the time Estie made it inside, Penny had already

disappeared into the bowels of the ER. "Is she okay?" Estie asked the attendant at the check-in desk. "Can I see her?"

"She's with the triage nurse," the attendant told her. She looked all of fourteen. She pointed at a little seating area off to the right. "Maybe you can wait there."

Estie obediently moved to the waiting area, which was a couple of rows of padded metal chairs. There were only a handful of people there—an older woman talking loudly on her phone, a man leaning his head against the wall, a towel wrapped around his left hand, another man in a black jacket coughing into a tissue. She chose a chair in the back corner and tried to position Rosie for feeding without flashing anybody, feeling weak with relief when Rosie finally quieted down. She slumped back and tried to get comfortable—why did none of the chairs have arms? "I told him not to clean the gutters by himself," the woman on the phone was saying. "And now this." The man in black snorted and cleared his throat noisily, and Estie found herself hunching over Rosie protectively as if she could physically shield her from the man's airborne germs. An ER was no place for a baby. A parked car was no place for a cat. For a moment, she worried she was going to lose it completely, but then she pulled herself together, because what choice did she have? Dress for the job you want, she told herself, not the one you have. She stood up, keeping Rosie nestled against her chest, and walked back to the front desk, where she looked the attendant in the eye and asked, "Should I be calling her husband?"

The attendant gave her an appraising look. "Let me check." She disappeared through the double doors behind her, returning a few minutes later and signaling Estie to follow her. She led her past a nurses' station to a small exam room with dingy blue walls, where Penny was lying hooked up to an IV, a fetal heart monitor strapped around her middle. But at least she was awake.

"Sheesh," Estie said in what she thought was a fabulous imitation of composure. "What's all this?"

Penny shrugged. "Fluids. I guess I got a little dehydrated." She was, Estie noted, already looking a little better, less pale, more alert. "But the baby's moving okay."

Finally, finally, Rosie let go of Estie's nipple, her head lolling back in a pleasant milk coma. Estie fastened her bra, pulled down her shirt, and moved the plastic bag of Penny's belongings that was taking up the only chair in the room. Then she sat down, suddenly exhausted. "What now?" She supported Rosie's head with the thumb and forefinger of her right hand and bent her forward, patting her back with her left hand. Rosie burped like a pro, then spit up all over Estie's jeans. "Really?" Estie asked her. Through the window of the exam room, she saw the man in the black jacket shuffling by, still wracked by coughs. She had to get Rosie out of the ER, but she couldn't leave Penny alone in some dinky hospital either.

A nurse in green scrubs walked in, or at least Estie figured she was a nurse even though she looked even younger than the desk attendant. "I'm Madison," she introduced herself. "How are we feeling?" She was wearing, Estie noticed, a perfect smoky eye and purple Crocs.

"Is there nobody at this hospital old enough to buy beer?" she asked Penny after Madison checked her vitals. "What kind of place is this?"

Penny smiled wanly. "I'm sorry."

"As if," Estie said. "If anyone here should be sorry, it's me." Now that it seemed unlikely that Penny or her baby were going to die, a weird calm settled over Estie, as if she were observing herself from a safe, measured distance. She knew what she had to do first, then second, then third, and so on, each subsequent step magically revealing itself as she completed the one before it. The first step was to call Jack, who, exactly as Estie expected, immediately got in his car and headed their way. According to Google, it would be a little over two hours before he arrived. The second step was to get Rosie out of there, which was a little more complicated, except that here too Google pointed out a solution: the small town where Dan lived was less than fifteen minutes south. Estie looked through her email and found his phone number, then called and explained the situation. "Please," she said, "just until Penny's husband gets here?" Dan agreed, because of course he did, and so Estie took Rosie outside and waited for him in the parking lot, feeling all glamorous in her spit-upon clothes and finger-combed hair, all the while reminding herself that this meant nothing, that it wasn't about her, that any decent person would have done the same. "Right, baby?" she asked Rosie. She'd gotten the stroller out of the trunk of the car, but she kept Rosie pressed close against her, rocking lightly from side to side, glad for something to do, for Rosie's warm weight in her arms.

Dan pulled up a few minutes later in a staid blue sedan and parked in the space next to Estie's. He was wearing jeans, a gray fleece jacket, and a red stocking cap, and it was clear he hadn't shaved that morning. "Hey," he said. "Estie. You look exactly the same."

"Right," Estie said, before catching herself. "Thank you."

"Not me," Dan said. He removed his cap and rubbed a hand across his shaved head, then slipped his cap back on. He gestured at the baby. "And this must be Rosie." There were laugh lines etched at the corners of his mouth. "How's your friend doing?"

"Penny," Estie said before remembering, with a pang of guilt, that by the time she and Dan had started dating, she and Penny had no longer been friends. "She's okay. Dehydrated. Her husband's on his way."

Dan held out his hands and leaned toward her, and she carefully passed Rosie to him. "Well," he said, transferring Rosie into the stroller, "you don't have to worry about us. We'll just go for a little walk and wait for your text."

"Thank you, really," Estie said, and then she was blinking back tears again. The two of them were, for all practical purposes, strangers, and he was probably fucking Alice most weekends, and still, he felt so familiar. Why hadn't she followed him to Boston, where he'd gone to get his CPA, all those years ago? If she had, she might not be in this mess with Penny, and she definitely wouldn't be in this mess with Alice, and Owen would have found some other woman to lie to and impregnate. "Seriously. Thank you."

Dan smiled and patted her shoulder briskly, as if they were teammates about to take the field. "No worries." He smelled, Estie noticed, the same as he always had, tart and clean, a scent that made the hairs on Estie's arms stand on end.

Back in the ER exam room, Penny had turned on the small television mounted on one of the walls and tuned it to one of those reality shows where women in microminis tried to sell real estate. "There's nothing on," she told Estie. "Just this or a show where women try on wedding dresses."

Estie sat down. "This is good." While the Realtor, a slender woman with gigantic breasts, lectured a man with sleeve tattoos about down payments, Estie watched the monitor next to Penny's bed track her pulse along with the baby's. "What is a normal maternal heart rate?" she asked Google. "What is a normal fetal heart rate?" At least as far as Google was concerned, everything looked good.

"Don't worry," Penny said. "We're fine. I already feel so much better."

"I'm so sorry," Estie said. "We didn't even look at any baby furniture."

Penny shrugged. "That's fine."

But was it fine? Had Penny's getting sick erased Estie's horrible behavior over the last two days and back in high school? Was this one of those moments where you were supposed to realize that nothing was more important than your health, that there was no point in sweating the small stuff? Estie reached for Penny's medical-device-free arm and squeezed her hand. "I'm still sorry."

"It's okay," Penny said. "I'm fine. You're fine." She said it again: "You're fine."

But Estie wasn't fine: the crushed sparrow, the deer, and now Penny. She was a harbinger of destruction, if not outright death. Who would she harm next without meaning to?

Penny pressed down on her belly, a gesture Estie recognized from her own pregnancy and the way she'd braced herself against Rosie's kicks and rolls, pushing back against them in a kind of acknowledgment: *I feel you.* "I can't stand the suspense," Penny said, her voice breaking. "How will I make it until December?" On the monitor, her heart rate accelerated slightly.

"I don't know," Estie said, because the truth was that she didn't know how she would make it herself, and her baby was already out in the world, already working her way into a life apart from Estie. "I guess we just keep going."

Jack arrived a good twenty minutes before Estie had expected him, bursting into the exam room just as Estie was unwrapping a six-pack of tiny donuts that she'd purchased from the vending machine and which she'd saved until Penny dozed off so that her gluttony could proceed without comment. Jack, though, caught her with white sugar on her hands and lips and sprinkled across her jeans. She couldn't think of anything to say, so she gestured toward sleeping Penny and whispered, "Want some?"

Jack waved her off. "I drove ninety," he said, looking a little proud, and then he knelt over Penny, his expression so concerned and tender that Estie almost started crying. Here it was, finally, a big love, Penny's eyes fluttering open, her relieved smile, the way Jack buried his face in her neck and then looked up, his eyes wet: "I was so worried."

"I'm fine," Penny said. "Really. It was just food poisoning."

Estie stood up and tried to brush the sugar off her clothes, but managed only to grind it into the fabric. "Okay," she said, "I better get going before Rosie gets hungry." She hugged Penny and then Jack, then stopped in the restroom to try and make herself presentable. It was no use—even after washing her face and toweling off her clothes, the nicest thing you could say was that she looked disheveled, her shirt wrinkled and stained, her skin all blotchy, her hair a frizzy halo. "Whatever," she told her reflection. "Whatever, whatever." She pulled out her phone and texted Dan that she was done. She headed outside and began walking in the direction she'd seen Dan go earlier, and sure enough, after a few minutes she spotted Dan and Rosie in the stroller making their way toward her.

"Thank you," she said. Again. "This was a huge help." And then, because Alice was right, and she was obsessed and could never tell when enough was enough, she pointed at Tony's Pizza across the street. "I'm starving. Can I buy you lunch?"

19

THE INSIDE OF TONY'S PIZZA was all plastic red-checked tablecloths and dark faux-wood paneling. A sign advised them to seat themselves, so they headed for a booth upholstered with red vinyl that was peeling at the seams. The restaurant was empty save for two old men who were seated at a yellow laminate countertop, doing a crossword puzzle together, and the server who handed them menus and offered a booster seat for Rosie, who was still months and months away from being able to sit up.

"Are you still all about the green pepper and onion?" Dan asked as he studied the menu.

Estie tried to remember what Dan liked on his pizza, but she couldn't, not until he ordered: pineapple and Canadian bacon. She felt weak with nerves—what on earth would they talk about for an entire meal? "It's so weird to see you," she said, which was what Penny had said when they'd run into each other at the Creamery, "and also not weird at all."

"I know," Dan said. "First Alice, and now you." He unwrapped his silverware. "So what happened with your friend?"

"Um," Estie said, choosing her words carefully. "Food poisoning." Then the server brought out their drinks—Dr Pepper for Dan and water for Estie because, well, it was important to keep up appearances—and by the time she'd unwrapped her straw and taken a sip, Dan had moved on: "How did you find my blog? Did you google me?"

Estie felt herself flushing in embarrassment. "Maybe?" She deflected a second time: "Did you google me?"

"I google everyone."

"And?" It came out sounding coquettish, and Estie tried not to cringe. *Do not flirt*, she told herself. Only sociopaths flirted with their babies by their sides and their friends in the hospital across the street.

Dan waved his straw in the air like a magic wand. "You're married to an English professor. And you still work at Big Earth."

Estie swallowed. "He's not really an English professor anymore."

"I know," Dan said. "I googled him too."

Just like that, Estie's eyes filled with tears.

Dan looked stricken. "I'm sorry," he said. "I didn't mean to—" He began jiggling his knee, an old habit, one that meant he was either nervous or having trouble staying awake. Without thinking, Estie reached under the table and placed her hand on his knee, another practiced gesture, signaling him to stop moving. Dan stiffened, and Estie hastily pulled back.

"It's like muscle memory," she said apologetically. "Like time travel."

"Old habits," he said. "Blah blah," which, Estie supposed, was another old habit as well. "Anyway," he continued, "I got married too, but then we got divorced. We have a kid—he's three. Henry." He pulled out his phone and showed her the lock-screen photo of a curly-haired boy in a field of sunflowers.

"What a sweetie," Estie said, mostly because it was what people said about photos of other people's children. Dan smiled, and there, suddenly, was his double dimple, as deep and charming as ever. The image of Dan pressing Alice up against a wall, his hands in her hair, her stroking his face with the tip of an index finger, flashed before her eyes. She was too late. The whole thing was hopeless. She forced herself to glance at Rosie, who had managed to pull off one baby sock and was now clutching it and staring at the ceiling fan. "So hey," she said as if she'd just thought of it, "Alice told me you two matched on Tinder. Bizarre, huh?"

"Yeah," Dan said. "I had no idea she was in Chicago, but I recognized her right away."

"She really hasn't changed," Estie agreed.

Dan nodded, his expression neutral. He shifted in his seat, and under the table, his knees bumped hers. "Sorry."

Another thick silence settled over them while the server brought over their pizza and Dan busied himself sprinkling his slice with hot pepper and powdery parmesan cheese. As she watched him, Estie could feel herself starting to panic. "I'm sorry. I don't know what I'm doing here. I thought I would see you—not just you, Alice—I just saw her too—and I would know, and everything would magically click into place."

She waited for Dan to issue some sort of platitude about how life is messy or having children is hard, but he just sat there, watching her, his expression unreadable. She grabbed a napkin and used it to dry her sweaty hands. From the corner of her eye, she could see that Rosie was growing restless and starting to root around—on top of everything else, she was going to have to nurse her in front of Dan. She couldn't have been less desirable if she tried, although, in a way, this knowledge came as a relief. She cleared her throat and forced herself to keep going. "I know I don't have any right to ask this, but it would mean a lot to me if . . . if you didn't fall in love with Alice."

Dan blinked. "What?"

Estie thought she might be sick. "Please don't fall in love with Alice. Anyone else is fine, just not her?" She started digging through the diaper bag to see if she had anything to cover up with while she nursed Rosie, but all she could find was one of the swaddling blankets they'd gotten from the hospital, or maybe just taken as revenge against the evil nurse who had yelled at Estie about losing the baby's hat. By now, Rosie was squawking, and so Estie had no choice but to reach under her shirt, unsnap her nursing bra, and then squeeze her nipple between thumb and forefinger so that Rosie could get a good seal, all while Dan pretended to be fascinated by the ice in his drink. "All set," she said once Rosie was finally in position, and then suddenly Dan was leaning toward her, speaking in a low voice as if he were afraid the men at the bar were listening: "Are you really telling me who to have sex with?"

"I'm telling you who *not* to have sex with. And it's only one person." She sighed. "I really, really love her, and"—here she squeezed her hands into fists, then released them—"I really, really loved you, and I just . . . I just can't."

"What?" Dan said again. He was doing that knee jiggling thing again, shaking the whole booth, or maybe it was just Estie shaking. Either way, her arms were full, so she couldn't reach his knee to make him stop. "It almost killed me," she said, "the way you disappeared after college. It felt like I'd gone missing too." She felt woozy with the relief of finally saying it. She looked down at Rosie, who was grunting between swallows. "I had to call your parents to find out you were okay."

When she looked up again, Dan was gaping at her. She felt a twinge of annoyance: Why was everyone always gaping at her? "Estie," he said, "why are you doing this?"

"Doing what?" Estie asked again.

"Acting like I'm the one who ghosted you."

"Because you did."

Dan shook his head. "You could have come with me, and you didn't."

"Because it was just for a little while," she pointed out, "just until you got your CPA."

"Two years," Dan said. "And I didn't finish. I hate accounting."

"All the more reason."

"Why?" Dan sounded incredulous.

Estie opened her mouth and closed it. What could she say? That she'd loved her job at Big Earth more than she'd loved Dan? That certainly hadn't been true, and yet she'd held on to her job anyway, forced herself to be practical, because who would she have been if she'd followed Dan to Boston all blind and in love? A barista? A receptionist? The kind of woman who gave everything up for a man and, ten years later, ended up crying in the bathroom while her daughter stood outside listening? "People have long-distance relationships all the time," she said finally. "They have long-distance relationships, and they get through it."

"Yes," Dan said, "but not because one of them is sitting around waiting for the other one to be worth moving for."

"That's not what I was doing."

"Then what *were* you doing?"

"I was waiting for everything to be perfect."

Dan shook his head. "And how did that work out for you?"

"Well," Estie said, trying to keep her voice from wobbling, "it didn't. It didn't work for shit."

They didn't talk much after that, mainly because Estie was crying too hard. A stolen hospital swaddling blanket, it turned out, was just the right size for hiding your face from a horrified server and an even more horrified Dan. "Stupid hormones," she told him. She flagged the waiter, who packed their leftovers in a single container, because who wouldn't assume that Estie and Dan shared a fridge?—and then presented Dan with a bill, which he and Estie promptly divided between them.

Out in the parking lot, they awkwardly hugged each other goodbye, the weight of Dan's chin pressing against Estie's shoulder in the exact same way it used to. She waited for something resembling grief to hit her, and it did, but it wasn't grief for letting Dan go, but grief for herself, for her friendship with Alice, for her marriage to Owen.

"Good seeing you," Dan said, and that was the end of that, which was just as well, because apparently Herbert had spent the last few hours pooping all over his carrier, and to make matters worse, before Estie even managed to strap her into the car seat,

Rosie blew out her diaper. Estie hoisted Rosie on her hip and ran into the hospital to find a restroom where she could clean Rosie up, then again for a wad of paper towels to wipe out Herbert's carrier while he hissed and spat and swiped at her. *God, everybody was turning on her,* Estie thought, before reminding herself that she deserved every last bit of it.

By the time she got home it was nearly six, and Owen was sitting at the kitchen table in front of a stack of student papers, a forty-four-ounce Slurpee by his side. When he smiled, his teeth were pink and tongue bright red. "Hey," he said, looking pleased, "there's my girl." He was, Estie realized, talking about Rosie, whom he scooped out of Estie's arms and asked, "So how did you like Chicago?"

Estie left him there and went to retrieve the rest of her belongings from Penny's SUV. She would have to take it to get detailed or something just to get out the smell of cat and baby shit, but she was too tired to worry about that right then. She hauled her luggage and the diaper bag upstairs to the duplex, then returned for the cat carrier and the litter box.

Owen blinked. "I thought Alice was taking him."

"Well," Estie said, "she didn't."

"Why not?"

Estie shrugged. "She's not a cat person."

"Okay?"

"Spare me the disappointment," Estie said, suddenly furious. "You knew this would happen. You knew it would be awful, and it was awful, and Alice doesn't want to be friends anymore, and Penny got sick, and, yes, I brought home the cat, so you can go right ahead and hate me too."

"What on earth are you talking about?" said Owen.

"You knew what would happen," Estie said. "You knew. And you let me go anyway."

This was the part where Owen was supposed to sit down next to Estie, apologize, and pat her back soothingly, but he didn't. Instead he rubbed his right hand over his face and, sounding tired and resigned, said, "I didn't *let* you go anywhere. You're an adult."

"Fine," Estie said. "I'm an adult." She stood up and retreated to the bedroom, slamming the door behind her like the adult she supposedly was. She flung herself on the bed and lay there fuming, reveling in the heat of her breath, her pounding heart. *Fuck everybody*, she thought. *Fuck them all.*

She heard the creak of footsteps followed by a soft knock on the bedroom door. "Estie?" Owen said, his voice soft. "Um. I think Rosie might be hungry."

Estie threw her hands up in despair. She wanted so badly to be left alone, to just lie there and stare at the ceiling and feel sorry for herself, but Rosie's needs were bottomless and never-ending, and already her breasts were throbbing and she was cramping up, her own body calling out to Rosie's, never mind what Estie wanted. *And fuck you too*, she told her reflection in the full-length mirror that hung on the wall. *Fuck you most of all.*

She opened the door and took Rosie from Owen, then headed to the living room and switched on the TV, where a frantic mother was pacing back and forth in her kitchen while she waited for someone to call in with a ransom demand. "Sit down," the grizzled detective told her. "Have some coffee. Don't tire yourself out."

Estie felt a pang of wistfulness, followed by a flood of guilt. What would she be doing in the frantic mother's place? Would she be able to muster the requisite fear and sorrow, or would she, as she suspected, be feeling something closer to relief? With Rosie gone, Estie would be able to sob without appearing weak or selfish, without having to stop to change a diaper or start the dishwasher or sort laundry. Police officers would make her coffee. Social workers would ask if she was all right. Her mother would squeeze her hand lovingly and urge her to eat something to preserve her strength.

Except that none of that was good enough for the TV mom. She locked and loaded her husband's shotgun. "I can't just sit here," she explained, her eyes wild. "I have to do *something*." The TV husband puffed his cheeks out in concern. "Don't you go being a hero," he warned. "You know nothing about guns." But what did it matter what the frantic mother knew? Motherhood, by its very nature, infused women with superhuman powers: the ability to sense that, against all odds, their child was still alive; the strength to track down and wrestle their child's burly kidnappers; the stamina to rise up again and again even after being shot, one hand plugging the wounds in their sides. There was, it seemed, no greater story than motherhood, no greater bond than the one between mother and child. And yet, hiking into the woods fully armed and in designer boots, the frantic mom seemed so desperately alone, so abandoned, so reckless in her grief.

Estie turned off the TV and transferred Rosie, now drowsy, her belly taut with milk, into her crib. She set up Herbert's litter box and made sure there was kibble in his bowl, then headed for the shower. She made the water as hot as she could stand it, then stood under the stream, rocking back and forth on the balls of her feet. Where was *her* superhuman strength? Where were *her* stamina and insight? What kind of mother imagined her baby's death as relief? She turned off the water and wrapped herself in a towel, then went to check on Rosie, suddenly afraid that she'd find her lifeless, Estie's punishment by a vengeful God. But there was Rosie, swaddled tight and still breathing her little baby breaths. Estie watched her for a while, then double-checked the windows and doors, all the while knowing her fear was misplaced. She had no reason to fear strangers, or illness, or dogs in the park, not when the real source of danger was the kind of woman who weighed her baby's well-being against her own, against her desire to sleep, or bathe, or gallivant with childless friends. No. The real source of danger was Estie's fatigue, her distractedness, her inattention. The real source of danger was Estie herself.

20

IT WAS HARD TO COME home to find everything exactly the same. So Estie had lost Alice. So what? Lost friendships didn't merit time off for mourning, and neither did babies, nor Owen's students, who needed their papers graded in a timely fashion. "Can't you assign less homework?" Estie wanted to ask Owen. Instead, she sat grimly on the couch, watching TV and using her foot to rock Rosie in her bouncy chair while Owen sat at the kitchen table, sniffling and blowing his nose. Even though she'd asked him to before she left for Chicago, he hadn't moved the laundry from the washer to the dryer, and now the washing machine smelled funky, which wasn't his fault because, as he noted pointedly, it wasn't as if he could smell anything anyway. He also didn't beat her, or keep teenage girls chained in the basement, or set her bed on fire like the husbands in the made-for-TV movies she kept streaming. She had no problems, Estie kept reminding herself, or at least no problems that she hadn't created almost entirely on her own.

That Monday, after Owen had gone to work, Estie brought Rosie to her bed to nurse. It had been another bad night, Rosie refusing to sleep for more than an hour or two at a time, and so they'd both fallen asleep before Rosie was done with the first side. Estie slept lightly, her body curved around Rosie's, and dreamed that Rosie somehow got tangled up in the curtain cords and that she couldn't find any scissors. After a while, her dream self gave up looking: Owen would cut the baby loose when he got home from work. Estie awoke with a start, turning to check on Rosie, and for a moment she wasn't sure what she was seeing. Had her mother been right about this, of all things, and the cat was sucking out Rosie's breath? Estie bolted upright, and Herbert looked up at her casually, his tail thumping twice. He hadn't been sucking Rosie's breath, Estie realized, he'd just been lying next to her, a small spoon to Rosie's even smaller spoon. Rosie was breathing. Everything was fine. Even so, Estie couldn't shake loose the fear she'd felt when she'd seen him there. What if he'd accidentally suffocated the baby? Could Estie have even begun to pretend that she hadn't been warned?

She shooed Herbert off the bed, transferred Rosie to her crib, and went to get a glass of water, Herbert trailing her like he always did. Now that she and Alice weren't friends anymore, what did it say about Estie that the most constant presence in her life was a cat? And a mother who always seemed to intuit when Estie was at her most vulnerable? There she was now, calling Estie's phone, then calling again when Estie sent her to voicemail, and again when Estie just let it ring. Estie sighed, then picked up—at least this way, she'd get it over with.

"You've got to answer your phone when I call," her mother said. "You know I worry."

"I couldn't," Estie lied. "I was on the phone with Penny."

"Oh, yeah? How's she doing?"

"Fine," Estie said. Then, because she had to say something, she said, "She has a cold."

Her mother didn't respond, and Estie could feel herself getting riled. Where were her mother's "Oh, poor dears" and pots of homemade chicken broth? Why couldn't her mother be like other moms in at least that one way? "Well," Estie said, "are you going to say something or aren't you?"

"What do you want me to say?"

"I don't know!" Estie said, exasperated. "You called me."

"I see I caught you at a bad time."

"They're all bad times." Estie felt desperate—they were never going to understand each other, were they? "Oh God, Mom," she burst out, "what happened? How did we turn out like this?"

"Like what?"

"I don't know," Estie said. "Like us."

Her mother exhaled loudly in what Estie couldn't help but think was disappointment. "There's nothing wrong with being like us, Estie."

That's it, Estie thought. She was finished. She was going to pack everything up and move to Florida, show up at Mara and Carol's doorstep and offer to bunk with the tortoise. Then she'd hand Rosie over and say, "Show me how it's done," and they would start her out on something simple—maybe caring for an iguana—then gradually move her up the evolutionary chain until she finally understood how to be a mother to a human baby, or maybe even a mother to herself. Of course, by then, Rosie would be twelve, and Estie would have missed out on her entire childhood.

"Mom," Estie said, "I've gotta go."

Why didn't cell phones come with cradles so that you could slam the receiver down when you were upset? Hitting End Call just wasn't as satisfying, especially now that the other person could follow up with a text and still get the last word in: "One day Rosie will hang up on you, and you'll find out how hurtful it is." Or maybe that wasn't quite the last word, because Estie texted her back: "Stop it." Why couldn't her mother say something positive about the future for once? Her phone vibrated, signaling the arrival of another text: "Everything would be easier if you stopped expecting it to be easy." Estie swiped left and hit delete.

In her crib, Rosie was sucking sleepily on her bottom lip, and Estie found herself wishing that she could pick her up and hold her without waking her up. She leaned over her and examined Rosie's sharp fingernails, her long eyelashes, those funny rolls of fat on her thighs. How many other moms were standing over their sleeping babies right then, thinking, *How can anything be so helpless? It would be so easy to be free.* Maybe this was the secret of motherhood, that you could lose your children at any moment, that you could *choose* to lose them, that you *would* lose them if it weren't for all the rules and restrictions and the certainty about what Good Mommies did and didn't do, rules designed to keep you hovering over your baby's crib, believing there was no greater joy. Estie felt overtaken by a sudden wave of pity, and not just for herself but for the younger, more bewildered version of her mother. If Estie was this lonely, this lost *with* Owen, then how lonely her mother must have been, sitting by herself on the edge of the bathtub, knowing that in a minute she would have to stop crying, dry her eyes, and go back out there to face her disengaged husband and apathetic kids and every other goddamn person out there, who, for all she knew, was just as miserable as she was and hiding it too. Except if that was true, then what hope was there for the future? Why even leave the bathroom at all?

Rosie slept on, and Estie sat in the kitchen eating dry cornflakes straight from the box. She needed to do something, stop waffling, take stock, but she couldn't even manage to keep Herbert off the counter. "Get down!" she hissed and clapped her hands sharply, and when that didn't work, she grabbed him and pushed him off. He landed on the floor with a thump, dust particles—probably dander—rising up around him, then immediately jumped back onto the counter, practically leering at her. God, Estie thought, she was so done with him, done with his yowling and vomiting, his middle-of-the-night sprints, his quiche-stealing, Owen's snot rags, Owen's allergies. She hadn't asked for a cat, had only agreed to take him because of Alice, had only kept him for the same reason she'd kept Alice's loathsome toothbrushes hidden away under the bathroom sink, which was that one day Alice might arrive for a visit and note everything that was missing and decide Estie didn't appreciate her enough.

But now it was clear that Alice wouldn't be visiting, and Estie owed her nothing, and just looking at Herbert filled Estie with hot shame. How was it possible that in all this time, Estie had never once paused to consider whether it was cruel to keep a pet that made her husband ill? What kind of wife worried about her best friend's approval more than about her husband's well-being? No wonder Owen hadn't told her about his Ph.D. How could he have when she'd made it clear over and over that her loyalty, her devotion, lay elsewhere, at the feet of a woman who actively disliked him? Well, fuck that, Estie thought. She imagined retrieving the toothbrushes and doing something dramatic, stomping on them, smashing them with a meat tenderizer, even setting them on fire, except that the toothbrushes were beside the point—they bothered nobody, they made no one sick, they kept no one from taking care of the baby. They weren't, right at that very moment, looking her straight in the eye while they sharpened their claws on the back of the couch.

For a long moment, she and the cat glared at each other, and then Herbert strutted off toward the bedroom, unmoved. "Fine," Estie said. "Whatever." She pulled out her phone and googled the local animal shelter. Giving up your cat, she discovered, was called surrendering, and required filling out a four-page form full of questions about your cat's personality and litter box habits. Was your cat friendly? Did he scratch up furniture? Did he bite people? Did he prefer clumping litter or sand? A more feeling person, Estie suspected, would have wept as they filled out the form, but not her. The main thing she felt was numb, an absence of emotion she didn't want to look at too closely. Or maybe what she felt was a rage so powerful she had to mute it, tamp it down. She waited for Rosie to wake up so she could change her diaper, then feed her, then change her diaper again, then buckle her into her car seat bucket, then bundle her up against the cold. Then, once Rosie was ready, Estie spent half an hour chasing Herbert around while he yowled plaintively at her from under the bed, under the dresser, under the couch before she managed to force him into his carrier and carry both him and Rosie down to Penny's SUV, which still needed to be cleaned and aired out.

And then, after all that, after driving to the animal shelter and hauling in both baby in bucket and cat in carrier, after standing at the front counter trying to ignore the dingy tile floors and the smell of Lysol and all the barks and meows that were coming from the back, the man who worked shelter reception told her, "You should've called. We're all full up."

"But I really need to surrender him," Estie said. "My husband is super allergic."

"How long have you been married?" asked the man. And when Estie told him, he said, unsympathetically even, "They've lived together this long—what's a couple more months?"

"But—"

"Look," said the man, "even if we could accept him, odds are he'd end up euthanized. Is that what you want?"

"Of course not."

"Then try Craigslist or something," the man advised. "Although make sure to charge money to root out all the Satan-worshipping weirdos."

Estie nodded obediently, consoling herself that, anyway, Herbert had never been good at being boarded—the other animals, their smells and sounds, overwhelmed him to such an extent that he'd return home with bare patches of skin where he'd anxiously groomed himself bald. No, Herbert would have suffered at the shelter during the days or weeks that passed until they inevitably decided to euthanize him. She would go home and put an ad on Craigslist and go from there.

By the time she got back to the car, however, she was no

longer sure that putting Herbert down wasn't the best option. The Craigslist route would take forever, and besides, nobody in their right mind would adopt a cat who required leather gloves and a sedative just to get through a routine physical—"He's not a beginner cat," the vet had observed after Herbert left yet another gash on her forearm. "I guess you just got lucky." But Estie didn't feel lucky, and anyway, she needed to do something quickly before her resolve wavered, something immediate and huge that would not only demonstrate a fundamental selflessness on her part but also force Owen to acknowledge her despair, to admit that he wasn't the good guy in this scenario either. She steeled herself and dialed up the nearest vet's office—there was no way she could face Herbert's actual vet—and cleared her throat as she listened to the phone ring. "I need to euthanize my cat," she told the receptionist when she answered. "Do you have any openings?"

"Oh," the receptionist said in what must have been her most comforting voice. "Oh no, you poor dear."

The vet's office was located in a small strip mall, nestled between a nail salon and a cupcake shop as if it specifically catered to women who had just received bad news. "Let's have you pay in advance," the receptionist instructed Estie before leading her, Rosie, and Herbert to an exam room that reeked of bleach. "Do you want cremation or burial? Cremation is more economical."

Estie studied the price menu, then handed over her credit card, trying to ignore the trembling in the carrier. "Cremation, please," she said. She'd expected more questions, more judgment, maybe an argument with the vet about putting Herbert on kitty anxiety meds, but the vet, when she came into the exam room, had simply asked, "Are you sure? Do you want to discuss alternatives?"

"I can't," Estie said, gesturing vaguely at Rosie. "I just can't."

"How old is she? Two months?"

"Just about."

"And the cat?"

"Almost ten."

"I have a two-year-old," the vet told her. "A boy." She flipped the ID she was wearing around her neck to show Estie a photo of a child hugging a black Lab. "It's not unusual for people to rehome a pet after they become parents."

"You didn't rehome yours."

"No," the vet agreed, "but I'm a vet."

"Please." Estie wanted to say more, felt she *ought* to be saying more, but she couldn't. "Please?"

Estie expected the vet to sigh in disappointment, or roll her eyes, make some small gesture to make clear she was accommodating Estie's foibles against her better judgment, but all the vet did was flip her ID back into position and say, "Do you want to be with him when it happens?"

She did, Estie realized. Here was a death she knew was coming, a sacrifice even, and she wanted to be present, eyes open, making sure nothing slipped past her, at least this once. "I do," she said in what felt like a grim exchange of vows, although Estie wasn't sure exactly what she was promising.

"What about her?" The vet indicated to Rosie. "I can have one of the assistants watch her if you don't want her to see."

Estie considered this for a moment, considered all those neural pathways Rosie was forming even right at that instant as she kicked out her legs and cooed at the wall, which was also stainless steel for easy cleanup. It wasn't as if Rosie would remember any of this, let alone understand what was happening, but then Estie thought about how she would tell it later and how much worse it would sound with a baby in the room.

The vet took the carrier away, returning a few minutes later with Herbert unconscious but still breathing, and Estie found herself wishing his expression were more dignified: tongue in his mouth instead of lolling, eyes closed instead of slitting open. A tech came in behind the vet, her eyes thick with mascara, and picked up the baby. "We'll be right outside," she told Estie, and then they were gone, and Estie could hear the tech in the hallway asking Rosie in what was no doubt her talk-to-pets voice, "Who's a pretty girl? Is it you? Is it you?"

"Don't worry," the vet assured Estie. "He won't feel a thing,"

Estie placed a hand on Herbert's warm back, resisting the sudden urge to thrust him into his carrier and bolt out of there, leaving the baby behind and heading south, just her and the cat and the bathing suit she'd buy at a Target along the way. Cut to: Owen warming formula at three a.m., Rosie crying in the next room; Owen changing diapers, dark circles under his eyes; Owen dozing off over a stack of papers that needed grading. Except that all that oxytocin meant Estie couldn't leave Rosie behind, and taking the baby with her would defeat the purpose of the whole exercise. Besides, who was she kidding? Even with Herbert out of the picture and Owen awake and alert, she'd still be the only one with the boobs and the milk.

"Okay," the vet said, picking up the syringe. "You ready?"

"I'm ready," Estie said, moving her hand out of the way so that the vet could inject whatever it was into Herbert's thigh. By the time Estie reached again to stroke him, he was gone, his breathing stilled, the heat draining out of his body.

So this was death, Estie thought to herself. One minute you were breathing, and then you weren't. Already—or maybe she was imagining it—Herbert's fur felt coarser, cooler, fake like stuffed-animal fur. She wondered if she was going to cry, but she didn't. She wasn't sad, and she wasn't relieved. She felt distant, as if she were observing herself with a kind of clinical detachment: *Huh. Well.*

"You can stay with him as long as you want," the vet said, her brown eyes sympathetic. "I know how hard this can be."

"No," Estie said. "I'm fine." She retrieved Rosie, then made a run for it, ducking the judgy gazes of the three dogs, two cats, and one bewildered ferret in the waiting room, who, with their sensitive animal hearing, had probably listened to the whole thing go down.

Out in the parking lot, Penny's SUV felt cavernous now that Herbert wasn't in it, and Estie found herself thinking about the multitude of sick and dead animals strewn in her wake, which now also included Herbert, whose death she'd planned and witnessed and paid for in advance, as if taking charge of this one death would make up for all the unintentional others. All that dying, and for what? Estie didn't know. *Good riddance,* she reminded herself, then climbed into the driver's seat and gripped the steering wheel firmly, with conviction, and waited for her hands to stop shaking.

21

THE PROBLEM WITH SWEEPING DRAMATIC gestures, selfless or no, was that not everyone considered them to be sweeping or dramatic. "Oh, Estie," Owen said when she told him what she'd done, "finally," as if he'd known all along that, one day, she'd do exactly that. It was, after all, the kind of thing that spouses routinely did for each other. Then he asked, "Are you sure?"

Estie shrugged. "It's a little late for that." She handed him Rosie and took the litter box out to the trash can. It took two more trips to dispose of all the cat's belongings: his food, his ratty little mouse toys, his fur-clogged brush, his heartworm meds. "We could probably donate some of that stuff," Owen pointed out, but Estie ignored him. A clean break was important. She stripped the bed and shoved the sheets in the hamper, then pulled the vacuum cleaner out of the closet.

"Are you sure you're okay?" Owen asked.

"I'm fine."

The vacuum was the fancy, pet-hair-busting kind, with a sealed bag and special HEPA filter. It was heavy, and using it always made Estie sweat, but rule number one of pet allergies was that the allergic person didn't do the vacuuming—it stirred up too much dander. Or maybe that was rule number two, and rule number one was, "Don't live with animals you're allergic to." Or maybe *that* was rule number two, and rule number one was, "Don't marry a person who won't give up their cat for you," which would make the whole thing Owen's fault for not knowing better.

She put the vacuum away in the hall closet, then plopped herself on the couch, only to realize it too needed vacuuming. She sighed and stood up again. In the bedroom, Owen was asleep on the bare mattress, Rosie wriggling at his feet. Thirty more seconds, and she would have ended up on the floor. For a moment, Estie imagined just leaving her there, on the edge of the bed—natural consequences were important, if not for the baby, then for Owen—but she wasn't that far gone, at least not yet. She picked up Rosie and took her to the living room, where she set her on her belly in the middle of the rug for some tummy time while she vacuumed the couch. All that vacuuming, and still, after she was done, Estie found cat hair on Rosie's chin and on the front of her onesie. It was hard not to feel taunted, as if Herbert's ghost had somehow already made it back to the duplex and was floating around whispering, *You can't get rid of me that easily.* As if on cue, Owen started snoring throatily in the bedroom. Estie tried not to think it, but she thought it anyway: She'd euthanized the cat; surely Owen could have at least put a clean sheet on the bed. Or moved laundry to the dryer. Or emptied the dishwasher. Something. Why couldn't he have done *something*? *You can't get rid of that either,* Herbert's ghost whispered in her ear, and Estie felt herself tear up. She'd had a plan. She thought she knew what she was doing, and she'd been wrong.

It wasn't fair. *Stop being a martyr*, Herbert's ghost whispered, *and go and wake him up already.*

And so Estie stood at the foot of the bed, Rosie cradled against her left hip, and repeated Owen's name until his eyes fluttered open. "Not only is Herbert dead," she informed him, "but Big Earth is moving production to China."

"What?" Owen said. "What are you talking about?" He rolled himself into a sitting position.

Estie filled him in, watching closely for his reaction—Horror? Panic? The realization that they'd already burned through a good portion of their savings and had no plan for moving forward?—but Owen just looked blank. "So?" she prompted. "What are we going to do?"

Owen shrugged. "We'll figure it out."

"How?"

"I don't know." He held out his arms, and she handed him the baby.

"But—"

"Trust me," Owen interrupted her. "We'll be fine. Don't worry."

Estie realized she was swaying from side to side as if she were still holding Rosie and forced herself to plant her feet and stand up straight. "How?" she asked. "How are we going to be fine?" After that, the rest came easily: "I have no job. You're adjuncting for hardly any money. And you did this to us. You did this to me. You lied to the people you work with, and then you lied to me about your lies, and then you got me pregnant even though you knew you might lose your job at any second, and then *you lost your fucking job*. And now we have this"—she gestured at Rosie—"*baby* that we're going to have to take care of forever, and we're stuck together, trapped, and we'll never be free again. And you want me to trust you?"

By now, Owen was standing up too, Rosie in the crook of his elbow. Estie couldn't read his expression—he was stone-faced, looking beyond her so that she couldn't meet his eyes. Was he just going to stand there in silence until—until what? Until she got so mad she started punching him with those weak-girl slap-punches? "What are you thinking?" she demanded.

Owen blinked, then slowly turned to look at her. "I'm thinking," he said, "that we chose to get married. Both of us. I'm not holding you hostage—"

"The baby is!"

"I'm not holding you hostage," Owen said again, "and neither is Rosie. And I've never lied to you about anything that didn't have to do with my job, and that was only because I was so ashamed." He swiped at his eyes. "I don't understand what's happening," he said. "When did you become so helpless, so . . . *dependent?*"

Here, finally, was Estie's turn to gape. "Are you fucking serious?" She started pacing. "You knew I wasn't ready to have a baby, and you held me down and got me pregnant anyway."

"You wanted a baby too. You said okay. You said, 'Let's do it.'"

"So what?" Estie said. "I wasn't ready."

"Then you should have said so!"

"You shouldn't have asked me, not in the middle of sex."

Owen set Rosie down carefully on the bed and turned to face Estie, placing a hand on each of her shoulders and making eye contact like a pro. "I'm sorry about Herbert," he said. "I should have come with you." This was beside the point, of course. If Owen had been the sort of husband who went with his wife to the vet, there would have been no need to euthanize Herbert in the first place. Estie closed her eyes and imagined Herbert in some kind of biohazard dumpster with all the other animals the vet had euthanized over the past week or month: gerbils, parakeets, bunny rabbits, chinchillas. And for what? Owen didn't understand. She couldn't make him understand. Not that this mattered either, because Rosie was starting to fuss, and by the time Estie was done with nursing and changing and swaddling her, Owen was stretched out on the couch, eyes half closed—again!—a frozen pizza in the oven. "Come here," he said as if their fight hadn't happened, and pulled her and Rosie down next to him. The three of them lay together for a while, Rosie squirming in Estie's arms, Owen stroking Estie's hair absentmindedly, Estie bristling. He was so calm, Estie thought. So . . . *complacent*. The word appeared in her mind in bright white letters, like those words of the day on *Sesame Street* that were superimposed over a shot of a New York block. What kind of person listened to his wife shriek at him that everything was his fault and that he'd forced her to get pregnant, then acted as if she'd said nothing at all? *Had* she said nothing at all? She tried to remember. "Do we need to talk?" she asked him finally, and he said, "Sure. About what?"

Estie felt herself tense up. "The part where I said everything is your fault?"

"You were upset," Owen said matter-of-factly. "People say things all the time when they're upset. And don't forget, you're awash in all these weird hormones."

"Awash?" Estie repeated. "Hormones?" She twisted away from him and moved beyond his reach. "I'm not an irrational freak."

"See?" Owen said. "That's what I'm talking about, right there. No one said you're an irrational freak. Having feelings doesn't make you a freak. There's just a lot going on."

She glanced down at Rosie, who was practicing facial contortions, and for a moment, their eyes met, Rosie's eyes a deep blue-gray that would eventually turn brown like Estie's. At moments like these—more and more—Estie felt that she was being watched not just by infant Rosie but also by a future Rosie, the version of Rosie who, one day, would have to decide whether to pierce her nose and whether it was okay to let the future bigheaded Joseph Van Vranken feel her up because prom was a special occasion. Now Estie wondered what she would advise the future Rosie to do when the person who was supposed to love her most, except for maybe her parents, dismissed her anger as something hormonal, an awkward new-mother phase that could safely be ignored.

She stood up and handed Rosie to Owen. "I need to get out of here," she said. "I can't breathe."

"But the pizza—"

But Estie was already slipping on her sneakers and grabbing a jacket and the keys to Penny's car. "When's my car going to be ready?"

"I thought you were taking care of that."

She couldn't believe it. "When, exactly? With what free time?"

"I don't know," Owen said. "I mean, you're the one who keeps going on road trips."

"Fine," Estie said. "I'll take care of the car. Enjoy your fucking pizza." And then she was out of there, her only regret that their front door wasn't the kind that was easy to slam.

22

ESTIE DROVE AROUND FOR A while before finally pulling into the Southside, a diner that was all chrome and vinyl and seven thousand hot dog toppings. She ordered a banana split because she was alone, and because she'd never dared to order one before, and then she sat there watching the whipped cream melt into the hot fudge and thinking about the time she and Alice had gone rappelling and how frightened she'd been of transferring her entire weight to the ropes. She remembered hesitating at the edge of the overhang for what felt like three hours but was probably only ten minutes, her heart hammering against her ribs, while Alice, who was already more than halfway down, encouraged her to push off. Once she finally did, the ropes had held as expected, but still, she'd been so proud of herself, so grateful to Alice for pumping her up and cheering her on. What a fool she'd been to believe that she was achieving something by overcoming obstacles she'd chosen herself, obstacles that appeared risky but were perfectly safe. She was like her mom with her elaborate schedules and her unwavering belief that if only she followed the plan, she'd never be caught off guard.

She didn't know how long she'd been sitting there, absentmindedly stirring all that glop with a spoon, when someone approached her table and pulled out the seat across from her, someone who, when she sat down, turned out to be Estie's mother, her nose wrinkling at the sight of all that wasted ice cream, or maybe at the fact that Estie had ordered a banana split all on her own.

Estie blinked. Surely this was one of those illusions that pointed to Estie's inevitable descent into postpartum psychosis. "Mom? What are you doing here?"

"I stopped by to see Rosie, and Owen told me about your fight."

"He did?"

"He was upset, poor guy." Her mother lowered her voice. "And then he told me about Herbert, and then I *knew*."

"Knew what?"

Her mother shrugged. "That you needed me. I mean, you loved that cat." She turned and waved the server over. "Can we get the check?"

"I'm still eating."

"No, you're not," her mother said. "I'm taking you home." She was already fishing her wallet out of her purse, pulling out a couple of bills to leave as a tip. *Whatever*, Estie thought: it wasn't as if she had the energy to fight anyone, let alone her mother, who had never lost an argument in her entire life.

Out in the parking lot, Estie's mother led her to the shiny Subaru she'd recently purchased. "We'll come back for your car later," she said.

"I'm fine to drive," Estie said. "Just tired." But she got in obediently and leaned back in the passenger seat. She tried not to cry, but the streetlights blurred in front of her. She probably had thirty minutes until Rosie started getting peckish. She closed her eyes for a moment, then opened them, startled, when she heard the pop of gravel under the tires. Estie's mother wasn't taking Estie to the duplex with its cracked concrete driveway but to her own house, the house she'd moved into after the divorce.

"No," Estie said once she understood what was happening. "Take me home."

Her mother didn't answer. She parked the car, then took the keys out of the ignition and unlocked the door. "Come on."

Estie didn't move. "Why are we here?"

"Because you're sick."

"I'm fine."

"You loved that cat," her mother said again. "This isn't you."

Estie tried hard not to start shouting. "Of course it's me. This is who I am now."

Her mother got out of the car, then walked over to the passenger side, opening Estie's door.

"Please," Estie said. "Take me home."

Her mother shook her head. "You need me," she insisted. "You need your mom." And then she was helping Estie, who seemed incapable of resisting, out of the car.

"I'm fine," Estie mumbled.

"I know," her mother said soothingly. Then she put her arm around Estie's shoulders—when had she last done that?—and led Estie up to her old room, which still smelled like dryer sheets and perfumed issues of *Cosmo*.

"Rosie's going to be hungry soon," Estie said, but her mother was already pulling back the covers on Estie's narrow twin bed and, somehow, compelling Estie to lie down.

"I got this," her mother said, tucking the sheet in around Estie.

"I don't think I can sleep." Estie felt stiff, immobilized by tension. She tightened and relaxed her muscles, then tightened them again. At some point, her mother left the room, and Estie could hear her murmuring on the phone. Then she came back, carrying the small plastic footstool she used when she needed to reach the high shelves in the kitchen, and placed it near Estie's bed.

"I'm sorry," Estie's mother said, taking a seat on the stool. "I knew things were hard, but I hadn't realized they were this bad. Owen's going to watch Rosie and you're going to sleep, and we'll see how things look in the morning."

Her mother was lying, Estie knew. How could Owen, with all his sleep deprivation and essays to grade, manage to watch Rosie when Estie could barely handle it? "I know I'm not a good mom," Estie said, "but you don't need to keep me away from Rosie." She was slurring her words, as if even her own lips and tongue were working to keep her there, safe from harm or harming. She clenched her jaw and pushed forward: "I've been feeding her and changing her diapers just fine. And Owen's just going to sleep through her crying." For the four millionth time that day, Estie teared up, and because her mom never approved of anything she did anyway, this time she didn't even try to stop herself. Let her mother see her ugly crying, her swollen red eyes and blotchy face. It felt good to admit that she wasn't a good mom. It felt right. Something was wrong with her, something she'd no doubt inherited from her mother and would now pass on to Rosie, who was supposed to have been born a boy precisely so that she wouldn't turn out like Estie, awkward and perpetually dissatisfied, the kind of woman who euthanized her pets when she tired of them.

Estie's mom got up from her stool, her knees creaking, but instead of leaving, she turned off the light, then sat back down. Even in the darkened room, Estie could make out her mother's tight expression, her nearly invisible lips. Estie rolled over onto her side so that her back was toward her mother. She braced herself for a lecture about peasant women and bucking up, but her mother stayed silent. Instead, after a moment, Estie felt her mother's fingers in her hair. Estie froze under her touch, releasing her breath slowly. Had she ever felt anything so wonderful, so comforting, as her mother tugging at her hair just then? *Don't stop*, she found herself praying, focusing all her concentration on her mother's hands. *Please, God*, she prayed. *Please. Please don't let her stop*.

And maybe God heard her, because her mother kept stroking her hair, leaning forward so that her mouth was near Estie's ear, her breath warm and steady. "You're a good mother," she said in the same soft way she used to tell bedtime stories. "You're taking good care of Rosie. You've got this. You can do this. Nobody's taking your baby away."

Estie slept hard and dreamlessly, waking up to discover that her shirt was soaked with milk. Holding the fabric out so that it wouldn't cling to her, she tiptoed to her mother's room, hoping that the old floorboards wouldn't groan and give her away before she found a different shirt to wear. But the floor did creak, and Estie heard her mother stirring in the kitchen, then padding up the stairs. She felt her skin prickle: Which mother would show? The loving mother from last night or the regular mother who liked telling it like it is?

Whichever mother she was, she seemed uncomfortable. "Are you feeling any better?" she asked Estie, then walked over to her dresser and pulled out a T-shirt, handing it over without a word. Estie recognized the shirt—it was the baggy one with her college's logo, which was peeling at the edges. It was soft from hundreds of washings and smelled clean. "This isn't about being fat," Estie told her reflection in the bathroom mirror after she'd changed. "She was being kind." And maybe her mother was being kind, because even before she'd gotten pregnant, Estie had no hope of fitting into her mother's daytime clothes. At least this way she didn't have to go through the humiliation of trying.

"Owen's on his way over," Estie's mother told her once Estie was suitably dressed and seated at the kitchen table. She opened the refrigerator and pulled out a carton of milk and some eggs. "French toast?"

Estie nodded, watching her mother take a braided challah from the breadbox on the counter, then scramble some eggs. "I don't know if you remember," her mother started, "but I used to be depressed."

Estie scoffed. She couldn't help herself.

Estie's mother blinked. "I guess you do remember," she said lightly before continuing: "I was blindsided by parenting—maybe because my mom had already passed. All those nonstop demands from you and Sammy and your dad seemed to come out of nowhere—all of it seemed to come out of nowhere. That's why I tried to prepare you, to be honest with you about what's involved. That way, when things got hard—because they always get hard—you'd know that it's normal and you wouldn't run away just because Rosie says she hates you or because Owen or whoever tells you a little lie."

"It wasn't a little lie."

"Don't shout," her mother said. "And yes, it was. There are so many worse lies out there."

"God, Mom," Estie burst out. "Isn't there one positive thing you can say about the world? Something that isn't about how everyone's awful and how much you hated parenting? I'm sorry Sammy and me were such a disappointment to you, but weren't there good moments too?"

Her mother opened her mouth, no doubt to argue, but thank God this was when Owen and Rosie made their appearance, and Estie and her mother quickly resumed their standard roles of Moderately Loving Mother and Daughter: her mother placed more egg-soaked challah into the pan and Estie sprinkled the steaming slices on her plate with powdered sugar. Owen resumed his role too, the role of Caring Husband of Psychotic Wife, shrinking away in anticipation of her next blow even as he tried to pretend everything was normal. He didn't have as much practice at it as Estie and her mother, as Estie and her father, as Estie, and, it seemed, just about everyone in front of whom she needed to pretend that she was well-adjusted and 100 percent on board. *Well,* Estie thought, *at least nobody was going to call her bluff about Rosie—stupid letdown.* Estie's body didn't lie, and neither did her voice, which immediately rose up into a coo: "You hungry?" she asked the baby. She crouched down and released Rosie from her bucket, then carried her into the living room and settled into her mother's tasteful if uncomfortable Queen Anne couch. Rosie immediately turned her face to Estie's breast, nuzzling her shirt and grunting like the small mammal she was. "Patience," Estie told her. She lifted up her shirt and unclasped her nursing bra, and then Rosie was on her, still snuffling and squeaking, first tense and then gradually relaxing into a steady, meditative rhythm. Estie grasped Rosie's left hand in her right, pressing on her palm gently with her thumb. Rosie's fingers bloomed open one at a time, then curled back shut as if they belonged to some tentacled underwater plant. And all of it—the letdown, the nursing, the too-sharp fingernails—all of it a big stupid reminder that human life—all life—was nothing more than a series of stimulus and response.

When Rosie was done, Estie returned to the kitchen, where Owen immediately whisked Rosie away. "I got her," he said, settling her on his lap. He supported her with one arm and leaned her forward with the other, noisily forcing the air out of her. "That's my girl," he said when she burped, and set her back down in her car seat. He looked at Estie and smiled a tight-mouthed smile. "I brought the pump," he said, his voice apologetic. "Then we can see how you're feeling tonight." He cleared his throat. "You already look much better."

"Yes," her mother interjected, "a little vacation will do you wonders, don't you think?"

But what kind of vacation was it, alone in her mother's house with a pump? The pump didn't cry or blow out its diaper, sure, but—and this fact wasn't lost on Estie one bit—it also wasn't vulnerable to smothering or shaken baby syndrome. "I thought you said no one was taking Rosie away," she accused her mom.

"Nobody is," her mom agreed. "You just need some time to recharge. Your needle's hovering at zero. You need to take care of yourself before you take care of the baby."

"I'm just tired," Estie said. "I just need to snap out of it."

Owen sighed impatiently. "Fine, then," he said. "Snap out of it." But instead of meeting Estie's eyes, he retreated to a safer position behind her mother, the human shield.

For a moment, the three of them glared at each other, and then her mother forced a smile: "For heaven's sake, Estie, let me take care of you," she said. "I know you better than anyone. Let me do for you what nobody was around to do for me." Her expression was earnest, her eyes moist, and Owen was nodding from his hiding place behind Estie's mother's left shoulder, as if to say, "She's your mother. She loves you. Just do this one thing."

And all of it, all of it, felt deceptively easy: return to your mother's house, replace your baby with a machine, be coddled by the mother you've always wanted. Had Estie's mother made a similar offer to Sammy and his wife when their kids were born, to Sammy after his divorce? Estie didn't have to ask to know that she hadn't. This was a daughter thing, a hormone thing, a deal you made with female progeny so that in another decade or two, when you were too old to do so yourself, she'd clean you and diaper you and feed you with a spoon, the daughter turned to mothering, the mother turned to child. No wonder that Estie's mother was so invested in Estie's success as a parent.

"Fine," Estie said. "I'm going back to bed." She really was reverting to her teenage self, stomping up the stairs, trying to slam the door behind her, except that this was another door that wouldn't slam. What was it with all these doors? Estie tried a second time—she distinctly remembered slamming the door multiple times when she'd been younger—but apparently the frame had shifted over the years. She stomped off to her bed, arms crossed in front of her chest, a teen with giant lactating boobs she didn't know what to do with, and threw herself onto her narrow twin, a move that only served to remind her that it wasn't just her boobs that had changed since she was sixteen, but also the rest of her: she grossly misestimated the space she had, bashing her head into the wall with enough force that, once she'd sufficiently recovered from the blow, she saw that she'd managed to dent the drywall. She felt her scalp, but other than a bit of tenderness, there didn't appear to be much damage—certainly no blood. For a moment, she felt a twinge of pride: talk about hardheaded, no fainting spells, no trips to Oz. Then she felt foolish. She wasn't a teenager. This wasn't her bed. This wasn't her home. There was no wand her mother could wave that would return Estie to high school, where she could start over knowing what she knew now and actually do things the right way. Not that any of that mattered. She remembered her college career counselor looking over her résumé: "So you were hot shit in high school," he'd said. "So what? In the immortal words of Janet Jackson, what have you done for me lately?" And wasn't that really the heart of the matter? Without a husband she trusted, without the job she'd held for years, who was Estie now? A mom, yes; a denter of walls. But what else? Surely there was something else. And she certainly wasn't going to find it in her childhood bedroom.

23

BY THE TIME SHE GOT downstairs, Owen and Rosie were gone, but her mother was at the sink, filling a water bottle. Estie cleared her throat "Can you give me a ride back to the Southside?"

Her mom looked up. "I would've killed for someone to force me to rest. I wanted it to be different for you."

"It *is* different for me," Estie said. "And I'm sorry. I'm sorry you were so alone."

Her mother didn't respond, only turned off the faucet. "I have Pilates," she said, patting the outside of the bottle dry with a dish towel. "I can drive you after."

"Please," Estie said, "can't you just drop me off on the way?"

"It isn't on the way," her mother pointed out, "and I don't want to be late. And you need to rest." When Estie opened her mouth to object, she added, "I'm done doing things on other people's schedules. I think I've earned at least that courtesy."

Here she was, Estie's mother: her hair was streaked with gray and her face was showing the first signs of wrinkles, but her arms were strong and wiry, her thighs were muscular, her posture straight. If she wanted to be on time to Pilates, who was

Estie to stop her, to judge her for putting herself first for this one thing? "Okay," she said. "No problem. I think a walk will do me good."

The three-mile walk from Estie's mother's house to the Southside Grill was unpleasant, most of it on a busy street lined with strip malls full of fast-food joints and nail salons with names like Happy Nails, and Joyful Nails, and Blissful Nails. Estie marched along on the crumbling sidewalk, traffic roaring in her ears, wondering about the women who could afford to pay a stranger to exfoliate their feet in the middle of an October workday. Where were their jobs? Where were their babies? She sighed, wishing she'd thought to wear sneakers the previous evening instead of the ratty flip-flops that now made her feel like a flat-footed clown with freezing toes. Whatever. It felt good to walk, to move forward, even if all she was doing was retrieving Penny's SUV. She wasn't a child or a surly teen. She was a woman walking with her head up high, a woman pretending that she wasn't peering into each car that came up behind her, hoping that the driver would turn out to be someone she knew, or rather, someone who knew her, who knew what was happening and had spent the last thirty minutes driving up and down the roads near her mother's hoping to find her and make sure she was fine. "I was worried about you," the person would say after rolling down their driver-side window. "Need a lift?" And Estie would say, "Oh, God, do I," and thankfully climb into the person's car, adjusting the passenger seat so that she could lean back and close her eyes. Or, she thought after the fifth car inched past her only to make a left turn into a Taco Bell, she'd settle for some car simply mowing her down, not to kill her so much as to put her in the hospital for a week or two, where everyone she knew would visit and tell her how lucky she'd been to survive until she began believing it too, and believed it so deeply that, by the time she was discharged, she'd be raring to go, ready to stop complaining and able to face whatever came next.

There was a car wash around the corner from the duplex, so this was where Estie headed after retrieving Penny's SUV from the Southside. "Human or pet, body fluids are extra," the manager warned her, and she nodded—what choice did she have? She left the car, then walked home, hoping that Owen wouldn't be there, and that Rosie somehow would be. She got half her wish: the duplex was empty, dirty dishes piled on the counter and unwashed baby bottles in the sink, some still full of defrosted breast milk. Herbert would have had a field day if only he hadn't been euthanized. She set down her purse and dutifully began separating the nipples from the bottles. At least she wanted to see Rosie. That felt like a good sign.

Once everything was clean, she texted Owen, "I'm back fyi." Then she dug a pile of dirty baby onesies out of the hamper. She'd just started a load of laundry when she received Owen's response: "Took Rosie to class. Home soon," along with a photo of a pretty blonde—no doubt one of Owen's students—cradling Rosie in her arms.

While she waited, Estie swept and mopped. She checked their credit card balance and moved more money from savings to checking, she typed "jobs near me" into Google and then, to suppress the panic welling up inside her, she watched three episodes of a reality show in which women were ambushed on the street and given makeovers. It didn't work. Her breasts throbbed. The pump was still at her mother's. "Happy Nails," she whispered to herself. "Joyful Nails. Blissful Nails." The words felt a little like praying: if only she were earnest enough, Our Lady of the Blessed Manicure would intercede on her behalf. But there was no Our Lady of the Blessed Manicure, and when Owen and Rosie finally got home a little while later, instead of admiring the sparkling floors, Owen looked around disapprovingly. "I was going to wash those bottles," he said. "You have to give me a chance."

"I *am* giving you a chance."

At the sound of Estie's voice, Rosie began to wriggle and coo. "Yes," Owen confirmed, "it's Mama," and handed her over to Estie. He looked so disappointed—In Estie? In Rosie?—that Estie felt her mouth go dry in what she guessed was a must-make-my-husband-happy reflex. She settled herself and the baby on the couch, then lifted her shirt and unfastened her nursing bra. Owen watched her for a moment, then shook himself out of his stupor. "I forgot to tell you," he said. "Rosie's smiling."

"She is?"

Owen pulled out his phone and opened his photo app. "See for yourself," he said, handing it over, and there Rosie was, smiling a broad, gummy smile at the blond student who had been holding her earlier. The shot was in profile, and the student was holding Rosie up straight in front of her so that their foreheads almost touched. "That's Stephanie," Owen said. "She's a sophomore. She's offered to babysit."

Estie flipped to the next photo. Stephanie was still holding the baby, but this time, Owen had taken the picture head-on so he could fully capture the joy on Rosie's face, the amusement in her eyes. Estie felt her stomach clench—weren't babies supposed to smile at their mothers first? "Huh," she said. "She must prefer blondes."

Owen reached over and took his phone back. "She smiled at Stephanie because Stephanie smiled at her first."

"I smile at her—"

"No, you don't," Owen interrupted. "You don't smile at anything. Not since the baby. Not anymore."

Estie stared at Owen. If she hadn't been literally attached to the baby, she would have jumped to her feet, maybe even throttled him. "Are you seriously asking me for service with a smile?"

"Yes," Owen said. "Because that's all you are to me, some kind of maid."

"Fine," Estie said. "Will there be anything else?"

Owen threw his hands up in the air. "You know I didn't mean it." And then, because apparently even he couldn't leave well enough alone, he added, "Nobody would put up with this kind of shit from a maid."

Estie considered spending the night on the couch, or maybe in the rocker in the baby's room, but wasn't this what couples did before they got divorced? For a moment, she tried to imagine life without Owen, just her and Rosie and all of Rosie's needs. Who was she kidding? She wasn't going anywhere, at least not on her own, not anytime soon. Alice had been right at least about that. Estie felt herself tear up. Wasn't it enough that she'd grown up subject to her mother's unpredictable moods? Did she really have to go through all that again, this time with an infant? Yes, she'd known that babies weren't easy—God knows her mother had warned her enough times—but she'd always assumed that she wouldn't mind, that she'd take one look at her baby and feel a love so intense that all that work would be worth it. But becoming a mother hadn't made Estie more selfless and nurturing, it had merely recast her desires as distractions and then shamed her for them. She cared about Rosie, sure, but even now, she wasn't in anything that resembled love, not really, although she suspected that she was getting closer, that all that love was there just beyond her reach, like a forgotten word on the tip of her tongue. All those studies were true: with enough proximity, you could learn to love anyone.

And so Estie had gone to bed next to Owen like a normal person—if nothing else, she was an optimist. Even so, she didn't fall asleep until after Rosie's four a.m. feeding, and when morning came, she was only vaguely aware of the shift of the mattress as Owen woke up, the clink of his spoon against glass in the kitchen, the jangling of his keys in the front door. When she finally did get out of bed, she looked for a note but all she found was a shopping list, on which Owen had written "frozen pizza" and "gum." Fine, she told herself. She didn't really need a note. She didn't really need anything except to get Penny's SUV back to Penny.

Once Rosie was up and fed and diapered, Estie packed the stroller in Penny's trunk, bundled up the baby, and drove over to Penny's house, which turned out to be maybe twice the size of Estie and Owen's duplex, with a deep front porch and an actual porch swing, its front yard shaded by hundred-year-old maples. She expected Penny to be at work, had even brought an envelope so she could stick the keys in the mailbox, but to her surprise, Penny was home. "I had a doctor's appointment earlier," she explained, "so I took the morning off."

"And?" Estie prompted.

"Everything's good. Strong heartbeat. Good levels of amniotic fluid." And Penny really did look much better than she had at the hospital, rosier, more awake. "I was just folding laundry," she told Estie. "Want to see the baby's room? Rosie could test the crib."

Estie retrieved Rosie from the car, and the two of them trailed Penny through the house, Estie gaping at the stained-glass panels in the living room, at the *two* wood-burning fireplaces and polished oak floors. She did her best to disguise her envy as admiration, but God, she was so jealous she couldn't breathe: even before Owen had lost his job, they would have never been able to afford a house this lovely.

"I really can't believe it either," Penny said, as if reading Estie's mind. "It's kind of like winning the Lotto, the difference in price between here and California. The house we had there was maybe nine hundred square feet and cost three times as much."

Estie nodded, then followed Penny upstairs to the nursery, which was large and sunny, the walls painted a citrusy yellow.

All the furniture matched. A framed cross-stitch featuring the baby-to-be's name—Oscar—hung over the cherrywood crib. "My mom made that," Penny said when she saw Estie looking. She lowered herself with some effort into the glider and resumed folding an enormous pile of little baby clothes. "She went a little nuts at Babies'R'Us," she said, holding up a blue kimono-style onesie.

"You're not going to want those right away," Estie told her. "Not until the umbilical cord falls off. Otherwise, the fabric just pulls on it." Already, it felt as if she were talking about something that happened long, long ago, something she could barely remember. She started to set Rosie down in the crib, then immediately thought better of it. "It's like birthday cake," she explained to Penny. "Oscar should be the one to use it first."

Penny patted her belly. "How's he even going to get out of me?"

"Believe me," Estie said, "the hard part comes after." Immediately, she wanted to kick herself. "Ha," she said. "Kidding."

"No, you're not," Penny said. "You haven't exactly been a walking advertisement for the joys of parenting."

Estie's face grew hot. "I'm doing my best."

"Of course you are. I didn't mean to imply that you weren't."

A long, sticky silence descended upon them. Estie didn't know where to look, so she looked at Rosie, who was kicking her feet happily on a rug shaped like a lion. "La," Rosie said. "Ga."

"Ga yourself," Penny told her.

"She's started smiling," Estie told her. "At blondes. I'm still waiting."

Penny pushed the laundry basket aside, suddenly serious. "Estie," she said, her voice low, "are you sure you're okay?"

"Sure," Estie said automatically. "Why?"

"I don't know. The whole trip to Chicago, the way it played out. It's like you're going through something, something that isn't just the baby."

"Well," Estie said, because she had to say something, "Big Earth is moving production to China."

"Oh no," Penny said. "What will you do?"

"I don't know." For a moment, Estie considered telling Penny the rest of it too, the parts about Owen lying, about Dan, about Alice, but in her head it all sounded so ridiculous, so low stakes, especially compared to the news about Big Earth—*Oh, boo hoo. My husband doesn't have an advanced degree. Oh, wah, my friends from college are having sex.* Maybe her mother was right all along and Estie was overreacting. "I guess I'll be a stay-at-home mom."

"Is that what you want?"

"I don't know." Not that what she wanted mattered. "I want whatever's good for Rosie."

"No, really," Penny said. "What do *you* want? Don't *think* about it, just say the first thing that pops into your head."

"It's not that easy—"Estie began, except that it was: she wanted not to have to go back to the duplex, not to be in charge of the housekeeping, or forgiveness, or the future of her marriage. She wanted not to be in charge of anyone except herself. And that wasn't all she wanted: She also wanted not to have married Owen in the first place, not to have settled, or at least not to feel that she'd settled. She knew all this without a doubt, with the same clear-cut intensity she knew she wanted to erase Joseph Van Vranken's sweaty hands on her boobs, on her thighs, in her underwear all those years ago. But she wasn't seventeen anymore and stuck in someone else's car: she was thirty-two and certainly independent enough to say, "No, I'm not ready, I think we should wait." But she hadn't said any of that, she hadn't said anything. And she couldn't say anything to Penny now either. Instead, she felt her face changing colors, the bile making its way to her throat. "I think I'm going to throw up," she said. Hand over her mouth, she dashed across the hall, but nothing happened, except that after a moment Penny joined her, kneeling down beside her and rubbing her back.

"I'm fine," Estie said, scooting away from the toilet so she could lean against the wall, the white wainscoting cool against her back. If only Penny wanted out of her marriage too, she thought. Then Penny would get the house in the divorce—didn't women always get the house and the children?—and Estie and Rosie would move in, help with the mortgage, split the cost of the nanny who would stay with the babies while Penny and Estie went off to fabulous and fulfilling jobs that paid them as if they were men. They'd adopt cats, and dogs, and tortoises, go on vacations to places with hairy spiders so large they could eat entire birds. And then, years later, after Rosie and Oscar went off to college or even married each other, Estie and Penny would convert their rooms into guest suites and open a bed-and-breakfast that specialized in soon-to-be single moms who needed a place to stay while they gathered up the courage to strike out on their own, to ignore all the rumors that divorce not only made you poor but transformed your children into junkies who stole your cash and sold your laptop, then bitched about you during the group sessions at rehab.

Estie opened her eyes. She had to give Penny something. "I want—" she began, hoping the sentence would finish itself for her, but it didn't. She couldn't do it. "I want to go home. And you need to go to work." It was nowhere near "I want us both to get divorced so we can be roommates," but it was the best she could do. She stood up and pulled Penny's car keys out of her pocket and handed them to Penny without meeting her eye. "Anyway," she said, "I brought back your car, fresh from the car wash."

"You didn't need to do that."

"Sure, I did," Estie said. "Everything smelled like cat shit."

"Poor Herbert."

There was no avoiding it any longer. Estie swallowed hard. "Just so you know," she said in as steady a voice as she could muster, "Herbert died. I mean, I had him euthanized. I mean," she tried again, "I just couldn't . . . I couldn't deal with him, with Owen's allergies, so I had him killed. I killed him." There was relief in putting what she'd done into words—into accurate words—but saying them out loud also brought a kind of clarity. She was ridiculous. She was a horrible person. She'd broken her promise not just to Alice, but to Herbert. There had been no reason to euthanize him, and there certainly had been no rush: she could have taken her time, could have asked Penny if she wanted a cat, or asked her mother, or even Mara, but instead she'd opted for the drama, for the supposedly grand gesture that—was there any other way to see it?—served as an elaborate Fuck You to Alice, who didn't know and didn't care, and to Owen, whom she was supposed to love and honor, and whose allergies she'd ignored right up until the moment they'd inconvenienced her. And so she'd killed a small, helpless animal. According to most movies, that made her a psychopath/serial killer, or, at the very least, a villain. No wonder nobody believed her when she insisted that she'd never harm Rosie, a human baby more helpless than

Herbert had ever been, whom Estie was expected to care for until one of them died (*Please, God, please, let Estie be the first to go . . .*). Even if you ignored the tens of millions of peasant women popping out babies on their lunch breaks—if they even got to go on lunch breaks—and trading one kind of labor for the other, there were still the fewer but also millions of women out there who, like Estie, had the money and access to medical care that turned them physically weak and morally flabby—at least according to Estie's father, sitting in his fucking golf cart—women who, despite their privilege, were capable of raising their babies into adulthood *and* walking their dogs three times a day, uncomplainingly cleaning up both human and animal waste without blinking.

"Oh my God," Estie heard herself exclaim in something that resembled awe, "I think I'm actually going crazy."

"You want to go to the ER?" Penny asked cautiously. Her face was somber, and she met Estie's surprised look head-on with the sheepish air of someone who'd been working up to the question for a while.

Estie paused, tamping down the urge to mock Penny's earnestness, to say something equally hurtful back. "I'm good. I'll just call my doctor."

Penny nodded, and Estie could tell by the way her mouth seemed to soften that she was relieved. "Okay," she said. "Good." She watched Estie pull out her phone and dial her doctor's number, then announced, "Gotta pee," leaving the room to give Estie some privacy, returning with a batch of Kool-Aid only after Estie hung up.

"Oh," Estie said, tearing up. "Oh. You didn't have to."

"No big deal." Penny handed her a glass. "I had extra. Did they give you a referral?"

Estie nodded. "They even made the damn appointment for me. For tomorrow. They're squeezing me in." Being a new mother who might, at any minute, descend into psychosis and harm her baby apparently had its advantages.

Penny raised her own glass with a flourish. "You did it. Yay you."

"Yay me," Estie echoed. No doubt about it, Penny was a much better person than she was, and yet somehow, despite all their years together, this was something Estie had managed not to notice, or maybe to ignore, until right then. "I'm so sorry about Chicago," she said. "I was awful to you, and you were so patient. I've always been awful and you've always been patient. I don't know how I'm ever going to make it up to you. How can I make it up to you?"

"Don't be an idiot," Penny said and took a sip of Kool-Aid. "Just get better."

24

BACK WHEN SHE WAS YOUNGER, before her father had moved to that golf course in Florida, Estie had believed that if she and Sammy stopped asking their parents for things, stopped making mistakes, washed dishes without complaint, they could fool their parents into believing their family was happy, that everyone got along. This plan hadn't worked, of course: "I can finally breathe," Estie's mother announced after her father moved out. "You don't know how good it feels." And by the time the divorce was final, her mother was doing yoga three times a week and knitting socks with complicated Fair Isle patterns that she gifted to the other members of her book group. She kept herself so busy that sometimes Estie worried that she was divorcing not only Estie's father, but Estie and Sammy as well. But when she finally worked up the courage to bring this up, her mother said, "This divorce has nothing to do with you two. It's just between me and your dad."

"That's what everyone says," Estie countered.

"They say it *because it's true*."

But how could it be true that divorce had nothing to do with children? If Owen and Estie's marriage ultimately ended up falling apart, some large chunk of it would have to do with Rosie, with all the sleepless nights and diaper changes and Estie's grief over the loss of the woman she used to be—at least theoretically—a woman who reported to no one, was accountable to no one, was free to decide when to even bother to think about others, let alone do anything for them. There was no end to parenting, no time off, no graceful exit, just guilt and more guilt, worry and more worry. Estie's mother had needed medication to get through it. Estie's father had to leave the state.

And yet. And yet. And yet here was Rosie, sighing sweetly, her eyelids fluttering in sleep when Estie set her down in her crib. Maybe, Estie tried to convince herself, if she acted like a loving wife and mother, she would eventually become a loving wife and mother. The kind of passion Estie had felt for Alice and Dan was a rare and precious thing, yes, but the world needed ordinary lovers and middle managers too, people who were fine being good enough rather than exceptional. And that, Estie thought, was something she might be able to do, or at least be able to fake. She would turn herself off and think of England. She would close her eyes and push her way through. And in eighteen years, after Rosie left for college, she'd have finally earned her freedom. She would finally be free to catch her breath.

"I've been giving it a lot of thought," Estie told Owen the following morning, "and I don't need therapy. Really. I'm like those cars that miraculously repair themselves right before you take them in to the mechanic."

"Good thing I canceled class," Owen said, his voice flat. He picked Rosie up off her bouncy chair and started buckling her into her car seat. "You're not backing out. I'm driving."

Estie felt herself bristle. "I can drive myself. You stay home and watch Rosie."

"I can drive you *and* watch Rosie," Owen said, his hands on his hips, "so stop arguing."

Estie stopped arguing.

The therapist's office shared an unremarkable office building with a bank and some mortgage lenders. There were a handful of other women in the waiting room, some massively pregnant, some bearing telltale postpartum belly flab and dark circles under their eyes—all studiously holding clipboards and filling out health histories and depression questionnaires. Except for the whirring from a couple of noise machines, everything was quiet, the women careful to avoid eye contact, as if everyone there had tacitly agreed not to see each other, not to bear witness to each other's failures as mothers or mothers-to-be. After Estie checked in, she followed their lead, hunching over her own clipboard and dutifully circling *Rarely* and *Never* for questions about how often she wanted to die and whether her appliances talked to her. After she turned in her paperwork to the receptionist, Owen reached over and took the hand closest to him in his, and Estie's fingers automatically interlaced themselves with his without Estie deciding to do so, more stimulus and response—she had no self-control. She leaned back, resting her head against the wall behind her, and watched the woman who was sitting across from them blow her nose forcefully into a tissue, then examine the tissue—presumably for little bits of brain—before discarding it in a trash can. The woman shrugged apologetically and turned away, blinking rapidly, her eyes shining with tears, but before Estie could react, the therapist called her name, then stood holding open the door to her office. And Estie, good girl that she was and always would be, didn't want to keep her waiting.

Therapy had changed since Estie had last seen it on TV. There was no couch. There were no cigars. There was no notepad. Instead, there was an overwatered rubber tree in the corner, a pair of sturdy, hard-backed armchairs that reminded Estie of the ones used to furnish her dorm back in college, a desk with a computer whose screensaver alternated between touting the benefits of hand-washing and illustrating the appropriate way to sneeze. The therapist herself seemed to be in her late thirties: she was wearing a sheer scarf elegantly draped around her neck and a severe ponytail pulled back so tightly that it revealed a receding hairline. Plus her shoes needed buffing. "So," she said pleasantly, sitting down across from Estie, "what exactly is going on?"

Estie took a deep breath. "My mom and my—my partner think I'm depressed." The therapist didn't say anything, just looked at Estie expectantly as if she knew there was more. "Fine," Estie said. "I guess *I* think I'm depressed. Or I thought I was depressed, but I've been doing a lot of thinking, and nothing's actually wrong. I just need to do a better job of sucking things up."

"Well," the therapist said, "it's a plan, I guess, but not a good one. Sucking things up rarely makes anyone feel better, and it doesn't actually solve anything."

"It doesn't need to," Estie said. "I mean, fake it until you make it. It's an actual slogan and everything."

The therapist pursed her lips. "Surely you can aim a little higher than that."

"That's plenty high for people like me," Estie said, then trotted out the heavy ammunition: "One time, I dreamed that Rosie died, and I didn't even care. What kind of mom doesn't care that her baby's just died?"

"A mom in a *dream*," the therapist pointed out calmly. "Have you actually *tried* to hurt Rosie?"

"That isn't the point. Other moms don't have dreams like that in the first place." Estie leaned back into her armchair, triumphant: apparently she was a little depressed after all.

"Sure they do," the therapist said. "I can't tell you how many women have sat in this office and told me the exact same thing."

"Okay," Estie conceded, "but all the other moms you see aren't normal either."

The therapist smiled brightly, which Estie would learn was the way she showed disapproval. "I don't think *normal*"—here she used air quotes—"is a useful distinction here. Hundreds of thousands of women experience postpartum depression, and that's just in the US, so who's to say what's normal?"

Estie rolled her eyes. Part of her recognized the truth of what the therapist was saying—tabloids at the grocery store checkout line were forever running headlines in which depressed mothers either killed themselves or their children—but a bigger part of her knew that she wasn't like these mothers, that her own depression was mild, an excuse, a way to blame the baby and avoid the responsibility she'd taken on when she'd gotten pregnant. But when Estie tried to explain this to the therapist, all she got in response was a raised eyebrow and an "Are you even listening to what's coming out of your mouth?"

Estie tugged at her hair in frustration. She was a horrible person. What was the point in pretending she wasn't? She explained to the therapist about Owen, about Alice, about Herbert and her mother, and as she talked, she watched the therapist carefully, expecting to catch her suppressing a yawn or checking the time, but if the therapist was thinking that Estie needed to get some real problems for a change, she gave nothing away. Besides, was there anything that felt better than finally being given permission to luxuriate in your worst possible self rather than trying to suppress or disguise it? "There," Estie said when she was done. "See? I wasn't exaggerating."

The therapist shook her head in what Estie assumed could only be pity or ruefulness. "So how do *you* explain the fact that Owen is out in the waiting room and that your friend—uh—Penny—drove you all the way to Chicago?"

"She's a sucker."

"Because she did something nice for you?"

"She had no choice."

"There's always a choice."

The therapist just didn't get it, Estie saw now, didn't understand how truly manipulative and awful Estie was. Instead, she was giving Estie the benefit of the doubt, maybe because women like Alice and the therapist intuitively knew all the things that women were somehow expected to know and couldn't imagine a woman who didn't, a woman who wasn't considerate and pliant even as she set her own terms. These were important skills even if everyone pretended they were relics of a time when women couldn't vote and had no economic power. And now that she had a daughter, Estie was expected to pass on all those skills that she didn't have. Wasn't it enough that Rosie was going to have to deal with global warming and antibiotic-resistant bacteria? Did she really have to be burdened with all of Estie's failings as well? By now Estie was wailing—snot, sobs, streaming eyes, the whole deal. "Poor Rosie," she heard herself sob. "What if she ends up fucked up like me?"

The therapist handed Estie a tissue, then an entire box of Kleenex.

"You better not blame this on hormones," Estie warned between sniffles. "This is who I am. I should have never passed on my genes."

The therapist waited patiently for Estie to collect herself. "Now listen carefully," she said after Estie blew her nose one final time. "If Rosie ends up with depression, then you'll teach her to recognize the symptoms and get her help if she needs it, just the same as if she turns out to be diabetic or allergic to peanuts. And yes, maybe you passed on a tendency toward depression, but maybe you didn't. Children get sick for all kinds of reasons, many of which have nothing to do with genetics."

"How is that supposed to be comforting?"

The therapist took off her glasses and rubbed the indentation on the bridge of her nose, then flashed Estie another one of her bright smiles. "Don't you think it's comforting," she said finally, slipping her glasses back on, "to know that nobody, not even you, has that kind of control?"

"Well," said Owen, his voice tentative, as they walked back to the car, hoisting Rosie between them. "What did she say?"

"God," Estie said, "am I really all that scary?"

"Pretty much," Owen admitted. Then he said, "Kidding!" because everyone knew that you should never admit fear, unless it was of something meaningless like insects or clowns. "Did she prescribe something?"

"She did," Estie told him, "so you can go ahead and relax."

Now that she was officially depressed, Estie really did feel depressed. The duplex, when they returned to it, felt crowded, little tumbleweeds of Herbert's fur congregating in various room corners. They would never be rid of him: even if they moved, his fur would follow, clinging to their suitcases, to the bottom of their couch. Estie walked to the bedroom and looked under the bed: there was his toy mouse; there was his jingly ball. She retrieved both toys and threw them away, and then, because she apparently still wasn't sufficiently worked up, her mother called. "I'm glad you're getting help," she said, "but remember that antidepressants make you fat."

"Ignore her," Owen said. "I'd rather have a fat, happy wife any day of the week."

"Well," Estie said. "I'm already fat." And then, in keeping with family tradition, she retreated to the bathroom, first to examine her jiggly arms in the mirror, then to shed a horrified tear or two. If she kept up this behavior long enough, she told herself, Rosie would grow old enough to scribble out notes in crayon and slide them under the bathroom door just like Estie had with her own mother. What *had* Estie's mother done with all of Estie's notes from her pre-Prozac days? Were those even the kinds of notes parents were supposed to keep?

Estie blew her nose into some toilet paper and washed her face, then opened the door to find Owen sitting on the floor in the hallway, a Phillips screwdriver in one hand, the orange bottle of prescription medication in the other.

"I know it's childproof," she said between sniffles, "but you shouldn't need actual tools."

Owen didn't bother smiling. "If you start locking yourself in the bathroom," he said, "I'm going to take off the doorknob."

"I can install a fucking doorknob."

Owen scoffed as if he'd never heard of Google: "Then I'll take off the entire door." He twisted the top off the pill bottle, shook out one pill, and presented it to Estie. "I feel like I should be making a speech."

And he was right: the occasion felt formal, important, as if, instead of taking her pill with water, she should be downing it between sips of champagne, toasting the return to a safe, predictable, everyday life, a life unclouded by endless dissatisfaction, endless yearning, with only a minor risk of nausea and a moderate risk of weight gain. So why did Estie feel so defeated? *If this is really all there is*, she found herself praying with the same fervor she felt whenever a plane she was on hit turbulence, *then please, God, please. Please let it be enough.*

25

FOR THE FIRST WEEK OR so, the meds made it hard to sleep, and Estie lay in bed, marveling at the way her right eye was twitching. When she did fall asleep, she had strange dreams. In one, Owen was shaving his legs in the shower. In another, Owen's parents turned out to be circus acrobats. The worst dream, though, was the one where Estie came home to find Alice leaning over Rosie's bassinet, looking sorrowful. "I'm afraid that's not a baby," she said, then reached into the bassinet and pulled up one of those giant pads from the hospital. "See?"

By morning, the dream had faded, and Estie awoke to the baby's fussing. "Who's a bad person?" she cooed at Rosie as she picked her up out of her crib. "Who? Is it Mommy?" She was holding Rosie at arm's length so they could see eye to eye. "See, baby?" she said. "You're fine." Rosie looked at her with those serious blue eyes as if considering whether Estie could be trusted, and that's when it finally happened: suddenly, out of nowhere, she smiled a radiant, open-mouthed smile. Estie felt herself smiling back reflexively, almost against her will, even though what she really wanted to do was weep in some kind of weird, hysterical relief. She placed Rosie over her right shoulder, embarrassed by her gaze, and Rosie burrowed her face into Estie's neck, then relaxed against her as if, somehow, she already knew that Estie was her mother, that this was exactly where she belonged, that it was Estie who was coming in late to the game.

In the movie based on Estie's life, this would have been the epiphany, the tender moment of connection between mother and child that made all the hard parts of parenting worth it, and for a good half hour, Estie felt almost giddy, practically reborn, but then she took Rosie to the pediatrician for a checkup and had to pin down Rosie's arms while a nurse in Snoopy scrubs plunged four needles in quick succession into Rosie's thighs. For the rest of the day, Rosie was fussy and refused to be set down, her cries so grating that by the time Owen got home, Estie had forgotten all about the smile, which didn't come close to making up for the rest of that awful day. "Here," she said, thrusting Rosie into his arms. "She's impossible. I'm going for a walk."

It was late November, and cold, and there weren't many people out. Even County Park was empty, the trees bare, the sidewalk swept clean of leaves, and the only other people Estie saw were an elderly couple holding hands and a bearded man doing sit-ups on an angled platform. Estie did one slow loop along the fitness trail and then another. She and Penny had spent so much time here as girls, Penny doing cherry drops from the chin-up bar, that Estie half expected to round a corner and find her younger self standing watch and praying that no one from school would see them.

As for present-day Estie, she must not have been paying attention to where she was going, because suddenly she stumbled and nearly face-planted, startling two Canada geese picking at somebody's discarded sandwich. "Watch it," the elderly man called to her. "There's ice by the parallel bars." Estie nodded and picked herself up. At least no birds were harmed this time around, she told herself. She brushed off the knees of her jeans and checked her mittens for rips, remembering the injured sparrow, how light it had felt in her hand, how insubstantial. That time, when she'd fallen, she'd been too scared to check herself for damage, afraid to see exactly what she'd done, but then Penny was helping her up, steadying her, wiping something off her coat, maybe blood, Estie couldn't recall. What she did remember was how cursed she'd felt, how monstrous and lumbering, and how grateful she'd been that she wasn't by herself, that Penny had been there to whisper, "It's okay, it's okay," and put her arms around her and guide her home.

Estie blinked back tears. She thought about the woman sitting in the back of that ambulance that she had walked past after the car accident. The woman had been wrapped in a blanket, Estie remembered, and she'd been breathing into what Estie assumed was an oxygen mask. But the thing that struck Estie most as she'd walked past was that the woman had been rocking back and forth, ignoring the paramedic who was checking her blood pressure, his face calm and his movements sure as if he spent all his days taking the vitals of frightened women. When he was done, he adjusted the blanket around the woman's shoulders and gave her a squeeze, but the woman kept on rocking: having someone there to wrap you in a blanket and help you catch your breath still wasn't comfort enough. Just the memory made Estie sigh, made her aware of the way her lungs expanded and contracted within her chest. No, she definitely didn't need any help breathing. She stood for a moment, listening to the air rushing in and out of her body, to the grunts of the man at the sit-up station, to the wind stirring through the trees. Was this the point of it all, she wondered, the absolute knowledge that she was alive?

Later, Estie would think that this was the moment she began to understand, at least a little, how hard it must have been for Owen to admit defeat, to admit to himself he couldn't finish his degree, how desperate he must have felt when he decided that his best option was to lie and keep on lying, that the consequences of the truth were too much to bear. He'd come so tantalizingly close to making it, to living life as a more capable version of himself, a version with a degree, a version who had beaten out the countless other candidates for that very same job. People got away with worse—assault, robbery, murder—every day, it seemed, and yet here was Owen, unable to get away with something so simple, so harmless.

Yes, Estie had been deliberate and clear-eyed about choosing to get married. But so what? What did it matter how you loved someone as long as you loved them? As long as you had faith in that love to carry you through? Because Estie really had believed every little bit of it—the marriage, the babies, the happily ever after—and she'd have been perfectly content to go on believing if Owen's lies and Rosie's arrival hadn't forced her to come clean about the parts of her love she'd been withholding, and keeping safe, so that when their marriage failed, she wouldn't be blindsided like she'd been with her parents, so she wouldn't lose all that time falling apart and pulling herself back together.

These were all things that Estie would one day be able to think through and articulate to herself, to Owen, to the marriage counselor they would begin seeing once Owen found a new job. But right then, in County Park, all Estie knew was that she wasn't angry anymore, and that even though she still wasn't sure what she wanted, she needed an anchor, a hand on her shoulder, someone to remind her she wasn't alone. She checked her phone: Rosie would be getting hungry soon. There was no point in fighting it. It was time to go home.

After dinner, while Owen gave Rosie a bath, Estie flipped mindlessly through the stack of papers he was grading. "Mass incineration is a big problem in the United States," one student argued, and another had written, "For all intensive purposes, it's helpful to know the rules for coma splices." How did Owen stand it, all the references to *dinning rooms* and *passed lives*? This was, she thought, why everyone believed teachers to be devoted and selfless, people to whom you could entrust your children in exchange for some tax dollars and the hope that it wasn't too late, that despite all your shortcomings your children could still turn out to be doctors and lawyers.

In the bathroom, Owen was crooning to a towel-wrapped Rosie who was doing her best to get her mouth on his knuckle. "A boob isn't a knuckle," Owen sang to her gently. "A knuckle isn't a boob." He looked up at Estie. "Needs work, huh?" God, how could she have even considered taking Owen away from Rosie when he loved her enough to sing such sweet songs?

Owen adjusted his grip on Rosie and freed his left hand to reach for Estie's. "We'll get the hang of it eventually," he said, "this parenting thing."

"When?" Estie asked. Rosie was nearly three months old, and right then she was fixated on gnawing on Owen's shoulder because apparently when you were an infant, anything you put your mouth on could turn out to be a boob.

"A shoulder's not a boob," Owen half sang, half murmured. "A boob's not a shoulder." Rosie paused and turned her wobbly head in the direction of Owen's face, and then, before Estie or Owen could register what she was doing, she tensed her legs and flung herself backward and over, right out of Owen's grasp and down to the floor, where Owen tried to block her fall with his foot. Estie felt a guttural moan rise up from somewhere deep inside her, but by then Owen had scooped Rosie up, his face ashen. "Oh my God," he kept saying. "Oh my God."

"It's okay," Estie said. "She's okay."

Rosie gave a little warm-up sob, exhaling until she went silent, her face purpling with rage. Estie had seen her do this before, when Estie accidentally scratched her cheek with her thumbnail, at the doctor's earlier that morning, but never for quite this long. "Don't forget to breathe," Estie said when it didn't seem Rosie could possibly have any air left inside her, and then she braced for the next part, which was Rosie taking in all the air she could so that she could wail and wail and wail. She looked so stunned, so betrayed, weeping in that heartbreaking tearless infant way, that Estie found herself apologizing. "I'm so sorry, baby," she said, reaching over to stroke Rosie's thin hair. Then, because Owen was still muttering, "Oh my God, oh my God," she carefully lifted Rosie out of his arms and carried her to her room, where she wrapped her as snugly as she could in a swaddling blanket, then held her tightly against her chest. "I'm sorry," she said again. "I'm sorry." This time the apology worked. Rosie stopped crying and, after one last accusatory stare at Estie, took a long shuddering breath.

Owen, who had followed Estie into the bedroom, took a couple of shuddering breaths of his own. "I'm going to call the doctor," he said, then retreated into the front room, where Estie heard him ask the answering service for the nurse on call.

Rosie blinked, then started working her tongue and lips in the way that meant she wanted to nurse, which was just fine with Estie, whose own legs were trembling: she was grateful for the excuse to sit down. Holding Rosie firmly with both hands, she carried her over to the rocker and assumed the position. Rosie gave Estie one more glance before latching on and taking a couple of tentative mouthfuls. She sighed contentedly and closed her eyes. In the next room, Owen was saying, "I don't know, five feet? I tried to block her fall with my foot." The nurse must have said something, and Owen gave a perfunctory chuckle. "Yes," Estie heard him say, "like a hacky sack," but he didn't sound the least bit amused. "I don't know," he said again. "I think she's nursing."

"She doesn't think we need to come in," Owen told Estie once the conversation was over, "although we're supposed to wake her up every hour." He pulled up the clock app on his phone. "I think I'm having a heart attack," he muttered while he set an alarm. "Not a heart attack. Something." Then he knelt in front of the rocking chair, burying his face in Estie's lap, and started to cry. "Why is everything so hard?" he asked, his voice breaking. "Why is everything so hard?"

"I don't know," Estie said. She was feeling hemmed in, anchored down by the baby, by the weight of Owen's head on her legs. She knew objectively that Owen was wrong, that their lives were astonishingly easy, and yet it was also true that everything was hard.

"Do you think," Owen asked, still face down, his voice muffled, "that you could maybe touch me a little? Like maybe rest your hand on my head?"

Poor Owen, Estie found herself thinking. The last months had been hard on him too, with him never knowing what he'd find every time he returned home—Baby in crib? Refrigerator empty? Mommy dead in bathtub? And after all that, the only thing he asked for were her hands on his skin. How could she say no? She adjusted her hold on Rosie, then ran her fingers through Owen's hair, which was matted and damp with sweat, and kept her hand on his head, patiently waiting out his ragged gasps until his breathing steadied, until she was pretty certain that he'd dozed off.

By then, Rosie was lolling sleepily at Estie's breast, spacey and relaxed, a thin trail of milk dribbling out of her mouth, and, watching her, Estie understood that no matter what, she couldn't give up Rosie. She also realized what should have already been obvious to her before and wasn't: near-death experiences were a horrible way to figure out your feelings about someone. So what if it would have taken Estie another month or two to understand what she felt? Staking all your hopes on a rush of adrenaline was stupid, like dangling your wriggling baby over a pit of crocodiles just to see if you had the strength to hang on.

Even with the benefit of hindsight, Estie couldn't pinpoint the moment when she started feeling better. She'd been miserable to begin with, and then, one day, she wasn't miserable anymore. Everyday tasks like washing dishes and doing laundry took less time when you didn't have to cry about them first, when you weren't wasting your energy resenting your husband for the hours he spent sleeping or plowing through stacks of ungraded papers. Had she really been depressed, she wondered sometimes, or had the whole thing really been just a matter of snapping out of it? Either way, it wasn't as if Rosie had missed any milestones, so how badly off could Estie have been?

The relative ease of it all, Estie knew, was a matter of privilege. As long as she could afford visits to the therapist and her prescriptions, the most difficult thing Estie had to do in order to recover was to be diligent about taking her medication. If she was, then six to eight weeks later there would be a day when she'd finally notice that, in fact, she was fine, or at least good enough. And that was, pretty much, the end of the story, because it wasn't as if not being depressed changed anything important: Estie still had to do whatever needed doing.

But even once she was better, Estie still found herself flipping through any magazine that featured interviews with new-mom starlets whose own depression had been so severe and terrifying that they'd written memoirs about the days, if not weeks, they'd spent forgetting to eat and dreaming of hurling themselves and/or their babies off the roofs of their mansions. Then there'd be a dark moment on a cold tile floor, and then the recovery, and after that Estie would put the magazine back in the rack and try to ignore the glares from the grocery store cashiers. Reading about other people's depression made her feel ridiculous, as if she'd done the psychiatric equivalent of showing up at the hairdresser's with a picture of a celebrity and then gotten angry when she discovered she still looked like herself.

This was why, once it was over, Estie kept quiet about those early months of parenting in the same way she kept quiet about that night with Joseph Van Vranken, about her meeting with Dan. Still, sometimes, she scrolled through the pictures of Herbert on her phone and remembered that maybe she had been depressed after all.

But all of that would come later, of course, and right then, she was still holding Rosie, and Owen was still resting his head on her knee.

"I want you to stop adjuncting," she heard herself say even though she wasn't sure Owen was awake. "I want you to find a real job with benefits and normal hours. I want you to tell your parents the truth. I want you to never lie to me again." And then, for good measure, she added, "And I want to go back to school." "You do?" she asked the Inner Estie, and the Inner Estie answered, "Yes, I don't know. Maybe."

But Owen, it turned out, wasn't asleep, because there he was, looking up at her, his eyes still wet. He studied her for a moment, considering, something flickering across his face—hurt, annoyance, determination, hope.

"Okay," he said. "I will. I promise."

The night stretched out in front of them, long and dark, with its hourly alarms and baby concussion checks, none of which could be helped. But this was what people did for each other. They threw off the covers, and they got out of bed, and they made sure the people they loved were still breathing. They did this as often as needed. They did this again and again.

Acknowledgments

This novel has been a long time coming, but it never would have arrived if it weren't for the following people:

Ashley Miller, Sally Jordan, and Bridget Hardy, who read early drafts and encouraged me to keep going. Helena Mesa and Susan Finch, who offered commiseration and support. Krista Quesenberry, who cheerfully served as a sounding board. I am beyond grateful to have you all as friends.

Helen Rubinstein, who kept me writing through the pandemic and believed in me even when I didn't. Sorche Fairbank, who took me on and offered invaluable guidance.

The various Browns, who never once hinted that it might be time to give up: Mort and Raya, Alon, and Anna.

Everyone at Melville House Publishing who gave from their talents, time, and energy to this novel: Dennis Johnson, Valerie Merians, Katrina Weidknecht, Pia Mulleady, Kezia Velista, Michael Lindgren, and Karen Krumpak.

Michelle Capone, who saw this book for what it could be and helped me see it too—I can't even begin to express my gratitude. Working with you has been a joy.

Bill, who has stood by me through all the ups and downs of this novel, and Ziv, Nadav, and Shai, who have taught me to love more deeply than I knew was possible.